ONLY DEAD LEAVES FALL

VINCENT DONOVAN

Black Rose Writing | Texas

First printing

ISBN: 978-1-68433-798-9
PUBLISHED BY BLACK ROSE WRITING
www.blackrosewriting.com

Printed in the United States of America
Suggested Retail Price (SRP) $20.95

Only Dead Leaves Fall is printed in Plantagenet Cherokee

*As a planet-friendly publisher, Black Rose Writing does its best to eliminate unnecessary waste to reduce paper usage and energy costs, while never compromising the reading experience. As a result, the final word count vs. page count may not meet common expectations.

To Robin, who colors my world.

ONLY DEAD
LEAVES FALL

"Heaven has no rage like love to hatred turned, nor hell a fury like a woman scorned."

–William Congreve

CHAPTER ONE

The hubbub outside the ballroom suddenly mushroomed as the Yahoos began beating on the locked panel door. A violent rumble shook the room and Darlene watched the banquet manager do a faceplant on the head table. Before she could swallow her smile, Nico Pappas jumped up and clapped his hands three times. Immediately, the wait staff abandoned their various assignments and moved like magnetic particles toward him.

Darlene arrived first to the ad hoc meeting and held her breath. She avoided the permanent scowl on Nico's face and studied how his thin silver hair ran away from his face and congregated sloppily along the edge of a heavily starched white collar. *Stretches the saying "only a face a mother could love,"* she thought.

Nico began brushing off the shoulders of his black tuxedo jacket with such choreography, it looked like the beginning of a dance routine. The mood lighting captured the dandruff taking flight and grew in similar size to the cloud surrounding Pig-Pen from *Charlie Brown.* It also made her wonder which plate the dead skin might season tonight. The comic moment ended much too soon as the others arrived. The team wore a uform of crisp white button-down shirts, pressed black dress pants and shiny plastic shoes and were all last-minute recruits. They were all broke, tired, hungry; and united in their hatred of Mister Pappas, which by exchanging one vowel they secretly called Master.

The room shook with another frightful thud and the hired hands turned in singular fashion toward the door anticipating a breach by the hungry marauders.

Pappas snapped his fingers. "Pay no heed to our invited guests, boys and girls. Let them salivate and make tonight all the more memorable!" He slowly scanned the crew and verified all were paying attention before raising one hand like a conductor. "I'll begin by saying I'm quite displeased with the amount of prep time required for tonight's celebration." The poor performance review was followed by a shake of the head and a strange clicking of the tongue that sounded like a sick metronome.

Darlene glanced at the chipped red polish on her index finger. It would only take a few drops of her black magic before she could practice the art of taxidermy on his corpse. *Why, I'd even include a sprinkle of his dandruff too.*

"Weak managers might devote an hour and talk about lack of intensity," Pappas continued in an elevated voice, "but I don't believe in using a butter knife when an axe is required. I would therefore suggest a team field trip to Kelley library tomorrow. Form a line in front of the giant Oxford English dictionary and look up the word *sloth*." His eyes scanned the team. "Shall I spell it for you?"

"With all due respect sir," a high-pitched man's voice from the back of the group offered, we lugged thirty tables and a couple hundred chairs from the storage shed down the street. We were lucky nothing got stolen by all the hoodlums watching us. Set-up only took three hours. That's not too shabby if you ask me."

The five-and-a-half-foot manager stood on tippy-toes to address the rebel. "And you believe this feat belongs in the *Guinness Book of World Records*?" He worked his mouth like he was preparing to spit out a lemon seed as an exclamation point. "That I would consider your appraisal of anything is laughable beyond measure." He paused and bit his lip for a long moment. "Spell it with me now, Finn! S-L-O-T-H!"

Darlene's peripheral vision noted many heads hanging in resignation as the banquet manager's hand morphed from conductor to butcher and began slicing the air. "If you cannot show more hustle next weekend, don't bother showing up at all! There's a hundred hungry hoboes within a quarter mile of here that will work for half of what I'm paying for your laziness." He pointed at the bevy of tables outfitted with fine white linen, ivory China dinnerware and crystal glasses. "Five years ago, events like this would have been as special as grains of sand on a beach," he scoffed, "but at a thousand dollars a plate, we'll make all the papers from here to New York!"

Someone coughed and broke his vision of grandeur. "Let me remind you once again what you signed in your employment papers regarding the enforcement of the eighth commandment. For the heathens among you, that means *Thou shalt not steal.* If I catch you pilfering so much as a breadcrumb, I will retrieve it and leave the method to your imagination." He held up his baby finger featuring a long white nail showcasing the likely instrument used for such extractions. "Now before I find you more despicable that I already do, take your stations."

Everyone immediately scattered but Darlene hesitated and checked the bobby pins holding back her unruly red hair. She watched a burly policeman accompany Pappas to unlock the paneled door. Immediately, the excited crowd pressed forward, and the cop positioned himself in the doorway and used his bully stick as a turnstile. Pappas stood a few feet away behind a slim hostess stand and carefully inspected each guest's government issued identity card against the confirmation list. Once satisfied, he flashed his pearly whites and communicated their table number.

The process slowly repeated itself as classical music rained down from crystal chandeliers. The previous din was replaced by giddy laughter as champagne glasses were filled by the roving staff. Darlene poured a few dozen glasses without incident until a familiar looking, two-fisted drinker wearing a green plaid suit three sizes too small stood in her path. The bald guy in his forties chugged one drink but when he tried repeating the performance, he forgot how tricky gluttony can be and spilled half a glass of the expensive bubbly on the parquet floor.

The surrounding tables went silent. The hairless pig, however, was not fazed by the failed circus act and shoved both glasses in Darlene's face.

"Gimme more," he barked. "As God is my witness, I'll never be hungry or thirsty again!"

"Says the drunk Scarlett wannabee!" a woman yelled from somewhere behind.

The tables burst into laughter and Darlene suddenly recognized his red plump cheeks. *They were almost purple last January in the bitter wind. Mister Gimme cut the bread line and whispered something to the homeland security guard. A couple minutes later, he left with a whole tray of dinner rolls. When her turn came, they only had packages of stale oyster crackers.*

She finished refilling his glasses and watched him take one long gulp. *Better sterilize your system buddy, before I serve you dinner.*

She moved on to the next table and spied Pappas escorting a stocky looking man in a baggy brown suit and sporting a pair of John Lennon style glasses to a temporary stage. On the way, Pappas motioned toward the back of the room and the chandelier lights flashed three times as the music dried up. However, many of the guests were caught up in the festivities and ignored the call to order until the banquet manager rapped on the hand-held microphone. If looks could kill, the offenders would have been on their way to the morgue. The room quickly fell silent.

Pappas thrust the microphone into the chest of a man Darlene thought was the antonym for eye candy.

The guest speaker looked disappointed as Pappas left the stage. "Ah, good evening...ladies and gentlemen," he reluctantly began before a high-pitched squeal filled the room.

Pappas made a quick U-turn and motioned for him to move away from the speaker.

"Uh, let's try again, shall we?" baggy-brown-suit said with a short laugh. "For those of you who don't know me, my name is Paul Watson, and I'm the regional director of the Phoenix Project. Our New Hampshire office is located here in Salem on Stiles Road." Watson paused and waited an uncomfortable moment before the light applause gained enough traction so he could nod in appreciation. "While we gather tonight and celebrate the one-year anniversary of the end of martial law, we hope the days ahead further accelerate a return to normalcy and the technological marvels of the twenty-first century. I've spent my entire life in the "live free or die" state and believed we could overcome any threat whether man-made or from mother nature."

He hesitated as if reconsidering his faith. "Some might say the COVID-19 pandemic was a combination of both. Yet, no matter what transpired at the intersection of medicine and politics during that unique challenge, it pales in comparison to that mid-August day four years ago when a coronal mass ejection produced a substantial cloud of magnetized plasma."

Watson reached into his vest pocket and fished out an index card and glanced at it. "History is filled with abbreviations marking mammoth events that changed the course of history...D-Day...911...and the Great Solar Storm of 2023 is no exception. How that event came to be ironically memorialized as Sun-Kissed, will be debated for years to come."

Watson adjusted his Lennon glasses and Darlene thought he might break into a bad Karaoke rendition of *Imagine*.

"However, what is not up for debate," he continued, "is a twelve percent chance every decade for such a solar catastrophe. We missed such a superstorm in 2012 by only a few days. Until four years ago, only history buffs would have known about the 1859 solar storm known as the Carrington Event. Now everyone is familiar with it since the media constantly drones on and on about it. Dinner would long be over if I explained how Carrington and Sun-Kissed are like comparing apples and pumpkins—two great staples of New Hampshire I might add. Suffice it to say that besides the wonder of being able to read newspapers at midnight after both storms, the impact of our current plight has been far more serious. Tonight, we celebrate how we have met the greater challenge."

A voice from the back yelled "Live free or die!" In an instant the room started chanting: "Phoenix! Phoenix! Phoenix!"

Darlene leaned against a curtained wall out of view and rubbed her thin white forearm. *If government propaganda were food, everyone would be obese enough to modify the State's motto to "Live free or die Roly-Poly."* She started counting the empty champagne bottles in a cardboard box in the corner. *If I fill them with some of my homemade brew, maybe I could make a few bucks.*

Watson waved his index card as the chanting subsided. "The key point is how connected the world has become. Carrington mainly disrupted the telegraph system but Sun-Kissed upset almost everything." He cleared his throat and moved cautiously toward the front of the stage while keeping an eye on the troublesome speaker. "Thankfully, NASA had the foresight years ago and deployed an ACE satellite which prevented us from being totally blindsided. We had just enough time to shut down some communication satellites and re-route large swaths of the electric grid. This action saved almost a quarter of our transformers and kept us from truly returning to the dark ages. We fared much better than other nations."

The room exploded with claps and whistles.

Watson inhaled the adulation. "As captains of local industry, your continued leadership is needed to complete the critical task of rebuilding our connected world while ensuring America remains open for business. In the last century, innovation put man on the moon. Our current mission may be earthbound, but no less daunting as we work on rekindling the world. As with any crusade there will be critics saying we are not advancing fast enough; and yes, we continue dealing with rolling brownouts, no internet, and frustrating rations, but progress is real. One can look at tonight as a prime example. Six months ago, this dinner would have been by candlelight as the electrical grid remained unstable. Tonight, however, we meet under brightly lit chandeliers to feast on prime rib, mashed potatoes and from what I hear a very special dessert. So, without further delay bon appétit!"

The guests responded with a standing ovation as Pappas stood guard at the kitchen door.

Darlene took her position near the end of the conga line of servers as *Happy Days Are Here Again* blared through the sound system. Moments later she paraded across the dining room carrying a heavy tray and placed it on a stand. Like a seasoned ballerina where no movement is wasted, she began dispensing the salads while refraining from looking at the crisp lettuce, red onions, thinly shaved cucumbers and plum tomatoes neatly arranged like delicate bouquets on crystal plates. The smell of the balsamic dressing, however, proved too alluring and she began breathing through her mouth to tamp down the impulse of running out the back door with a plate. *Mom would be beside herself tasting nature's bounty like this. She might even forget the frown she keeps in her top dresser drawer for me... Maybe I should gift it to the nursing home administrator instead, and hope he gives me more time to pay up.*

She bit the inside of her cheek because sometimes that helped cork her thoughts. When she waited on tables before the dark curtain descended, many folks would merely pick at a salad and save room for the main course. Tonight, however, this bunch of locusts attacked every morsel while keeping one eye glued on their bread plate which featured a dinner roll and a thick pad of real butter. She took in the frenzied dance of forks and knives cutting and piercing and it resembled the medieval pillaging of a conquered city. *By the time the Baked Alaska comes, they will all look as plump as Violet Beauregarde from "Willie Wonka and the Chocolate Factory." Better to be guilty of sloth than gluttony.*

A loud and familiar cackle pierced her ears and reminded her of the hideous laugh track from one of her mother's ancient tv shows. She scanned the tables for the annoying oaf when suddenly an electric pulse ran from the top of her head to the ends of her toes. In that painful moment everything went numb. Only the horrible noise of two plates crashing on the parquet floor broke her catatonic state. Falling to her knees, she debated whether to stuff the gorgeous vegetables into her pant pockets or transfer the whole mess back to the kitchen and blame it on some drunken idiot.

Before she could decide, she smelled the foul cologne that must have been extracted from the gallbladder of a poisonous snake.

"What's the matter with you?" Pappas hissed in her left ear. "Those salads cost me twenty bucks apiece!" He grabbed her by the arm, but she resisted and contemplated slicing his hand with the broken plate. Pappas must have read her intentions and released the death grip and pointed toward the kitchen like the Grim Reaper. She left the garden treasure on the floor and gave a quick glance at the man that was her undoing. The demon continued laughing and chewing with his mouth open. *It's a wonder he can still laugh given my recent intercession.*

Pappas led the death march across the room, but no one noticed. The invited guests were too busy making up for years of want.

Darlene stopped in front of the double walk-in-stainless-steel coolers near the rear of the kitchen. It contained all the ingredients for tonight's gastro-feast and delivered by an armored truck. She braced for a tongue-lashing and hoped it would be over quickly so she could return and spy on her nemesis.

Pappas continued walking and opened a gunmetal gray door leading to the alley. She could make out a hedge of brownish evergreens that looked as thirsty as her.

Master took a deep breath as if summoning all his strength not to take off his black belt and beat her.

I can still feel the leather strap on the back of my legs and how it burned. Black lightning—that's what Daddy called it. The thunder that followed came with a whiskey infused wind.

"Get out," Pappas said almost in a whisper. He pointed at the dark alley.

"You can't be serious?" she asked in a small voice rarely used, not because she didn't feel desperate most days, but because vulnerability meant weakness. Her tears remained hidden like water in a cactus and she extended a pointed finger. "Look, I made a stupid mistake, and it won't happen again. Okay?" She almost smiled hearing the defiant undertone.

He gave her a once over like she should be discarded along with the dropped salads. "No, it won't happen again because you're fired. I'm also deducting the salads from your paycheck." He shot her a smile. "That should leave you a few pennies to buy some strips of toilet paper to wail into."

She eyed the silver buckle of his belt and remembered being fourteen and sneaking into the house past curfew... Daddy staggers out of the den guzzling the last of a bottle...Our eyes lock for a microsecond... He heads for the long leather strap hanging at the end of the hall—the perpetual reminder to submit to his will...Submit! Is there an uglier word?... But something wild and unexpected suddenly blossoms…I'm sober and have half a step on him and reach the belt first… He tries grabbing it from me and I take a step back and beat him about the head screaming, "No More!"

Daddy collapses on the floor and protects his face… I would have wailed on him until the scales were equal if Mom hadn't stopped me… No matter—the tyranny ended that night and none of his drunken tears would soften my heart.

A plastic tub of balsamic dressing on a side table beckoned. She drooped her head in resignation and Pappas smirked like he broke another peasant.

In one fluid movement, she grabbed the tub of dressing and threw it at his face.

The intensely flavored vinegar found its bombastic target. It greased his silver hair and burned the coal black eyes before running down his face and dripping on the shoulders of the expensive black jacket.

Pappas let out a high-pitched scream and swiftly retrieved a white handkerchief from his pocket. He worked feverishly on his eyes.

Dandruff and dropped salads will be the least of his worries for the next hour, she thought. "You better pipe down or the captains of industry might think you're being slaughtered for the main course," she commented above the cries. "And don't worry none about my paycheck, Master. It can go towards the dry-cleaning bill."

Pappas lunged at her and missed badly. As much as she wanted to wait around and see if he would melt into the floor like the Wicked Witch, she decided to leave before the flying monkeys arrived.

She followed the long alley to a parking lot full of newly minted cars and let her hair down. The coolness of the mid-September evening was a welcome relief. Fifty feet ahead, she spotted two men feeding a trashcan bonfire. With no moon or streetlights, they were the unofficial town lamplighters.

"Hey there, miss," one of them called out. "What are they serving the half-percenters tonight?"

She wondered why they were asking her and remembered the uniform. "Just greed wrapped in stale malarkey," she yelled back, "and whatever is left over will be in a stew tomorrow and cost you half your life savings, if you have any left." The legendary *Seinfeld* episode came to mind. "No soup for you!" she mumbled. *Come to think of it, that cook had the same expression as Pappas.* She closed her eyes. Tomorrow and all the days in the foreseeable future would be fueled by government supplied MRE's—meals ready to eat and fashioned after the military, except for taste and quality.

She heard rapid footsteps approaching from behind and turning around expected Master Balsamic-Face and a linebacker sized cop. Instead, Carl came huffing and puffing up the sidewalk with his blond-man bun half undone. *It's rather silly how hard he tries to be thirty-nine for like the fifth time.*

"Don't tell me you've been fired too?" she asked with a heavy sigh. "One of us needs to make some scratch, you know."

Carl looked dejected for a second before gifting her with a toothy smile that called attention to his eye teeth and regularly made her question whether his ancestors shared DNA with Dracula. Not that the bottom teeth were much better. They looked like a Nor'easter came through and badly twisted some of the fencing.

"No, Master sent me for another shirt. Everyone is buzzing about the accident and think you're the reason, but boss man won't say." He handed her a bulging white linen napkin and glanced at the barrel guys.

Darlene discovered a dinner roll swaddled in the linen. "Babe, how many times have I told you I'm not the type of girl that needs rescuing?" She reached in her back pocket and fished out two jumbo shrimp and watched his proud smile collapse. She laid them on top of the roll. "All we need now is a baked potato or some pasta. When you go back see what you can do. I can't stomach rice and bean puree from a plastic tube tonight."

"Says the hotheaded ginger that got fired." He searched her face. "Tina told me you fumbled the salad five minutes in. What happened?"

She shrugged. *Too much to process or explain.*

"Well, I know how much you needed this gig. How long before the nursing home puts your old lady out on the street?"

"I don't know, maybe a few weeks by the time they process everything. Her house has a lien on it and I spent my last fifty on this gothic uniform. This nickel and dime stuff isn't paying the bills—mine or hers."

Carl nodded. "I know some guys that are pretty well connected, but they warn me there's too much competition moving counterfeit stuff. You try and break in around here and you'll end up as dead as the beef Pappas is serving tonight. What we need is a mark. Like they say, there's a sucker born every minute." He looked up at the dark sky. "Sun-Kissed didn't change a good scam any."

The familiar cackle from the dining hall echoed in her ears. *Once upon a spring, I was his gullible fool and he fancied plucking my buds.* She turned away so Carl would not see her smile. *But now it's autumn and time for his fall.*

CHAPTER TWO

Todd Dolan ignored the red light and blew by the startled jogger in the crosswalk. Luckily, no police siren announced his infraction.

The rearview mirror highlighted a middle-aged runner pumping a fist in his direction. "Good morning to you too," he whispered as the BMW sped along a patchwork of stores in Rockingham Plaza.

He headed toward the end of the parking lot where a USDA sanctioned store would hand out five-pound blocks of cheese and MRE's beginning at noon. Todd didn't have to battle for a parking space as they were all empty. After checking his watch for the nth time, he jumped out and sprinted faster in dress shoes than the jogger could ever hope to match. The twenty-yard dash ended at a bank of refurbished pay phones located between the USDA facility and a newly opened pet shop serving the well-heeled.

The late September morning matched his mood: gray and threatening despite giddy rumors that the internet would make a triumphant return by the new year. He picked up the sticky black receiver wrapped in bright orange stickers promising the rapture would occur for sure this time on All Souls Day. Todd studied the announcement for half a second. "Well, it sure feels like the great tribulation is underway," he whispered. He fed the phone two quarters and punched in Brad's number while making a mental note to use a generous amount of hand sanitizer afterwards.

He listened to the long rings and likened them to the opening and closing bells on Wall Street. While everyone watched their portfolios disappear along with electricity after the solar storm, he made some quick moves when the market reopened six months later. To an outsider, he had a Midas touch but his strategy centered on a common-sense approach by investing only in technologies that accelerated the global recovery and shunning stocks which traded on the hopes of consumer spending. Although he never considered himself a day trader per se, the half million he pocketed this year felt more like a windfall from a casino if such state sponsored vices still existed. Consequently, continued success depended upon a delicate balance of opportunity versus risk and like gambling, knowing when to walk away.

Although patience was a virtue, this morning it felt more like a weakness. XRE fell twenty percent yesterday with no bottom in sight. He felt hung over from pouting about the stock all night and rubbed the tension in the back of his neck.

On the ninth ring the phone finally clicked, and he did not wait for a greeting. "Thanks for the hot tip, bro!" he half-shouted but refrained from the four-letter words he normally peppered their conversations with. Martial law might have ended, but the police worked on keeping major crimes down by enforcing minor offenses. Blowing through a crosswalk and disturbing the peace meant heavy fines these days.

"Bloomberg said XRE may suspend trading by the end of the week," he continued. "I'm calling from outside a pet store so you can dump my remaining shares. That way, I'll have a few bucks left for some rawhide to chew on. Better yet, maybe they'll have a fat little cat toy that resembles you. Imagine the fun I can have!"

The line remained silent for a moment before an exaggerated sigh followed. "Todd let's get three things straight before we begin again with you saying good morning. First, remember this call is on a recorded line, so you should probably refrain from threats. Second, we were only related through marriage and that's been over for a while now. Third, and most importantly, you can't dump that stock not now, not ever."

"Blah, blah, blah and don't forget the warning how past results don't guarantee future performance. With that out of the way, let me explain why you can say good morning and I can't." He held the receiver in front of his face so he could pretend to shout at Brad point blank. "It's not *your* money being vaporized! I'm beginning to think you and your sister have congenital hearing issues, so let me say it again real slow and a bit louder on the recorded line. Get me out of XRE!" The stickiness of the receiver was grossing him out and he looked around for something to wipe it on.

Brad cleared his throat. "I see now why you work for a company that has record sales but reverse stock splits. You have no spine and the patience of a spoiled toddler." He let out a short snicker. "From now on, I'll call you Todd-ler whenever you pull a hissy fit like this."

"Wow aren't you the witty one! Believe me when I say there won't be a next time. As far as nicknames go, want to guess yours?"

"Will you come down from your high-horse for a minute and listen to me?" I'm telling all my other managed accounts—you know, people with *real* money and substantial positions to hold. XRE corporate is releasing their reorganization plan this afternoon and things will stabilize. Research indicates the stock will rebound nicely once they launch the communication satellite next month. A year from now when you see the growth and the dividend, you'll thank me. So, stop the belly aching and sit tight. Man, you're such a control freak!"

Another day, another siren song: "Look my money is as green as the big guys so don't talk down to me like that. As a matter of fact—"

"Can you hold for a minute?" he interrupted. "I have another call." An instrumental rendition of *Fire & Rain* began, and Todd wondered why Mick Jagger wasn't belting out *God Give Me Everything I Want*.

A sudden breeze brought the first raindrops, and he wedged his face between the phone and the protective Plexiglas. He pictured his overweight ex-brother-in-law stuffed in a black leather chair. On the right top corner of his desk a neatly folded copy of the *Wall Street Journal* was prominently displayed for the few pilgrims still possessing a few bucks and hungry to participate in the gold rush for the well-connected. Todd remembered Brad discarding a huge pile of neatly folded copies into a recycle bin.

"What are you doing?" he asked.

Brad held up the unread copy and laughed. "Well, since we're family, I'll share a little secret. There's a certain amount of mystique around finance, especially since Sun-Kissed torched everything. I found having a copy of WSJ on my desk communicates a certain mystique like I'm related to Oz and know how to pull the levers behind the curtain. So, I pick up a copy every week or two and fold it, so the date doesn't show. Works like a charm, except for one smart aleck that asked why I had a week-old issue on my desk. He smiled a devious grin. "I told him some cockamamie story about researching a hot lead and charged him an extra processing fee for being a showoff." He nodded to himself. "Now, if I could I'd get my hands on one of those old-fashioned ticker tape knock-offs, I could change my name to the Grand Oracle."

This poor excuse for a medium and financial advisor however, had an expensive coffee fetish that could fund a WSJ subscription for three lifetimes. While coffee had been severely rationed for years, if the beans were not hand-picked from some exotic location, it never touched Brad's lips. He also believed Styrofoam was located on the table of artificial elements between paper plates and plastic utensils, so he outfitted his office with Lenox coffee mugs. That way the coffee snob could grind, brew, and sip all day and believe he reached the peak of self-actualization on Maslow's hierarchy of needs. Meanwhile, the rest of humanity foraged for the next meal.

He considered ending their business relationship after he and Stephanie divorced. His logic for maintaining the status quo centered on mutual rewards: handsome capital appreciation for him and advisor fees for Brad. Even so, the arrangement had become strained and this morning he felt like reaching through the phone and pulling off Brad's coffee-stained lips. He would hold them as collateral until XRE rebounded. The image of his ex-brother-in-law painfully sipping coffee through a paper straw almost made him smile.

The music on the line suddenly cut out. "I really have to run," Brad said in one breath. "If you can reign in your emotions, I might even let you in on something that's been percolating for a while." He let out a short laugh. "I'll say it again, that solar storm is the gift that keeps on giving for those of us in the know. The key is not obsessing about yesterday, because that's like playing records backwards and hearing weird messages. Just trust me on this. Okay? Before you answer, just remember why you're driving a luxury car when most folks are either

---

---

crammed in buses, hoofing it on foot or resurrecting so many vintage cars the country now resembles Cuba."

The words were like a shot of Novocain and made his tongue feel fuzzy. *What else can I say?* Trying to time the market even before these crazy days was a fool's errand, but that did not include their business association. Standing in front of a pet store intent on saving his net worth drove home the point.

"You better be right about this, buddy," he replied. "I'm really frightened this could wipe out half my gains for the year. Call me after the reorganization plan is announced." He hung up without saying goodbye and closed his eyes. *Why did I ever invest in a company that started with an X? That letter already defines too much of my world.*

He checked his watch and frowned. Miller would be looking for him by now, eager to pummel him about the upcoming budget presentation. Another tension headache began in both temples. *This side hustle is too consuming, but a few more hits will erase what I lost in the divorce.*

The sticky phone reminded him of the divorce settlement with Stephanie. Recoiling from the painful memory, he collided with something hard.

He turned to find a woman spread out on the pavement.

"Oh, my goodness, I'm so sorry!" he said with a gasp, realizing he had not checked anyone like that since playing ice hockey as a kid. Helping her up, he quickly scanned the body for blood or broken bones. Besides the embarrassment, he did not need another hassle this morning as synapses were already firing to calculate how long this accident might delay him. Any minute now, Miller would invade his office and begin pawing through the files on his desk and editing project notes on the whiteboard.

The injured party stood up. "Nice way to greet me," she said with a sarcastic ring and hobbled sideways to retrieve a runaway black pump a few feet away.

Todd surveyed the familiar looking face still framed by shoulder length thick red hair. In the next instant, he clenched his jaw so he would not look like one of those popular Christmas carolers with frozen "O" shaped mouths. Memories flooded his thoughts, and a cerebral sump pump went into overdrive which made his ears ring. If the universe had any mercy left, it would be anyone but her.

"Darlene?" he asked softly hoping to be corrected.

She ignored the question and concentrated instead on brushing off her short black skirt and red satin blouse with the attention one might expect from a curator in a museum. She wore no rings and he kept his gaze away from the mid-section that once held new life. He managed a shallow breath as his eyes continued downward and found her shapely legs still connected to overly large feet.

The ghost in front of him seemed imperious to the morning's frustrated drizzle and wore no coat. Satisfied with the restoration, she glanced at the pet store behind him. "Are you here walking the dogs?" she asked with a quizzical look. "I remember how much you liked the bitches."

The comment felt like a tripwire and he didn't move a muscle except for flashing a weak smile. She gave him a once over which automatically made him suck in his stomach. While still possessing most of his hair at forty-three, the shower drain would certainly be full tomorrow.

She gifted him a small smile acknowledging the shock and awe campaign achieved the desired results. "It's usually much less painful running into people I know." The tone sounded more like an indictment than an olive branch.

Todd peered into her bottomless eyes and recalled how blue resided between green and violet on the spectrum of light. In her case it lived in the chasm between jealously and needy. He also knew that somewhere within the charcoal centers of those pupils were the scars from his teenage stupidity.

She took a small step toward him which ended the examination of conscience. "My goodness Darlene, how long has it been? Twenty-five years?" The second the words left his mouth he knew he sounded like an infomercial with too much gusto and rushed to counterbalance the question with an exit strategy. "I'm in a terrible rush this morning, but we should catch up some time." He planned on having a full calendar for the next millennia. No doubt the feeling was mutual.

He took a step backwards to begin the strategic retreat and checked the sky hoping the lousy weather would help end this surreal encounter.

Darlene matched his step and cocked her head. "Are you blowing me off sweetie? After all these years all I get is a quick-howdy-but-gotta-run disappearing act? If I let you escape, I won't see you again." She pointed at the cloudy sky. "Who knows what's lurking up there?"

He looked past her at the sticky phone and found himself suddenly rooting for the rapture.

She folded her arms waiting for a reply and when none came, rolled her eyes. "How about giving your jilted teenage lover a big hug?" She stepped forward and grabbed his right arm. "You haven't forgotten how to wrap your arms around me have you?"

Todd heard the familiar sting and opened his arms for a light embrace. He concentrated on the sidewalk display advertising scented cat litter as Darlene pulled him in close. She held on long enough, coincidentally, for him to smell the floral perfume he remembered far too well. *Does she still wear White Shoulders? Impossible!*

He pulled away. This time, he took two steps back and planned on keeping a safe distance even if she was one of those close talkers. *Thirty seconds of small talk and I will politely excuse myself so she can disappear back into the oblivion she crawled out from."*

He licked his sudden dry lips. "Why are you here so early?" he asked and pointed at the middle of the strip mall. "There's bargains at the State liquor store seven days a week, and few lines." He smiled wide to show off his whitened teeth. "Strange that booze is the only thing not rationed these days. Probably because it keeps the masses mellow about the slow recovery." He looked at her thin arms and could almost taste his shoe leather.

Taking a step sideways he tried to recover. "Last I remember you traded our little patch of heaven for upstate New York."

Darlene's hands found her hips. "Traded?" she asked as her face contorted. "That's an interesting description. I think exiled would define it better, don't you?" She let the comment hang for an uncomfortable moment. "What are you doing here anyways? Taking care of the dogs or," she smiled, "running one of those pitiful security outfits keeping the zombie apocalypse at bay?" She pointed toward a boarded-up window. "At first it was neighbor helping neighbor, but after a few months in the dark, not so much. Survival of the fittest, I guess. The new normal feels a lot like the old one, except on steroids."

The Hindenburg consumed in flames flashed in his mind. A lot of desperate folks wanted to burn it all down and start from scratch. "It's been a long road back for sure, but I think we're getting there." He pointed at the pay phone and laughed. "Hopefully in a couple years cell phones will appear like a great tidal wave too. In the meantime, we're all slaves to land lines. That's why I'm here and running into you proves timing is everything."

Darlene's gaze moved to the top of his head like she was watching him sprout horns. The throbbing headache he felt might be the birth pains. "I don't recall you spewing tired clichés like that back in the day. Let me guess," she said pressing one finger to her forehead like a clairvoyant. "You called home to help little Johnny with a stubborn math problem he struggled with over breakfast." She took a deep breath. "They used to say breakfast is the most important meal of the day. Now everyone just wants to break fast."

He knew he should ignore the fishing expedition. At the same time, he wanted her to know he turned out as successful as planned and luckier than most during the multi-year calamity. "Actually, I had to call my financial advisor about a substantial equity opportunity," he said imitating Brad's arrogant tone. The words tasted like dry flakes of uncooked oatmeal.

Darlene listened and her eyes narrowed. "That's interesting since you never liked games of chance."

Todd wrestled with the muscles of his face to keep them from twitching. "Well, this one is a sure thing."

"So, you're Tanned?"

Todd hated the description. Although the government refused to acknowledge it, Sun-Kissed vaporized political parties too. Democrat, Republican and Independent were meaningless labels now. People defined themselves as "Burned" or "Tanned"—meaning the solar storm made you either a peasant or a lord. It obliterated the middle class.

Time represented the last lifeline and he studied his watch for a millisecond and let true worry overwhelm his face. "Yikes! I'm really late for a meeting."

She looked unimpressed and took a deep breath. "Do you smell it, Todd?"

All that kissed his olfactory nerve was some ammonia mix the mall washed the windows with. It also diluted the smell from ticked off people that relieved themselves on commercial buildings as a protest against hopelessness. "Smell what?" he asked.

"September!" she responded almost breathless. "This month always smells of anticipation. Remember the wild days of summer back when the world was a different place? In late August it would turn a bit cooler and you could smell school in the air. Then Labor Day would sneak up faster than Sister Mary chasing you in sixth grade. I still can't believe you stole the girl's Phys-Ed book." Her expression went blank. "You wanted to read all the chapters in Braille and that's where I came in a few years later." She looked at her feet. "You read me over and over that summer."

He looked away. *This is too much.*

She walked to the edge of the elevated sidewalk and pointed toward the horizon. "Look at those maple trees way over there." She glanced back at him to make sure he was paying attention. "Notice how a few of the leaves at the top have already turned red? Soon all the trees will be dressed in their true colors. The same goes for people. Most try to blend in, but who they really are eventually shows." She searched his face for a reaction. "Am I right?"

Todd looked at the green canopy that reminded him of broccoli florets which he hated. He searched the parking lot with its spaces so faded they were hardly recognizable: one ancient looking Ford Escort with a cracked windshield sat a few spaces over from his black BMW. They made an unlikely couple.

He pointed at the old junk car that were the norm since Sun-Kissed fried the electronics in newer models. "Is that yours?"

She looked at him like she was confused by the question. "Can you give me a lift to the depot?"

He slowly nodded. *Okay...no coat...no car. Did she just fall out of the sky?* He looked at the pay phone again, willing to embrace the sticky receiver and call her a cab.

Darlene watched him. "Hope I'm not making things too difficult given your schedule."

He smiled and remembered how she used to play him.

"Why don't you wait here while I get my car?" he finally offered.

She stepped off the curb with him. "And lose you for another quarter century? That's not in the stars my dear," she said grabbing him by the arm.

Walking toward the car, Todd eyed the jogger searching a dumpster at the end of the strip mall. He thought about locking him in the trash receptacle as pay back for the quick manifestation of whatever curse he sent his way.

CHAPTER THREE

Todd discovered the main gate of Deputy Dynamic Defense blocked by a convoy of repurposed school buses transporting per diem workers employed in the fabrication of rubber bullets and police batons. Across the street from the three-story cement block building secured by a twelve-foot-high barbed wire fence, a half dozen women knelt behind a sign that read *"D Cubed = D Clubbed."*

A security guard directed him to the rear gate which added to the frustrating morning. He finally escaped Darlene after dropping her off at Federal Bank, but not before she extracted his phone number. On the short drive to work, he consciously willed himself from mulling over the unfortunate episode as there would be plenty of time for that later. Now all available brain cells were engaged for the upcoming battle with Monster Miller.

He dashed through the lobby and tackled the stairs two at a time before speed-walking down a long hall flanked with gray cubicles. The few coworkers he encountered simply nodded or muttered a quick hello as if fearful of guilt by association.

He no sooner booted up the archaic computer when he heard footsteps in the hall. The heavy shuffle meant F. Stanley Miller, the lumbering Cyclops and CEO, was on the prowl.

"Good afternoon!" an impressive voice boomed from the office doorway.

Todd never cowered like the other lemmings in the company. "Morning Stan," he replied in a hurried voice. "Sorry I'm late and won't bore you with the ugly details." He let out a long sigh for dramatic effect hoping he would move along.

The bald giant hesitated for a second before his hips swiveled girl-like toward the visitor chair in front of the metal desk. "Can I ask you a question?"

The superficial request felt like hitting your funny bone, except this numbing tingle ran between his ears and represented the beginning of a torturous cross-examination. Over the years, he tried different tactics short of jumping out the window. No matter how he answered the seemingly polite request, that leading question represented a gigantic sinkhole that makes you wake up in the middle of the night crying for Mommy.

Before replying, Todd studied the six-and-a-half-foot giant's nasal bridge—a trusty barometer of his mood and basis of the underground consensus: *"white all is right; but red means trouble ahead."* This morning the double wide fleshy honker glowed magenta. Although this made his pulse quicken a tad, he weathered enough epic outbursts over ten years at the company and quickly battened down the mental hatches. During these meltdowns, he realized how he never felt at ease with his boss and always kept his guard up. Not that he wanted more in their relationship, but it would be nice at quarter end to acknowledge another thirteen-week marathon. After all, they spent more time together than with anyone else in their sorry lives, especially with the plant running 24/7 to keep up with demand. When the Red Sox regrouped after a three-year hiatus, he even made a few overtures about taking the leadership team to a game and only received a blank stare in reply.

"So, can I ask you a question?" Miller repeated, evidently anxious to begin this morning's maiming.

If he asked me the same question twice, isn't the second one THE question? Maybe I should just say no and enjoy the fireworks." Instead, he nodded and hoped XRE made a killing so he could seek parole soon.

The executive nodded and sat back in the chair. Todd watched the CEO's mannerisms enough to liken him to a modern-day tyrannosaur. At the office, Miller loved making the earth shake and would bellow and rip flesh ad nauseam, but drop him in an environment requiring any social interaction and this reptile was in the tar pits. On the rare Monday morning when they traded tales of weekend activities, Miller would launch into an animated monologue about some "all you can eat" rib fest he and Mrs. Rex discovered at some government sanctioned cafeteria. He would even wave his skinny dwarf arms while explaining the bounty. Todd considered installing one of those hot dog rolling grills in his office just to mess with his primitive taste buds.

"So where are you with the budget presentation?" Miller finally asked.

Todd had a few half-baked spreadsheets he could use for show and tell but little else given the ups and downs of Wall Street. Before the solar storm, the annual budget was built over a few weeks with many late-night sessions from the convenience of his home office. With the internet burnt toast, however, the bulk of the work had to be accomplished in the office with refurbished computers backed up with generators. *The first draft isn't due for another day, so no need to panic,* he thought. Still, he hated looking unprepared, especially since his performance review dinged him on lack of initiative.

"I'm still reviewing the cost roll from manufacturing, so it's a bit premature. We can meet tomorrow afternoon and review the preliminaries if you like," he said reaching for a manila folder on the corner of his desk.

Miller stood up and made his way over to a file cabinet in the corner. Todd watched him pick up a fluorescent yellow tennis ball used for plantar fasciitis relief. His boss threw it against the wall and surprisingly, caught the return. Miller repeated the athletic trick two more times before Kent, the office busybody, strolled by to assess the carnage. Todd assumed an office pool was underway on how long he could withstand the barrage before begging for mercy.

"For giggles, why don't you pull up the PowerPoint template and we'll take a look at what slides you have so far?" Miller pulled the visitor chair close to the monitor.

Todd knew his boss was a pro at finding the weak point in a defensive line and capitalizing on it. Sometimes his target would become so unnerved by the assault they would assume the deer in the headlights look. This allowed decapitation from a distance and kept any stains off the CEO's perpetual white shirt.

Todd breathed rapidly through his nose instead of gulping for air. He clicked through a long list of presentation files, looking for a life raft. Unfortunately, none would support his weight.

The CEO sat down and worked a bony finger into his starched shirt pocket and retrieved a small piece of paper. "Perhaps you should ask your friends at Embassy Financial for the file," he announced, before placing the paper on the keyboard. "From the outgoing call report, it appears you work with them more than anyone here. Maybe I should cut out the middleman and ask them for next year's budget."

Todd scanned the activity report with Brad's number highlighted in yellow a dozen times and struggled to keep his expression calm. *How dare he check-up on me like I'm some entry level kid... With cell phones, this sort of thing would never happen.* Staring at the indictment, he took it as further proof to axe his ex-brother-in-law. *Why should I always be chasing him so I can stay whole?*

He realized the only option at this point was a heavy dose of subterfuge. Miller knew about the painful divorce and he could say he called his brother-in-law for regular counseling, which was true. Throw in a spoonful about being disappointed over lack of trust and maybe Stanley would clutch for his raisin-sized heart. Then Kent could do the mouth-to-mouth resuscitation. If he sold pictures to the protestors, he could pay off his house.

Suddenly, there was a small knock on the office door. Instead of Facilities rushing in with a box so he could pack up his personal belongings, Darlene appeared holding an arrangement of daisies in a thin glass vase.

"Please excuse me," she cooed in a velvet voice.

Todd considered seeking cover under the desk because Miller would not reach for the tennis ball this time. Last week he got so angry at the head of quality control, he tried out one of the new electric batons on the poor soul.

Instead, the CEO turned in his chair and with his lifeless dinosaur eyes drank in every centimeter of the visitor's satin blouse and skirt combo. Then he glared at Todd concluding the reason he was late.

"Darlene?" Todd blurted out in more of a plea than a question.

She set the vase down on the desk and gave her full attention to the giant carnivore. "You must be Mr. Miller."

T-Rex extended his short thin arm. "And you are?"

"Darlene Connolly." She shook his hand and held on. "Did Todd tell you how he rescued me this morning?"

Miller looked embarrassed holding hands and wriggled free. "No, but can I ask you a question, Miss Connolly?"

Todd rolled his eyes but the woman from his past looked unfazed. "Sure, but please call me Darlene."

Miller looked toward the hall before pointing at the badge hanging from his leather belt. "How did you up here without an escort?"

Darlene rubbed his arm. "Escort? Why, what kind of business are you running here?" she replied with an exaggerated laugh. "Seriously though, please don't blame Frank at the reception desk. I told him I was your sister and brought flowers as a surprise. Have to say, the look on his face was priceless! Guess you don't have many women bringing you goodies. I'm sorry for barging in like this but wanted to apologize for making Todd late this morning. I was in an awful state after my car broke down. I literally bumped into Todd and begged for a ride. He wanted to find a pay phone and call in to explain, but I was in a crazy rush to make a meeting with the bank. After he dropped me off, I realized my insensitivity." She fingered the vase for a second and shot Todd a quick glance. "Remember how daisies were my favorite in grade school? They represent innocence and purity, and like this morning, new beginnings."

Miller forced a painful smile and stood up. His nose remained pretty red. "Todd, we'll talk later about the budget." He leered at Darlene one last time and lumbered out of the office.

Darlene waited until Miller was out of range before starting to giggle. "What's with crab cakes, or should I say crab tree?"

Todd remained stunned and unsure whether to praise or curse her. "This really wasn't necessary," he began. "You already thanked me when I dropped you off."

"But I closed on my new house! Promise me you'll stop by this evening and celebrate my return," she said holding up a set of house keys. "I'll get going so you can get that budget done."

She stopped at the door and turned around. "Smell September now, Todd?"

CHAPTER FOUR

A throaty noise that could pass for Paul Bunyan gargling filled the Adirondack General Store. Proprietor Jennifer Pearson rushed out of the back room and found the frozen drink machine overheating again. She purchased the soon-to-be-doorstop a month before the solar storm hit when she was bamboozled by a handsome sales guy that linked skyrocketing profits to drooling kids spending their allowances on flavored frozen beverages. She did not realize he was making her a sucker green one that day.

She unplugged the machine and realized it would be many more summers before breaking even and that depended on locating the strategic reserve of fruit syrup concentrate. The stainless-steel contraption looked out of place against the knotty pine shelves and white and black speckled linoleum, a throwback to her father's era when Lake George campers stopped by to purchase a six-pack of Schlitz and a pack of Winston's. Now the shelves and standing coolers held a selection of USDA approved foods and beverages: block cheese, tubs of peanut butter, saltine crackers, generic beer, soda, bottled water and a smattering of ready-to-eat meals in plastic pouches which tasted like baby food. Toiletries like one-ply toilet paper and bars of unscented soap filled out the standard offering. The prime inventory for the vacationing Tanned crowd such as tuna, beef, chocolate, wine, and cigars were kept in a locked display unit near the register.

The cape-cod shingled building with the two-bedroom apartment upstairs represented her father's passion for family and entrepreneurship. Growing up, she would watch Dad plan all winter long for the spring invasion of city-folk, black flies and mosquitoes and wonder aloud which were worst. Come Memorial Day, families would arrive in droves professing a desire for simplicity, but more often seeking to replicate their urban lifestyles in the string of vacation homes and dude ranches that ringed the Queen of American Lakes. Jennifer amused her parents by pinching her nose and mimicking the vacationer's summer epiphany: *"My darling, it's absolutely fabulous having dinner together as a family. I thought I knew everything about the children from their text messages. Who knew they were only the CliffsNotes?"*

Even though the crowds were only a fraction of pre-Sun-Kissed days, throw in a few rainy days and smiles still shriveled into the same pouts they had for decades. *"Is there a theater nearby?"* both young and old would inquire, even if all the movies were reruns.

Jennifer eyed the worn keys on the old-fashioned cash register. She tried honoring her father's tradition of closing at 9 p.m. sharp Monday through Saturday and keeping the sabbath holy. Her resolve broke, however, after a twenty-something-year-old guy knocked on her door last month. Before the wild-eyed man opened his mouth, she knew his request would fall within the alphabetized need list of the wealthy: antacids, aspirin, beer, cigarettes, chocolate, snacks, or wine. Most were unavailable or commanded a fortune in luxury taxes if she had any. When he asked whether he could buy some food for a feral cat, she caved and let him in. He immediately forgot the starving feline and made a beeline for a brand beer which ran seventy-five bucks for a twelve-pack. When she balked, the guy shrugged and said the cat needed something to lap after its Sunday dinner. Since times were brutal, she decided on bending the rules and opened the store from 1 to 5 p.m. on Sunday's.

The store remained eerily quiet; the result of a late afternoon thunderstorm that eradicated hikers, bicyclists, and other roaming nomads. Most would call it quits for the day, but Dad drilled consistency into her.

"If a tree falls in a forest and no one is around, does it make a sound?" her fifteen-year- old impetuous self, asked her father after surveying the empty store. *"Who's going to know if you close a half*

hour early other than Mom who thinks you keep time like an atomic clock?" Dad paid no attention and cupped a leathered hand around his oversized ear. A few seconds later, the cowbell on the front door dinged and goofy-looking Mr. Hunter, who had a perpetual hankering for canned sardines came rushing in. "Thank goodness you're still open!" he gushed. Dad shot her that knowing smile of his and she forever questioned whether Hunter's last-minute visit was pre-planned as a lesson of consistency in business.

She wondered who Dad would send tonight if she locked up a few minutes early. Last she heard, poor Mr. Hunter died when he was carjacked before reaching Boston and the underground insulin he needed.

Jennifer meandered to the front window and admired the familiar derriere of a man bent over a fifty-gallon trash can in the parking lot. Watching the headless man, she remembered their first encounter a couple months back near closing time.

Tall, blond, and thin, he was in his mid-twenties like her. He wore the standard getup of a ranch hand: plaid shirt with pearl snaps, wranglers, dusty boots, and a black hat. He paced nervously around the store, eying one shelf after another, pretending to browse even though the inventory was identical to every other store in the state.

The cowboy suddenly cleared his throat and rushed toward the counter.

She felt for the metal pipe underneath the register and remembered her father's words when he became too ill to work. "They will beat their swords into plowshares and their spears into pruning hooks...and here I am doing the reverse," he said in a whisper before handing her the smooth silver pipe. "I hope you never need this, but there's so many desperate folks now." His eyes began to water. "You gotta make folk without souls understand you're no pushover or they'll take everything including the wood shavings around the wood stove." She accepted the weapon hoping things would get no worse than a lone Grinch attempting to steal a crumb on Christmas Eve. The mobs that came didn't have the kind of hearts that could grow. If they had not joined a neighborhood alliance that possessed some serious firepower, the store would have been ransacked in the first month after Sun-Kissed.

"Can I help you?" she asked the cowboy in a strong voice.

He must have realized how he came across and his shoulders slumped. Tipping his hat back a bit so she could better see his boyish face, he asked in a surprisingly small voice and with some degree of hesitation, "May I have permission and fish in the barrels?"

Even though cell phones were nothing but pretty relics, Jennifer noticed how Tanned kids still carried the dead devices around in their pockets like some sort of status symbol. At least once a month some kid would show up crying about a lost phone. Then there were the annual rumors that some Tanned geezer had an I-Phone that still booted up and contained a dozen games and he planted it in the woods as a scavenger hunt.

"Fish for what? I-Phones?" she asked.

"No, for redeemable cans and bottles. They command a nickel apiece." Color rushed to his cheeks. "Soda and bottled water cost more than a bit, but people around here don't seem to mind. I notice you stock quite a bit."

When she agreed, the cowboy stopped by every few days. As the weeks progressed, she looked forward seeing him. His muscular frame and good looks were easy on the eyes, no matter the angle.

Jennifer ran a hand through her long blonde hair and tucked her white t-shirt into her jeans. She smiled thinking this was the most she ever prepped for a guy.

When she walked outside, she noticed how clean the air smelled after the rain. Better yet, the evening felt very warm, which was rare this time of year.

"Hi Cotton," she called out.

"Good evening Miss Jenny," the trash barrel echoed back.

"How's the fishing today?"

The cowboy stood up with two soda cans in one hand and transferred them into a bulging green trash bag. "Well, the boys and I caught a few keepers this morning. Largemouth bass."

She laughed. "No, I mean how many empties did you snag? We had a bus from the "Y" stop by this afternoon. Every kid must have chugged two drinks apiece given the line for the restroom."

Cotton scanned the trash bag. "Well, looks like most preferred Orange Crush if they had the five bucks. Those that didn't drank plenty of spring water." A grimace crossed his face and he reached into the bag and held up a crushed plastic bottle. "I know a guy named Ted that uses a garden hose to fill these … I can assure you it's not from any spring. Let's hope those rich kids had their shots and are blessed with good kidneys. If not, you might think of selling antibiotics too."

"Gross! What brand is it?"

The bottle disappeared into the trash bag. "Rather not say. These are tough times, and it makes people do crazy things. Who am I to judge?"

She folded her arms. "They're still my customers and I won't sell stuff that makes people sick." She took a couple steps closer and he closed the bag tight.

"Okay, I can tell you're not a fink and that's honorable. No worries. I'll wait for your next dive and take a look myself."

He cocked his head. "At least you gave me a warning."

They both stared at the trash bag.

Jennifer looked up. "We'll come back to the stalemate later. You've been coming around for a while now and haven't said much about this strange vocation."

He flashed a smile happy to change the subject. "Nothing very exciting. Just trying to eke out a living like everyone else and appreciate your generosity. At the other places I fish, people tell me to get lost or try and steal my catch after I do the dirty work of pawing through the trash. That gets me worked up because some of the stuff I dig through is pretty disgusting. No wonder people have ulcers after surveying what they eat and drink." He shook his head. "Then there's the Preppers up on the hill. I only go there when all the other barrels are dry. They don't say much but paint me with a green laser just in case I have other intentions."

"I don't get their paranoia. Once the state politicians began twisting arms, Homeland Security designated this whole area as a regional respite for hard working families—which translated means a fortress vacationland for the rich. After that things calmed down pretty quick."

He shrugged. "Crazy times makes for crazier people."

She glanced back at the store. Since her father passed away last year it had become the yardstick of her independence. "I'm sure you're sick of the question but humor me. How did you get that nickname of yours?"

He reached down into the depth of the barrel and pulled out a dented ginger-ale can. "Pretty simple. I was a towhead when I was young, so my mother called me Cotton. Guess I'm lucky she didn't pick Q-tip," he said quickly as if the joke came automatic now. "Anyways, Cotton stuck and it's a lot better than my real name."

"Which is?"

He hesitated for a moment. "Emmett, and Rufus is my middle name. I was named after my maternal grandfathers. Never met either of them, but Momma says they made quite a combo. That might be true, but you understand my predicament."

Jennifer held back a laugh. "Hey, a lot of bygone names are back in vogue now, so there's hope. If they ever let Hollywood make movies again and one of the characters is named Emmett or Rufus, you'll graduate to cool overnight. Don't feel too bad. I think most people would rather have other names. I like Jennifer okay, but wished my parents named me Victoria, even if it's too royal sounding for the Adirondack General Store. I can hear my regulars now: "Hey, Queen Victoria, what's the price on the beef jerky?" She let out a laugh. "I'm sure everyone would call me Vickie, and that has the same ring as Jenny."

He shrugged. "I like Jenny better."

She pointed at his leather boots.

"You're working at a ranch too?"

"Yeah, at High-Top." He rubbed his forehead for a moment as if lost in thought. "I was working construction up in New Hampshire when the lights went out. My momma, she knew a few ranch hands back in the day and I thought I'd give it a shot."

Momma knew a few ranch hands? She wanted to know more but like the bogus spring water planned to cycle back later. "Is the dude ranch what you thought it would be?"

He hesitated. "I like the horses. It's the guys that can be tough living with some days."

She eyed the bulging bag of bottles and cans. "Except for payday's, right? That's when there isn't enough home-made beer or hand-rolled cigarettes for all the poker games around here. I've been watching you collect all these empties. My guess is you joined some of those rambunctious cowboys one Friday night and they taught a New Hampshire boy a thing or two about losing. It reminds me of that old English proverb: A cat has nine lives. For three he plays, for three he strays and for three he stays. In your case it's plays, strays, and pays. Now you're fishing for empties to pay off the debt." She folded her arms and smiled.

Cotton rolled his sleeves back down and buttoned them. When he looked at her, the shy demeanor was gone. His eyes narrowed as he adjusted his hat downward.

"My nana loves quoting Yogi Berra. Every time I thought I had something figured out she'd say, "You can observe a lot by just watching.""

"So, did I nail it?"

He shook his head. "No, but that would make a great story. Granted, I've been tempted at erasing a few smug smiles with a hand or two; but been there, done that. Winning, Miss Jenny, is too fleeting. It feels great in the moment, and if you're really lucky maybe you can extend the streak, but there's always a day of reckoning."

"A reckoning? Sounds like the Preppers are rubbing off on you or maybe one of those Doomsday groups that parade through town chanting the end of the world is near."

He took a red kerchief out of his back pocket and wiped the stickiness from his hands. "Then call it an accounting of sorts. I believe when things get out of whack, they must be brought back into proper balance. Growing up Nana taught me if you drop a dollar in the poor box at church, you'll get it back ten times infinity because God is love. My grandmother embraces faith and lives life sunny side up." His face relaxed for a brief moment like she was standing next to him. "My momma on the other hand, prefers everything fried and is a firm believer in an eye for an eye plus ten percent for good measure. You can pass the basket at church and not add a penny, but steal one, or abandon your responsibilities, and maybe the earth won't open up and swallow you, but you're marked for a reckoning."

She took it all in and nodded.

Cotton put the lid on the barrel and stuffed the kerchief in his back pocket. "I'm trying to take the best of both views. Pay it forward when no one is watching and embrace my responsibilities. The dragons come calling when I fail."

"Hmmm, that's an interesting outlook, but a bit too deep for a Friday night." She wanted to know why he collected cans and figured the answer would come in due time. "Tell you what," she countered. "I'm locking up in a few minutes. How about we head downtown for some bathtub moonshine. Who knows? Maybe it will delay the reckoning and the dragons until tomorrow." She was surprised how the invitation gushed out.

Cotton reached into the trash bag and tossed her an empty orange soda can. Its bright label and white lettering were clean of any spillage. She had a flashback of playing miniature golf with her mom.

"I'll cash in a few on the way in case we get the munchies. I know a few guys grilling up all sorts of things.

"Sure. As long as it's not Ted."

CHAPTER FIVE

Streetlights were too much of a drain on the fragile power grid which Todd blamed after missing the turn. By the time he realized the error, he was at the intersection of Route 28, a north-south route that cut through the heart of Salem. Once a gateway into New Hampshire and a shopper's mecca with no sales tax, most of the stores were boarded up or charred remains. Consequently, the major thoroughfare now served as an alternative route for armor-plated trucks escorting supplies into the state. He looked for somewhere to make a U-turn and wished he was headed home rather than honoring this commitment.

The parking lot for the Salem Food Pantry that once housed a popular gym, appeared a quarter mile ahead and he slowed down to navigate the one-eighty. The pantry sat in darkness and the car headlights called attention to the thick steel bars on the doors and windows. The added security proved unnecessary before they were even installed, as the catastrophe quickly overwhelmed the resources of local charities. After the looting and burning by roving bands of marauders led to martial law, residents were directed to a number of armed depots for supplies.

Todd drove below the speed limit on the watch-out for hitchhikers or pissed off Burned folks that threw rocks at new cars. It had been a tough day appeasing Miller after Darlene's visit and he glanced in the rearview mirror and noticed his bloodshot eyes. Although a pragmatist like his father, he had a smidgen of his late mother's superstition and believed life had a certain flow or rhythm as natural as the circadian clock. And sometimes for unknown reasons, the cosmic internet of everything would momentarily lose connection and cause consequences ranging from the merely irritating to heart-wrenching tragedies captured on the nightly news. High-minded commentators might write the latter off as random occurrences in the ebb and flow of the human condition, but he preferred ordinary people that wrote it off as being in the wrong place at the wrong time.

He bit his lip, knowing he possessed a morbid fascination with cosmic malfunctions, but believed such dysfunctions followed a specific outlier in the day. The hypothesis led him to follow specific rules designed to merge seamlessly from unconsciousness to wakefulness each morning, like a car accelerating onto the highway.

"Tell that creep Miller you're not feeling well and come back to bed and snuggle with me," Stephanie would plead after shutting off the battery alarm clock. In the early days after Sun-Kissed, it was so cold some mornings you could see your breath.

Instead of giving into the temptation, he would give her a quick kiss and jump out of bed. Stephanie would react by mocking him as the poster boy for OCD. What she threw at him next as an exclamation point depended upon what was within reach: pillows, books, slippers, candles, and water and wine glasses both empty and full. Sometimes the blowback would slow his progress, but he never surrendered and maintained a strict morning regimen: up at six followed by an established sequence: shower, shave, dress, and breakfast. Mental agility also played a pivotal role in the routine and he filled his mind during the ritual with chess like exercises pertaining to the day ahead, such as trade scenarios or corporate strategy. At seven o'clock sharp, he would briefly study himself in the hall mirror and steel his resolve before leaving for the office.

A vintage Chevy truck sporting a *Rolling Stones* hot lips logo on the tailgate passed on the left before cutting back too soon, forcing him to brake hard. The insult reminded him of the starving pack of dogs that ran through a busy intersection the week before causing havoc. Everything after that vignette became tainted. Even his portfolio suffered losses that day.

The traffic light up ahead let the erratic driver through, but skipped yellow altogether and turned red. Todd slammed on the brakes and

ONLY DEAD LEAVES FALL

while the seatbelt tugged snugly across his chest, it did not catch his thoughts.

The winter temper tantrum brought heavy wet snow and high winds. Inching his way home from the office, he berated himself for the lack of preparation and pictured his brown leather boots safe and dry in the hall closet.

When the car slid to a stop in front of the white split entry, he studied the two-foot-high snowbank which the snowplows built in front of the driveway. The BMW was newly minted so he hesitated barreling through the white cement. Instead, he sat there with the defroster on high and considered his options, all of which meant ruining his three-hundred-dollar tasseled loafers. In the process, he eyed two sets of footprints leading from the front door, down the driveway and terminating at the snowbank. Even in the storm he could make out some of the details: one small set with toes angled slightly outward which belonged unmistakably to Stephanie. The other pair were much larger. Who was the male interloper?

He rolled the window down and the wind blew a handful of snow across the dashboard, sweetening the new car smell. A moment ago, he would have rolled up the window and used a napkin from the glove compartment to pat the plastic dry. Instead, he sat flash frozen in place while the wipers worked overtime.

A strong gust rocked the car. He opened the car door and let the chime beat its warning for a good minute before shutting the car off. Abandoning the vehicle in the street, he began scaling the man-made mountain and immediately sank up to his knees. He repeated the frozen quicksand procedure a few more times before reaching the driveway. By now his feet ached and he moved parallel to the offensive tracks, adding his own steps in the opposite direction. At the front stairs, he knelt and inspected the stranger's set and noticed how the intruder's boot had a crescent moon impression embedded in the heel.

When he managed to open the front door, he found the electricity out and wondered if the storm was the culprit or the utility company shut the power off in an abundance of caution. Even before kicking off the wet shoes or retrieving a flashlight, he knew Stephanie had left. They had been struggling to make the marriage work for the better part of three years. When they first met, electricity flowed like oxygen, they held hands constantly and finished each-other's sentences. Now, electricity was synonymous with scarcity, their hands were paralyzed by their sides and they spoke fluent silence.

The house suddenly became much too small and he quickly slipped on snow boots and explored the driveway. The set of departing footprints were disappearing with the blowing snow and he concentrated on trampling the male set of tracks first with their insulting crescent moons. When he reached the street, he turned around and erased what was left of his wife's.

The wild wind bit at his eyes and he could not extinguish which tears belonged to Stephanie from those extracted by the ice whips. Looking skyward, he wished he could take all the snow and pitch it skyward so it could fall like a super-sized bottle of white-out and erase everything. Maybe then he and Steph could repeat the three one syllable words that melded their hearts before God. Minus that, all he had left was a blizzard of pain with no place to store it all.

He stumbled into the garage and retrieved a snow shovel and began methodically clearing the driveway so there would be no trace of those tracks of betrayal. If he could have located the pickaxe, he would have gladly worked on taking up the entire driveway and utterly destroy the departing path of betrayal.

The blare of a horn ended the flashback. He floored the accelerator intent on leaving the whole mess behind. The lingering pain, however, in never identifying who escorted his wife from their house remained forever in the passenger seat of his thoughts.

The road began a slow curve and he finally located Sunset Drive. He drove slowly past a long row of upscale houses on alert for the private security details neighborhoods like this one employed, which did not take nicely to visitors. What triggered the massive dysfunction today? Was it the heated call with Brad that conjured up this ghost from the past? Now he would see her for the third time today! This last visit was Darlene's classic style of overreach. He planned a quick visit and avoid dredging up the past.

Number thirty stood out from the other houses due to the radiance of solar powered lanterns. After navigating the long driveway, he parked behind a black Tesla. "What am I doing here?" he whispered and looked again at the scrap piece of paper she jotted the address on. He spent the day throwing it away and retrieving it. *So, what if she calls me tomorrow upset that I never showed? Like I care?* Their painful past overwhelmed any hope of having a normal relationship. A shiver ran across his chest guessing Darlene probably had a closet full of voodoo dolls of him too. The fight or flight response kicked in and he found his hand putting the car in reverse.

The retreat didn't get far when twin spotlights on either side of the front door suddenly came to life.

"Bagged!" he muttered and shut the car off.

The red front door on the massive blue colonial flew open and Darlene came out and began descending the stairs as if reading his intentions. Todd quickly exited the car and hurried up the driveway and noticed she wore the same outfit from their previous two encounters. Before he could wave hello, a man come bounding out of the house and appeared so intent on catching up with Darlene that he skipped the last stair altogether and jumped to the sidewalk.

"You were always so punctual," she called out, "that I began thinking I might have to call your boss and see what's keeping you." Mercifully, she only gifted him a quick hug this time before turning to introduce her out-of-breath escort. "Todd, I'd like you to meet my good friend and financial marvel Carl Michael. He's a partner at Toole, Cresch and Shaw in Boston."

Todd sized up the muscular, six-foot, middle-aged man with a deep tan and crooked smile and gave him a firm handshake. The dark blue suit looked first class, but he spied white socks married to beat-up brown shoes. Fashion faux aside, he hoped this was her significant other. *If so, I'll buy him a pair of nice wingtips in appreciation.*

Darlene monitored his reaction and put her arm around Carl. She gave him a quick squeeze. "If he weren't a whizz of a stockbroker, I'd marry him," she said with a quick laugh, "but, I'm afraid he'd put me out to bid."

"Fat chance!" Carl boomed in reply. "Why, if she were a stock, the investment research firm Eveningstar..." He stopped and his face slightly contorted like he forgot what words came next. He let out a short laugh. "Guess I'm a real lightweight when it comes to champagne!" He winked at Darlene and then touched Todd's arm. "What I meant to say is *Morningstar* would rate this lady a five-star investment that pays handsome dividends. She's not only smart but has quite a backbone. Any man would be lucky to have her."

"Aw," she replied and patted his arm.

Todd took in the smarmy lovefest as Carl reached into his vest pocket and offered a business card. The gold embossed lettering was brighter than the solar lantern.

"Our mutual friend tells me you were in the middle of a deal when you ran into her." The broker winked. "To hear her tell the story, you nearly knocked her out."

He kept his reply to a nervous laugh.

Darlene slapped him on the arm. "Now who's exaggerating?"

Carl nodded. "Maybe a tad." He looked at Todd. "What I won't kid about is the market these days. It's certainly not for the faint of heart. Any special areas of focus?"

Todd pointed at his stomach. "It may look like I attend trade shows featuring start-ups trying to compete with those horrific ready-to-eat meals, but you'd be wrong. The truth is, I prefer technology. Everyone is bent on rebuilding a new consumer driven world, but there's only continued disappointment. I'm not interested in the build back better philosophy because there's a ton of opportunity in reclaiming yesterday's infrastructure."

"Tell that to the ranks of desperados that want another revolution," Carl replied. His face turned inquisitive. "Capitalism rewards those willing to take risks. That's what this republic was built on and makes even more sense now. Getting off my soapbox for a minute, what's your favorite stock holding?"

I'm certainly not going to embarrass myself and mention XRE, he thought. "It's a no-brainer, really. I've done well with Canseco. They have been grinding out transformers in record time and the stock doubled over the past year. Things might slowly be getting back to normal here, but the demand in Europe and Asia is immense."

Carl nodded in agreement. "Conseku is a winner for sure." He touched Darlene's arm. "You have a modest amount of that stock in your portfolio. Next time we meet let's take another look. Maybe we should increase your exposure based on Todd's elevator speech, or should I say sidewalk sale?"

Todd smiled but wondered why this supposed whizz with two first names mispronounced the popular stock. While others might write it off to the large number of companies being tracked, maybe the champagne really did mess with his head. *If he's this buzzed, maybe I can do a little mining of my own.*

"Any hot tip you'd like to share with a friend of a friend?"

The crooked smile disappeared, and he turned serious. "I don't want to risk this timely introduction by offering some low hanging fruit." He took a step forward and Todd could smell stale tobacco. "As a favor to Darlene, I'd be willing to analyze your portfolio against some new modeling software we just developed. The analysis may provide you with a fresh perspective and some additional options. The cost is very minimal."

Darlene tugged on Carl's arm. "Do you ever stop trolling for clients? Todd's had a long day."

Carl laughed and checked his watch. "You know me well. I could drone on all night but don't want to risk upsetting a valued client and dear friend." He took a step back and looked her up and down. "And I wish it wasn't in that order." He kissed her on the cheek and held both her hands. "I'm running terribly late for a dinner meeting."

Darlene shot Todd a look and smirked. "Seems I've been having that effect on everyone today."

Todd offered his hand and noticed for the second time Carl's rough skin. He and Darlene watched as the broker walked to his car and appeared confused trying to unlock the door.

Darlene snickered. "You'd think he stole that car. Carl may be a genius when it comes to making money, but in other areas, not so much. He sure loves his toys."

"And that doesn't include you?" he asked before he could stop himself.

"Ah, there's the boy I know." She grabbed his arm, and they began moving toward the front door.

He scanned the front of the house and the manicured landscaping. *In the wild west of the new order, how could the poor girl he cast off so many years ago afford all this?*

CHAPTER SIX

Darlene escorted him into a large unfurnished living room. The silent flames from a gas fireplace cast a warm glow against the highly glossed hardwood floors. The crazy lady he bumped into this morning and the fast-talking flower girl at the office now appeared as a sophisticated and financially secure host.

Maybe twenty-five years is a deep enough hole to swallow up the past after all, he thought while gazing at the woman that could still turn heads. The sudden temptation made his throat tighten. He let out a small cough hoping to hurl the sentiment into the blue flames licking the fake log.

"I'm impressed Darlene," he said more to clear his mind than a compliment. "You've done very well for yourself."

Her eyes glanced around the room. "Considering how the rest of the world is faring, I've been extremely fortunate. I tease Carl lot, but it's his money skills that allowed me to afford this wonderful neighborhood. Now I can have some fun and get rid of the stark white walls and make it my home." She walked a few feet to a wall featuring a myriad of switches and dials and began experimenting turning on the recessed lights and ceiling fans. "Carl hasn't taken on a new client in some time," she said studying a dimmer switch, "but if you'd like, I'll call in a favor. He's putting together an exclusive opportunity regarding the Bad Creek Hydroelectric plant in South Carolina. When it comes back online, the return will be substantial. I can tell him to adopt you and let you invest."

Adopt? The word felt like a knife in the chest. *I banned the word from my vocabulary and yet she uses it without blushing… And why is she being so nice to me? I certainly don't deserve it, but would love exploring the opportunity.*

Darlene turned the overhead lights on high and watched him squint. "I also promise if you invest with Carl, you won't be chasing your advisor from a pet store or fear that boss of yours anymore."

The offer echoed around the empty room further amplifying her generosity despite how he treated her then and now. Trying to rationalize why was a riddle and he filed it away for additional thought. At the same time, his lust for gold nixed the plan of making this a ten-minute visit.

"That's very kind of you, Darlene," he said with newfound enthusiasm. "I appreciate the offer and yes, I'd be interested in continuing the conversation with him."

"Just remember Carl hates procrastinators. If he says it's a sure thing don't insult him by over-thinking it too much. That's why he stopped by this evening. He wanted my go-ahead."

He let his eyes wander around the vaulted ceiling while a nagging internal voice screamed, "*fire Brad tomorrow!*"

"This space is incredible," he continued and looked out a bank of windows and admired the golf-course-quality front lawn. "If I knew this house was on the market, I might have claimed squatter's rights. Next time I see Bob Olsen, I'll give him an earful."

"Who?" Darlene asked coming next to him.

He shot her a surprised look and pointed outside. "The guy with his mug on the sold sign? I went to college with Bob. I bet he drove you nuts with his interruptions."

Darlene nodded at the sign and stifled a yawn. "Thank goodness for Tricia. She's my new admin and keeps people like Bob at arm's length, especially these days when everyone is on steroids trying to make a buck." She pointed a finger at him. "You could use someone like her as a first line of defense with Miller. Just don't get any funny ideas about stealing her from me."

A halo of flashing blue lights appeared and they watched a police car speed by. "If Siri or Alexis were still around, I'd think they misinterpreted my comment about stealing Tricia and called it in," she added with a laugh.

"Touché! It's a constant worry though, isn't it? I bet if we stand here a few more minutes, we'll see shadows running on the street carrying a bunch of stuff." He shook his head. "Ever since martial law ended chaos is percolating again. At least when the National Guard were out patrolling, the hoodlums were afraid of getting shot. Now the sludge of society thinks if they get caught the reward is a bed, three squares and medical including dental."

"That sounds like a typical Tanned with the same bluster about law and order we've heard since Nixon. We both know the poor are just looking for some scratch to help their families survive."

"And money for their drug habits because it numbs the pain. C'mon Darlene! Open your eyes. You flog Nixon, but the government has more shovel ready jobs since Roosevelt. If people want to feed their families and heat their homes, they can get a job."

Her hands shot to her hips. "The majority of those jobs don't pay enough to cover rent at one of the federal dorms, never mind the exorbitant cost of electricity now. Is it any wonder most people are still scrounging for firewood so they can heat their homes? Plus, you have to be connected to get one of those plum jobs. Sun-Kissed didn't change that none."

Todd nodded and smirked. "Keep humming your liberal tune but look around. You're as Tanned as me." He began meandering around the room. "Let's drop the political stuff. Do you have enough furniture for this place?"

She followed him at a distance. "For the most part, if it isn't stolen by those crack-head desperadoes that scare you so. I may have to pick up a few pieces, but that shouldn't be too hard. Everything that isn't nailed down is on sale."

"True, but the really good stuff disappeared years ago. Now it's mostly worn-out junk," he said pointing outside, "or in the process of being relocated. Here's hoping that large opportunity with Carl pays off big so you can afford what you want." He looked at a twenty-four-pane window on the opposite side of the room. "What made you move back to Salem anyways?"

"Well, you know by now how much I despise clichés, but must admit life is a circle. After we broke up…" She stopped and moved sideways as if wanting more space. "I fell in love with microbiology at NYU, then did postgrad work at Cornell. After that I worked in monoclonal antibody research for some of the leading biotech companies. It was exciting chasing breakthroughs in cancer therapies until the solar storm changed my focus with the resurgence of infectious diseases." She looked at him. "Like you, I want the world to find yesterday."

"Well, your work sounds more interesting than being married to a calculator."

"Sure, as long as you like Boston, Research Triangle Park, San Diego and the Bay Area. Though, if I were adventurous, I'd move to Singapore, Bangalore, or Beijing where demand for expertise is high and the power grid is good. Who knows? Maybe I'll go abroad next. In the meantime, I have a nice opportunity for some consulting work nearby.

"I'm very impressed."

Darlene put her hand to her mouth. "All this time and I haven't offered you a drink! Where are my manners?" She walked across the room to a lonely glass tea cart in front of French doors leading to a red-brick patio.

Todd followed her and discovered the cart held enough top shelf liquor to support a family of four for a month. *And she gives me grief?*

"Is your mother still living on Main Street?" he inquired carefully like he was skipping stones and this one might be too heavy. "I'm surprised I haven't run into her." He could hear the rock go kerplunk.

She cocked her head and gave him a quick look like she wanted to check his expression. "Well, my mother's been in a nursing home since she fell and broke her hip two years ago. Otherwise, she would be living here with me. Her house needs a lot of work and the state has a lien on the place. I've been helping her out financially, but with the upside-down nature of things; the nursing home wants her out so they can move in some rich sucker willing to pay more. You'd think for the monthly price they charge she'd have gold threaded sheets and prime rib every night." She sighed. "The truth is Mom lives in flannel pajamas because half the time there are no clean sheets and has cornflakes on Sunday for a treat. Other than that, I have no strong opinion about the overpriced senior camp." She bent over and inspected the inventory. "Do you prefer red or white wine or maybe a shot of—"

"No, thank-you." The reply came automatic and rapid.

Darlene looked up puzzled. "How about a beer then? I think the previous owner left one in the fridge, but it's one of those no-name brands that gives you a headache instead of a buzz."

"I guess people will do anything to numb things." He waved her off. "Thanks, but I gave it all up."

She continued pawing through the tall bottles of vodka, gin, whiskey, and wine. "How long ago?"

He hesitated even if proud of the self-discipline. "It's been a while."

"Really? Ex-drinkers I know brag about the number of days they've been dry," she replied with a wink.

"It's okay to say alcoholic, Darlene. I've come to terms with it." He surveyed the tea cart looking for an alternative. "Seltzer water would be great."

"Hope you like lemon flavored." She poured some in a tall glass and added ice from a walnut bucket, before helping herself to a generous glass of merlot.

"So how about you?" she asked looking up. "Where's home and who's in your life besides the ogre you work for?"

Todd felt the probe. He considered a measured response while taking a sip of the seltzer and feeling the carbonation sting the back of his throat. "Well, I'm still in Salem as you discovered this morning." He took another drink before continuing. "Married for ten years. We divorced a short time ago."

"A short time ago?" she repeated. "For a man that lives by the numbers, you are pretty vague. So, any children? Try to be exact."

He avoided looking at her mid-section as any reply would be one short. She's so good with these zingers, she could make it big as a lawyer or comic. "No children," he replied quickly. "My wife and I were too career focused."

She studied his face like an abstract painting she didn't understand. "Another safe answer. If I hadn't met Miller this morning, I would think you're working for the CIA. Your boss not so much."

They both smiled at each other as if expecting a bell to announce the beginning of the next round.

"Ambition was always your first love," she said with a quick jab. "So, what does Stephanie do? Wait! Let me guess," she said pointing at her temple, "I bet she's in banking, or was until the ATM's were replaced with rows of colorful abacuses manned by tellers that had their smiles repossessed."

He held his glass high. "Now there's an image I can drink too." He shrugged. "You're half-right, though. My ex was in nursing until she came down with a terrible case of the gimme's. In her case, I'm afraid it's terminal."

"Says one side of the coin. I'd bet this house that she has a different take." She retreated into the wine for a long sip before coming up for air. "Sounds like bad karma."

He bit his lip. *I'd be willing to put up with an inquisition to learn more about Carl.*

"I bet she's blonde," Darlene continued.

"Actually, dark brunette, when she's not coloring it." *I'm tired of playing defense,* he thought and stared at her ring finger. "How about you? Married, divorced or just toying with Carl so he keeps impressing you with results?"

Darlene's eyes narrowed contemplating the multiple-choice question. "Actually, none of the above. Guess I'm that strange breed that takes intimacy seriously and learned the hard way it has consequences." The matter-of-fact tone sounded as automatic as his replies about drinking and divorce.

Another gulp of the seltzer went down the wrong pipe and he coughed.

"Take a good look around and rest assured I earned all of this. No matter my gratitude, Carl works for me." She stopped and let the pause grow intense before she gifted him with a slight smile. "Did you get your boss his report?"

Todd smiled in relief with the change of topics. "Just an installment, I'm afraid. Since everything requires hard copies these days, it's a wonder he doesn't give me one of those coupon books so I can keep a record of each payment."

She ignored the comment and came closer with her glass raised. "After all these years, is there anything you'd like to say?" She fixed her gaze on him.

Don't look back, he wanted to reply. He raised his glass. "I apologize I came without a housewarming gift. At a minimum I would like to toast your beautiful new house and wish you continued success."

Darlene held her glass in front of his. "That's rather bland. Let's toast to installment payments until the debt is paid in full."

They clinked glasses and Todd took a long drink wrapping his tongue around the bubbles, wishing he could find alcohol hiding in the fizz. He imagined inserting a straw in a keg of beer later.

Darlene retreated across the room and turned off the gas fireplace. "After twenty-five years I see you three times in one day. I would call that serendipitous, wouldn't you?" She let out a short laugh. "I usually only get to use that word in crossword puzzles. I hoped we could have dinner and catch up, but a last-minute commitment came up."

"No problem," he replied perhaps a bit too quickly as he never planned for a long visit. Nevertheless, he wanted more info on Carl and how he managed her portfolio but could not think of a good way to redirect the conversation without looking greedy.

Darlene led him to the front door. "Before you go…" She hesitated and eyed the floor. "What should I call you now?" She asked and then waved the question away. "We'll figure that out as we go along. For now, humor me and sign my guest log. It's a tradition wherever I move. My friends sign the book so I can remember all the good times when I move again." She glanced at the paper. "Looks like you'll be the first one to sign as Carl forgot. He will be so jealous," she remarked, handing him the book and a cheap pen. "It's an official record, so make certain you sign your full name, sweetie."

Todd thought it an odd request, but given the hostess, not unusual. He finished the entry and laughed. "Should I include my social security number too?"

She examined the signature and shook her head. "That won't be necessary because I know where to find you." She took the book and pen away and before he could move, kissed him softly on the lips.

"You still taste the same," she said stepping back.

Todd could taste the wine from her lips which mixed with the smell of her perfume pulled him back to a time he worked most of his life to forget.

He awkwardly said goodnight and walked to his car listening for the front door to shut behind him.

It never did.

CHAPTER SEVEN

Darlene held her breath as a hulk of a man checked for her name on a clipboard. Satisfied, he escorted her down a staircase to the *Best Kept Secret Speakeasy* located in the cellar of a local entrepreneur. Despite the crowd, she quickly spotted Brad sitting by himself in a corner, cradling a calculator in one hand and a whiskey tumbler in the other. He looked forty pounds heavier than the snapshot she received from the sorry slug of a janitor that cleaned his office and charged outrageous fees for a little reconnaissance.

It had been a long day and she fought the temptation of blowing off tonight's meeting. Back on-set, a six-jet whirlpool tub in the master bathroom waited. She longed for the hot pulsating water but confronted this last-minute temptation as a sign she anticipated every detail, even the desire to reschedule. Steeling herself against a mountain of procrastination twenty-five years high, she tightened her grip on a black leather clutch and thought how this ruse depended not only on guile but intense desire. In preparing for the ruse, Carl introduced her to the infamous "bag lady of the Merrimack Valley." The hip granny had so much premium makeup and designer clothes in two rolling suitcases, they should have been housed in a Brink truck. The black-market legend reported pink was the hottest color this season. "I thought green was the only color people cared about anymore," she commented before buying the ultra-pink lipstick along with a red satin blouse and black skirt. *So much for the five hundred in seed money she borrowed from Carl.*

Brad slipped the calculator into his briefcase and glanced up at a baseball game on a television set suspended from the ceiling. Even though the volume was off, a dozen guys at the bar provided the usual garden variety of vulgarities whenever the Red Sox played the Yankees.

When the rowdy bar fand cheered a strikeout, she took it as her cue and strutted across the room, hating high heels for the hundredth time today.

"Mr. Ponzell?" she asked in a sultry voice, remembering how she cracked up her friends as a teenager when she mimicked Marilyn Monroe.

The greeting worked its magic and the startled man almost dropped his glass. "Darlene?" he stammered and stood up so fast he nearly knocked over the small table.

She extended her hand and smiled after feeling a wimpy grip.

He grabbed a chair a few feet away and placed it close to his. "Please drop the formalities and just call me Brad," he said with a wink, "though some of my clients call me Magic." His face lit up with a camera-ready smile he must have perfected in grammar school pictures. "What can I get you to drink?" he asked while conducting a not too subtle body scan.

She bit her lip to keep from laughing at a skit worthy of *Saturday Night Live. A no name beer in here would cost twenty bucks and a glass of wine at least thirty.*

"Maybe later, as I don't mix business and pleasure." She sat down and continued profiling her prey. The gray suit would look fine on a regular sized guy, but not clothing an oversized block head with bulging eyes that looked like a relative of *Sponge Bob Square Pants.* Brad even managed to outdo the animated series character by wearing a gold stud earring in his left ear that really popped against his fuzzy burnt orange hair. She wondered the strength of the peroxide needed to achieve such unique color. *Where did he procure it in this busted economy? From an embalmer?*

"Sorry about playing phone tag yesterday," he said touching her hand lightly before flashing his pearly caps. After three seconds his smile evaporated and he reached for the leather briefcase next to the chair.

"Thank you for making time on such short notice," she began. "As mentioned, I'm looking for immediate assistance and a possible long-term relationship." She wished she had a radar gun handy.

She wasn't disappointed. Brad brought the heat and placed a brochure on the table. "I respect a client that doesn't waste time with small talk. That's why I think you'll be impressed with my firm. Before I explain why, are the funds we will discuss unencumbered?"

"What do you mean?"

"Sorry for the legalese, but it's a standard question. You teased me on the phone and provided few details. I need assurance you're not under any federal or state audits or involved in a civil suit. It's been a circus with the Feds seizing property under the Revitalization Act not to mention all the lawsuits since the world went dark."

She shook her head. *The feds wouldn't waste their resources sucking on the bones of a goldfish like me. As far as lawsuits were concerned, Nico Pappas doesn't know where I live.*

"Can I assume your funds are in U.S dollars and not the IOU's some states have been issuing?"

"Of course." *Blah, blah, blah,* she thought. *He sounds like Charlie Brown's teacher.* Looking away, she counted three dozen souls in the unsanctioned establishment. If she tallied up their cover charges and bar bills, Mom could make rent for the next couple months.

"Great, just had to get that out of the way." Brad pointed at the brochure. "My office is just up the street. I have tons of literature there on different product offerings; stocks, bonds and some special structured programs. This booklet provides an overview."

She stared at the dark green brochure with *Embassy Financial Services* in gold lettering and punctuated with small dollar signs running along the bottom of the cover.

He took a sip of his whiskey. "I can't wait for everything to get back on-line, because dragging all this paper around is a real pain in the butt." He stroked the brochure like it was man's best friend without the hassle. "Why don't we put the technicalities aside for a bit and have a friendly drink first? That way, I'll better understand your situation. You mentioned it was urgent on the phone, and we can meet tomorrow and formalize things. I have some of the finest coffee on the east coast and enjoy sharing it with my clients. Who knows?" he chuckled. "If we get a bit buzzed tonight, the java will clear our heads in the morning." He flashed another toothy smile. "I know for a fact they make the best margaritas here. Last time a client wanted top shelf—"

"Like I said business first," she said interrupting. "I'm interested in discussing something that promises high returns with minimal risk." She pushed her chair back and slowly crossed her long legs so he could notice, which of course he did. She fought the urge to roll her eyes.

"Do you know Todd Dolan?" she asked like a trainer trying to get an animal's attention.

The name immediately recaptured his attention. "Know him? Besides being a client, he's my ex-brother-in law. Don't tell me he referred you?" He let out a short laugh that made his square head shake.

"Todd and I go way back. I guess he never mentioned me?"

Brad snickered. "He isn't into sharing much of anything. If the situation were reversed, I certainly would have told him about you!" His eyes started wandering again."

"That's sweet." She touched his arm. "I learned a lot about the meaning of relationships with Todd and what happens when key ingredients are missing." She let it hang there. "Fidelity is key. Do you agree?"

"Absolutely." His eyes scanned her face.

"That's good, but I think it's strange Todd remains a client given the plight of your sister."

"You know Stephanie too?"

"Let's just say I know about the ugly divorce."

The easy smile disappeared, and he blinked a couple times. "This is an odd way to start a conversation about *your* financial goals, but okay I'll bite. Todd and my sister had a few good years before they suffered through their own solar flare up like half of all couples do." He glanced up at the tv as the camera focused on a man holding a banner that read John 3:16. "I've been married a couple times myself before I finally found my soulmate." He pointed towards the television. "Any relationship has its ups and downs. Ask the Red Sox. They had to wait eighty-six years before breaking the Curse of the Bambino. Now they're playing under lights again after being limited to day games for years. As far as Todd is concerned, sure I lost a brother-in-law, but kept a valuable client, even though he drives me nuts most days."

"Does your sister see it that way?"

He laughed and spun the liquid in his glass. "She got a nice settlement, even though she's still whining about it. I keep reminding her a good chunk of the money she received was based on what I did for her ex. So, from my perspective it's all good." Brad stretched out his arms wide. "Business is business as the saying goes."

Darlene reached across the table and using her index finger traced the top of his glass. Brad quickly became mesmerized. "I'm glad you can be so unsentimental because your ex-brother-in law and valued client plans on divorcing you too."

The warning broke the spell and the heavy man pushed back from the table and let out a belly laugh. "You think you're telling me something new, Darlene? Why, he's got more wind than a nor'easter and been threatening to leave since the day I took him on, but he's no fool. Todd loves greenbacks and I know where they're printed." He leaned towards her. "If you let me, I can do the same for you."

"Your confidence is admirable, but unfortunately, Todd will be trading up soon."

Brad looked at the tv in time to see the Red Sox get a man on first. "How do you know?"

"Todd's going to transfer a good portion of his portfolio shortly. When he does, you can take it as a sign he's thinking of moving the rest. Be prepared to kiss all the transaction and management fees goodbye."

A couple of businessmen in dark suits at a nearby table began yelling at the television. The sudden excitement seemed to irritate Brad. He took another sip of the whiskey and slammed the glass down on the brochure. "You're a prospective client, and this isn't a good start. To be honest, you're beginning to upset me a bit. So, why are you telling me any of this and how does it concern opening an account?"

"Let's just say Todd's needy past is catching up with his comfortable present. Since he has a nasty habit of betraying the people he should cherish, I thought you should protect yourself."

"How considerate given our long association." he replied sarcastically. "He can move his account tomorrow and suffer the consequences of meager returns. Out of sheer curiosity, though, what do you propose I do?"

"Turn the tables on him and take advantage of a unique proposition I'm offering."

He pointed to the tv. "One of baseball's biggest issues is the length of the game. They're too long—same with your elevator pitch. So, get to the point." He picked up his glass and Darlene noticed the round stain it left on the gaudy brochure.

"We both agree loyalty is important in a business relationship, and I have a small request that will build both." She opened her clutch and took out an envelope folded in half and placed it over the stain. "I need you to change the beneficiary on Todd's account tomorrow."

The finance guy smirked. "Let me guess, you're his next of kin too?"

"No, but his son is."

"Are we talking about the same guy? Todd doesn't have any kids."

She leaned in. "I'm afraid, that's another little secret he's kept from you and your sister."

He let out a low whistle. "Stephanie always wondered about all the late nights at the office but never had any proof. And I defended the bum!" He rubbed his flat forehead. "I'd give anything to see him changing diapers."

"Too late. His son is way past toilet training."

"Why? How old is he?"

"Emmett just turned twenty-five—"

"Wait a second," he said cutting her off. "Twenty-five months plus the pregnancy brings us back three years." He looked away. "I thought they were okay back then."

"For an advisor, you should listen more. By my math, we're talking three hundred months."

His face went blank for a moment. "You mean he's twenty-five *years* old? Are you kidding me? That's a lifetime ago!" He waved her off. "Look, I'm sorry if he got you in trouble at the beginning of the century and didn't live up to his responsibilities. But how dare you waltz into my life thinking you can use me in some sick scheme of yours." He reached for his briefcase. "You need a lawyer, not a financial advisor."

She nodded and pushed the folded envelope and the brochure toward him. Brad took the bait and after depositing the marketing material back into his briefcase, took the sheet of paper out of the envelope and studied it.

"Wow, I'm impressed you were diligent enough to even use our company form." He scrutinized the paper. "The signature looks pretty good for a forgery."

"It's not a forgery, it's his signature."

"So, you're a notary too? Kudos on the timing as everything is being paper processed like the old days." He slipped the paper back in the envelope and placed it on the table in front of her. "It's a remarkable effort, but I wonder what funny weed you're smoking thinking I would go along with this? Todd may be an immoral jerk, but I'm not losing my license over him."

His fat hand suddenly grabbed her knee. "Now, I suggest you accept that strong drink I offered and use all your assets in making me forget this unfortunate conversation. Maybe you can persuade me not to call the cops."

Darlene pushed his hand away. "As usual, it all comes down to choices, Brad. Will you help me with this small transaction or risk me making a call too?" She let the threat hang in the air. "Tell me, does Marcy know about that despicable underground paper called the Tablet?" She opened her purse again and pulled out a small piece of paper and gave it a once over. "I don't know if your wife will understand all the abbreviated lingo in your personal ads. If not, I'm sure she would understand the steamy pictures I have of you and Loretta at Hampton beach. I doubt they will join the family portrait on the mantle anytime soon."

She pushed the envelope in his direction. "Just process the change, sweetie. And if Todd asks your advice about investing in a hydropower plant, just blow him off."

Brad opened his mouth, but no words came out.

Almost home, she thought. "Do you think Loretta will make a good step mom to Bradley junior when you see him every other weekend? Maybe your ex-brother-in-law-and valued client will let you sleep on his couch and cry in your no-name beer. Oh, I forgot Todd doesn't drink so you'll have to get buzzed on that fine coffee of yours if you can still afford any."

"Let me get this straight. I met you like ten minutes ago and this whole meeting was about blackmailing me?" his voice squeaked. "I paid your hundred-dollar cover charge for this mugging?"

"Blackmail? I find that word awfully harsh." She extended her arms wide. "Like my new friend says: business is business. I'm just putting a deal together. Can't you see I'm working the close?"

Brad massaged the back of his thick neck. "I don't understand why you're doing this. Sue him and get what's coming to the kid; if that's what you still call the *little* man."

She reached over and grabbed his hand tightly and squeezed. "Todd would rather part with his left arm than recognize his son. There's a lot more to this story, but I won't bore you with the details. This is nothing more than an insurance policy in case his blindness is permanent."

"Don't treat me like a simpleton. This isn't about insurance. No, it's a mother-load payout to the beneficiary if he croaks. Is that in your plan too? Because if he finds out he can just change the beneficiary back."

"Brad, I'm touched by your heartfelt sentiment for a guy that pillaged your sister's life and is about to kick you to the curb." She took a deep breath. "I'm just protecting my son's interests and a father should understand that. So, process the change by midnight tomorrow. Make sure no confirmation is mailed."

"Do you know how much his account is worth?"

Darlene decided a simple smile would suffice.

"Of course, you do, and I don't want to know how." He thought for a long moment. "You said he's leaving me, so why go to this trouble?"

"Worry about your own future. In the meantime, answer none of his questions about outside investments."

"And if I do all this, what's in it for me?"

"Depends on what you want. Besides some shredded pictures, we can explore a new type of mutual fund—and the "d" is silent. You won't have to run any more of those pitiful ads."

Brad thought for half a second and then smiled. "I'll need twenty thousand for that level of risk, and a prospectus on the mutual fun." He moved his chair closer.

"Nice try, but you don't seem to understand what happens if you don't cooperate. So, while the processing fee is non-negotiable, I can address the other." She grabbed the lapel of his jacket and kissed him hard despite the fact his wet and fleshy lips almost made her gag. When she released him, he sat back in the chair looking a bit stunned, but still hungry. Darlene reached for his unfinished whiskey and drank the rest hoping to sterilize her mouth. When she looked again at Brad, she knew his brains were sufficiently scrambled.

"In the meantime, don't do anything stupid. Tell Todd or anyone else about any of this and you'll end up living in the Spicket River tent city. I also have a friend that's well connected and owes me a favor. Delay processing the change and the only financial instruments you'll ever sell again will be bingo tickets at the senior citizen center."

The patrons began screaming as the Sox loaded the bases and Darlene smiled. "Look around. Everyone is so into the game I could pickpocket all of them, but I'm not after their gold. Sure, I could have contacted you years ago, but patience is a virtue and Sun-Kissed provided the opportunity." She smiled and pointed at the television. "Nothing like a rally in the bottom of the ninth."

She got up and almost reached the parking lot before throwing up what little she had in her stomach. When she was done, she searched her purse for the prescription bottle with the little tablets that always calmed her nerves. She threw a tablet in her mouth and tilted her head back as the pill skipped down her dry throat.

The dark sky was minus stars. *How fitting,* she thought.

CHAPTER EIGHT

Opening the door, Todd noticed the red light blinking rapidly on the retro answering machine. He winced thinking it might be another invitation from Darlene. Instead, Carl Michael left his phone number, very interested in continuing their discussion.

"No wonder he's successful," he said. He took off his jacket and hung it in its proper place in the hall closet. He recalled Darlene's shocking offer of soliciting Carl on his behalf and rechecked the time stamp on the message and confirmed he was still at her house when the call came in. The message crystallized the contrast between a professional like Carl versus the fly-by-the-seat-of-your-pants operation Brad ran. It would be one thing if his ex-brother-in-law differentiated himself through communication and customer satisfaction, but they were alien concepts to him. The same was true about forecasting the market. Flipping a coin produced better results and XRE was a case study. Brad convinced him good times were moments away, but the stock fell ten percent after the highly anticipated reorganization plan underwhelmed the analysts.

He poured a glass of club soda and collapsed on the leather couch. The manifestation of Darlene's financial success nagged at his thoughts and underscored the old adage of getting what you pay for. She secured top shelf financial management and enjoyed a bumper crop of rewards. By contrast, he cultivated a small garden. He would call Carl in the morning and see what the wizard could do for him. Maybe he could get in on the large opportunity Darlene mentioned.

He stretched out on the couch and took a deep breath envisioning his mind's tachometer beginning to redline. If he did not relax soon, he would never find sleep tonight.

Todd stared at the ceiling and found Darlene's face surfing the plaster. No matter the venue today, she was a step ahead of him. *She stymied me twenty-five years ago with her sharp doublespeak and has upped her game since.*

Reaching for the *Eagle-Tribune* on the coffee table, he intended on finding a minute's peace by focusing on other people's missteps. Instead, he re-read the same sentence three times about some elderly gent getting run over by a bus. He closed his eyes and discovered Darlene waiting there too, wondering if the passing years had recorded his guilt like the rings of a tree. What did she want to hear? That he wore a suit of camel hair or volunteered at an orphanage as penance? No, he did what any sensible person would do and filed the mistake away with all the other regrets one accumulates in life and moved on. There was no sense beating himself up over something he couldn't correct. "Give me a break, I was young and dumb," he mumbled. "The blame isn't all mine...she participated too."

He searched the ceiling again. *Shame on her for coming back from the dead like some horror flick.* He countered the flood of negative thoughts with the million-dollar house she just bought. It appeared she moved on and pursued an advanced degree and had a meaningful career. She was living large.

He sat up and rubbed the stiffness at the base of his neck caused by hovering over too many spreadsheets. Darlene was very attractive— combine that with her education and career success, she should be fighting off multiple suitors. Why was she alone?

"Guess I'm that strange breed that takes intimacy seriously and learned the hard way it has consequences," she said. The words were razor sharp and he understood what she meant. After Stephanie left him in the snow that night, everything inside him had been shredded too.

Okay, I was her first and it had consequences, but in all the years since, was there no one else? He repeated the thought to counter the guilt she served with the lemon seltzer water. Language could be incredibly elastic and had become increasingly so since Sun-Kissed replaced political correctness with the age of euphemism. Maybe it was the same for Darlene and her definition of intimacy followed a torturous path.

Todd cradled his head in his hands as Darlene morphed into another face.

Caroline made his eyes ache and Todd hesitated thinking about her now. He had a good track record of keeping her hidden in the bell tower of his memory, where the doors were rusted shut and hidden behind a thick hedge of brambles. Given the appearance of Darlene today, however, he gave himself permission to endure the blood thirsty thorns of memory and unlock the door for a brief moment.

Not surprisingly, even after a quarter century, she still looked the same. The juxtaposition stabbed at his throat; he now middle-aged and graying, while she remained forever eighteen. Still, had she lived she would have aged gracefully, her blonde hair growing lighter with age; her Caribbean blue eyes warm no matter the season.

His cheeks felt hot recalling the awkward kid he was— and the innocent ways he tried to impress the new girl that transferred in for senior year. They would chat between classes and he would stumble over his words and nearly hyperventilate. This made her laugh and think he must be the class clown.

Sometimes in between the stammering and run-on sentences there would be a millisecond when he would catch a sparkle in her eyes and a connection that felt like an alternate reality. It represented such a simple and pure moment before the drive for riches colored everything that followed. Those days had a clarity of purpose; just secure a smile from Caroline.

Reality often uses a box cutter on the heart no matter the age, and he found himself just another suitor among many. While neither a star athlete or exceedingly good-looking, he clung to the laughs they shared as a beachhead until he could unfreeze his tongue.

He told his best friend about the predicament. Tom responded with teen logic akin to dropping a match in dry timber.

"The only way you'll ever have a chance with the girl of your dreams," he emphasized by drilling a finger into his chest, "is to make Caroline think you're in demand."

"How do I do that?"

"It's simple. Start going out with Darlene."

"Darlene Connolly?" Sure, she was good looking and had been chasing him since grammar school but he felt uncomfortable with the plan. He chalked it up to the way she always manipulated things. She would pop up as his secret Santa, chemistry lab partner and bring his mother pints of blueberries she picked. It creeped him out.

"I don't know."

"Are you an idiot?" Tom yelled for the first time in a week-long campaign. *"Have you ever heard of the theory of least interest? The one who has the least interest in a relationship also has the power. Darlene likes you more, so you're in control. Take Darlene out and Caroline will notice you're not some dweeb. Practice on her, or you won't have a clue if you ever do get a chance with Caroline. What's the big deal anyhow?"* he laughed. *"It's not like you're marrying her. Plus, they all look the same in the dark."*

When Caroline became involved with a college guy, he responded by going out with Darlene. As much as he enjoyed the taste of her fruit flavored lipstick, he imagined Caroline at the other end of his lips. As the relationship became more physical, he ignored all the speed limit signs along the way.

Todd stood up and walked to the window. The light from the table lamp caught the glass and reflected his tired expression.

He stumbled into a late summer party replete with spiked punch and a DJ. Surprisingly, Caroline was there alone and around midnight he asked her to dance. They held each other close. When the song ended, they kept moving in slow circles until she lost her balance and they fell on the damp grass.

He could still hear her laughing.

The rain began pelting against the window breaking the memory. He sighed, recalling how the constipated clouds withheld their assistance this morning with Darlene.

Water droplets raced down the windows with heavy heads sporting long tails and converged at the bottom of the pane. *The morning after the party he woke up hung-over, but still moving in rhythm to that slow dance. He was nursing a cup of coffee, when the phone rang.*

"I'm late," Darlene blurted out.

He repeated the four-letter word thinking it such a strange term for the possibility of new life. Late was a word his mother used when they were waiting for him at the dinner table or a teacher caught him sauntering in after class began. Now Darlene used the term as a warning of an approaching tornado. Suddenly, everything took on a yellowish hue.

The news sucked the air out of his lungs and fogged his brain.

"Did you hear me?" she yelled at the other end of the line.

That question would repeat itself in a string of desperate arguments.

"Did you hear me? Let's get married," she pleaded a week later, rubbing a still flat belly. "We can move in with my mom. She will gladly give up the master bedroom so the baby can stay in there with us. You'll go to college and I'll work nights," she said with a brave smile even if it trembled. "We'll be a happy little family." She touched his cheek. "I've loved you since second grade."

He backed away and she followed. "You said you wanted me, and I gave you all I had. Now it's your turn."

His replies were nothing but blundered attempts on providing emotional support, while skating the larger issue. He had a long-range plan and none of it included playing house. Darlene sensed it and as the days passed the urgent pleas grew in intensity.

Sharing the news produced more tears from Darlene's mother and a few obscenities he never knew a religious woman would keep in her repertoire. Confronting his parents had the opposite effect as they fell silent and hibernated for days in their matching recliners analyzing the issue. The rumor mill in town churned and the news soon reached Caroline, instantly extinguishing the promising spark. While he could understand the new distance between them, he needed to explain.

Tragically, that was one appointment he wished he missed. Dissecting the timeline burned into his very being the penalty paid when things get out of whack. If he had left the house five seconds later, or caught a red light on the way, Caroline would still be alive.

Instead, he arrived just in time to see her leaving the mall parking lot in her prized orange VW Beetle, apparently having second thoughts about their meeting. He made a quick U-turn and continued practicing the confession. As they approached a busy intersection, the traffic light turned red. Her brake lights came on, but strangely, the car kept moving.

Traveling south on Route 28, the driver of a tractor trailer hauling industrial steel pipe out of Maine grew tired of downshifting according to the police report. The thirty-five-year-old driver took his foot off the gas planning to coast so he could accelerate once the light turned green. Ten years of experience proved the strategy worked—if the other driver's obeyed traffic signals.

Todd watched as the Beetle swerved violently to the left. The rig turned hard in the opposite direction trying to avoid T-boning the small car and in the process spilled its entire load burying the Volkswagen.

Several good Samaritans stopped to help. They worked as a team, but the effort felt like standing on a hill of pixie sticks. They would roll a few pipes off the chaotic mess and the pile underneath would suddenly shift forcing them to jump off before being swallowed. When the police and firefighters arrived, they pulled everyone away. A half hour later they draped a white sheet over the crushed car.

At the funeral, lilacs surrounded the altar at Mary Queen of Peace, their sweet perfume competing with the incense. Father Healey quoted scripture standing behind a simple pine lectern and commented on the fragility of life. He went on to promise family and friends they would see Caroline again in a place absent pain or tears. He sat in the last pew, wanting a specific date so he could circle it on the calendar and mark off the days until it arrived.

The final prayers at the grave were said under grieving gray skies. Darlene didn't attend any of it. She was too preoccupied with the new life growing inside her.

The accident forced questions no Doctor of Theology could answer. Why did God let someone die with so much promise? He wondered about the purpose of life if a mistake measured in a millisecond could end it all. Little wonder he developed OCD tendencies regarding routine because life could be fickle. If you get out of sync even for an instant, it could turn deadly.

The days following the funeral felt as heavy and shifting as the steel pipes.

"You're smothering me!" he finally blurted out after the third call in an hour from the expectant mother.

"You're nothing but a modern-day Pontius Pilate," she shot back, "except you can't wash your hands and deny our baby."

"Except I don't want any of this!" He slammed the phone down. When he turned around his father was waiting, and they headed for the den where all the important conversations took place.

A few days later, Dad knocked on his bedroom door. "Everything has been resolved," he said looking exhausted. "Focus on your studies, but promise me you will never contact Darlene again. Understand?"

"No worries about that!" he replied. "But what's she going to do about the baby?"

His father got inches from his face and stared into his eyes for a long moment without blinking. "You think you're a man, but when your choices produced a life, you wanted to hide like a little boy. I stepped in like you asked and took care of it. That's all you need to know. Disobey me and you can put yourself through college."

The rain beat against the window like music specially composed for the cringe-worthy flashback. He embraced college and marinated his brain in accounting, finance, economics and found a comfort there. Numbers do not lie or manipulate. The digits line up in straight columns and when you have a variance, you analyze why and move on. Efficient and neat.

That same calculating philosophy defined his life. When Stephanie rejected this approach, he turned to the bottle for comfort. More than once he nearly drowned.

He grabbed his car keys, and headed for the door. The nearest licensed package store was a mile away and open 24/7. He rationalized alcohol as medicinal this evening. This time he would not repeat the mistake he made when Stephanie left those haunting footprints in the snow and he tried forgetting them with handles of rum. No, a six pack of no-brand beer would deaden him enough for sleep and hopefully keep Darlene from haunting his dreams too.

Opening the door, he could hear Darlene mocking his sobriety. He fell back and considered putting a fist through the wall in reply. But what would that prove? With his luck, he would break a finger and Miller would think he did it on purpose to get some extra time for the budget. *No, I must be smart and adopt a new tact. Analyze it like a business case.*

His proven approach centered on identifying opportunities and risks. The opportunity with Darlene was her financial success and how best to tap into her network. The risk was their past. He needed to find out what happened to the baby so he could plan accordingly.

On the way to the fridge, he began developing an action plan. He would return Carl's call in the morning and cultivate their relationship. The hydropower opportunity sounded like it would be in his wheelhouse. Next, he would suspend the automatic deposits into the brokerage account. Brad would be angry, but so be it. In the end, he was no better than his sister, who didn't have the decency of saying goodbye. He would never forget the abandonment.

He glanced at the ceiling and Darlene face was still there. "No worries, hon. This time what I want is between your ears," he whispered.

CHAPTER NINE

Brad believed protocol required knocking before opening a closed office door, but Loretta assumed their relationship bestowed special privileges. So, when the mahogany door flew open and Loretta hurried in carrying a small box wrapped in silver foil, all he could do was groan.

"The front desk received this package and it's marked confidential," she announced almost breathless. "I thought I'd be nice and bring it in."

His eyes narrowed because he ended up paying for these random acts of kindness. As much as he enjoyed watching her saunter around the office—and today was no different with her rust-colored dress accenting every curve and complementing silver blonde hair, the interruption still irked him.

"The way you burst in, I thought you were transporting an organ for transplant," he quipped, "and I don't understand why brainy kids dream of wielding scalpels anyways. I've learned there's less messy ways to extract things from people." He pointed at the overflowing in-box. "Since I'm focused on finishing today's transactions, why don't we live dangerously and save whatever that is for tomorrow's adventure in finance?"

Loretta always had a sassy retort and when none came, he glanced up and recognized her notorious pout. She continued clutching the box. "Look, if you think there's something in there that might spoil, you can always put it in the breakroom fridge."

Loretta ignored the suggestion. "By the weight, I don't think it's those make-believe blueberry muffins that pushy sales guy promised to send." She came around the desk and dropped the package in his lap. "What do you think?"

The bomb found its mark and Brad let out a moan. "What's the matter with you?" he yelled. He stood up and planted the package on the edge of his desk. "If this arrived in an envelope instead of a fancy box, you would have left it downstairs." He glanced at the package. "Maybe if I wrap myself up in foil like that, I'll get your attention too."

She rolled her eyes. "Not funny."

"Then why the drama over a stupid package?" He bit his lip realizing this wasn't a hill to die on and had already consumed too much time. "Okay, hurry up and open it if you must."

Loretta folded her arms. "Open it yourself or wait until tomorrow, I really don't care. I just wanted to point out before your meltdown that it looks like a present. Imagine that, somebody besides me thinking about you." She fingered the foil. "I haven't seen this type of wrapping in years. It makes me think of Thanksgiving and how my mother used yards of tinfoil wrapping up the turkey and all the leftovers. After raiding the fridge a few times, the foil would look crinkly like this."

I can't believe aluminum foil is now a rare commodity, he thought. *If I had known, I would have bought a warehouse full of the stuff and become the twenty-first century tin man, but with a brain.* He surveyed her anorexic frame. "C'mon Loretta, who are you fooling? Your family are strict vegetarians. What did your mother do? Put tofu in a turkey mold?" He shook his head. "It's crazy how people paid for reduced calorie foods before Sun-Kissed put everyone on a starvation diet." He plopped down in his chair. "When the holidays roll around this year, I don't care what it costs for a real turkey and all the fixings. Let the paupers suck on tubes of turkey flavored who knows what." He eyed her again. "Of course, you'll continue grazing from that hydroponic garden of yours."

"There you go again, making fun of me eating healthy and staying in shape, while you think the smell of money makes you some sort of hunk. The earth could stop spinning and your type would survive, just like the roaches." She eyed the package again. "Wrapping something like that takes time and communicates a level of care rarely seen anymore. Every present you give me is always in a paper bag. That's no way to woo a girl."

Brad rolled his chair toward her foot and regretted when she moved it out of the way. "How about the pearls I bought you last month? No one can afford luxury like that these days. Would you be happier if I gave them to my wife instead?"

She eyed him like she was considering the offer. "What's wrong with you? You've been a bear all day."

"Nothing." He rolled back to the desk.

"Then lose the attitude." She fingered the foil some more. "Well, are you opening the box or not? Maybe it's something that will give us both a lift. Heaven knows I could use it about now."

"Don't you want the pleasure?" When she didn't reply, he abandoned his chair again and hungrily tore at the foil and the underlying box. Inside he found a six-pack of beer. The green bottles identified it as a home brew, given all the watered-down-fizz-less suds the government pushed came in brown bottles.

He studied the label and how *Darlene's Wicked Ale* was fashioned in white Gothic font which really popped against the black background. In the bottom of the box, he found a small index card with a note written in red.

Brad—Thanks for demonstrating your willingness to do whatever it takes for your clients and proving how an "ounce of prevention is worth a pound of cure." You were so right; business is business! Look forward exploring the mutual fun we discussed after the transaction confirmation is received.

I'll be in touch shortly. In the meantime, I hope you enjoy this special brew. It promises quite a kick.

Very truly yours,

Darlene

Loretta scanned the card. "Who's Darlene? I don't understand any of this mumbo jumbo and why would she send homemade beer? It's so tacky."

Brad noticed black and white confetti inside the cardboard holder of the six pack. The pieces looked like shredded pictures, but certainly not *the* pictures because they would still be smoldering from that night of debauchery at the beach cottage. He glanced quickly at Loretta wishing he didn't have to shred her too."

"Brad, you look weird. Who is she?"

"Just a wannabee client," he answered quickly, "and like all the other desperadoes wants instant results." He picked up another bottle. "Champagne taste on a beer budget, I'm afraid."

"Let me get this straight. She just opened an account and is thanking you already?" She studied the card again. "Mutual fun?"

He glanced again at the card. "Careless typo."

She looked at him for a moment before cracking a smile. "Don't tell me I have to share you with someone else!" she said with a laugh. "Good luck to her. I hope she can divide by three."

She walked to the window and surveyed the street five floors down. "What's your plan on making me forget how much of a grump you were today?"

He grabbed a handful of the cut-up confetti and considered throwing it up in the air for the coming Academy Award performance.

"Sweetheart, I'm exhausted but have some more paperwork to tackle before I can leave." He faked a yawn and walked over and rubbed her back. "You're right, though. I've been a bear lately and we should make some plans and get away."

Loretta looked at him sideways and frowned.

He bit his lip and nodded. "Tell you what," he continued. "Why don't you go have dinner with Tina? You haven't seen your sister in a while. I'll stop by on my way home."

"That's you, Mr. Stop-by. When are you going to come clean with your wife?"

"I don't need any grief tonight," he said, and rubbed her back. "Please, honey."

"Funny, that's what you said last year, last month, and last night. You should have "please honey" tattooed across your forehead." She pulled away. "You better think hard about making it right. Maybe take a page from your new client and wrap up something expensive."

Brad pointed at the box. "Why don't I just re-wrap the beer for you?"

"You know I hate that stuff."

"Okay, okay. I'll give it some thought." He grabbed her arm. "C'mon, I'll walk you out."

"Let me log off my terminal first."

He pulled her in for a tight embrace and she giggled in surprise. "I'm sorry for being a jerk," he whispered. "I'll log you out. I know how you appreciate little things like that."

Her face lit up. "Easy now, honey. If you treat me too nice, I'll tell Marcy and she'll want equal treatment. I need to get my coat and purse."

He made her sit down in his chair. "Your wish is my command."

A minute later he returned with her things and escorted her to the hall.

Once the elevator door shut, he quickly patrolled the floor and only encountered a couple of elderly men from the cleaning crew. He took another lap before stopping at Loretta's cubicle. The ancient monitor waited.

This is too easy, he thought, and a few keystrokes later pulled up Todd's account. Tabbing through the profile, he noted how Todd made his father the beneficiary after the divorce and he felt a strong urge to restore his sister. Instead, he retrieved the folded piece of paper from his wallet and in rapid fashion, deleted Todd's father and carefully keyed in Emmett Connolly's name and social security number. He overrode the system so a confirmation letter would not be sent to Todd and submitted the change. Waiting for the transaction to process, he stared at multiple animal rescue posters tacked on the fabric wall. When the transaction number flashed on the screen, he jotted it down on the paper. "Thanks Loretta," he whispered, thinking how he just set her up and how painful it would be firing such a committed employee if it came to light. *She would freak out in prison, but so would I.* Before logging off, he did a screen print of the beneficiary page to exchange for the pictures.

He returned to his office and sought solace in a cushy leather chair. It was not Todd or Loretta that had him on edge. He rationalized more sinister deeds when required. No, it was the blackmail that really nagged at him. *Okay, so I changed his beneficiary? So what? Nothing changes unless Todd dies and I could put something in motion after I get the pictures back so he trips over it.* His mind raced thinking of possible options and then stopped. It would raise too many questions. Crazy Darlene had been right about Todd too. Loretta said he called in this morning and besides suspending automatic deposits, he was liquidating half a million. *I made him a lot of money and the gutless jerk didn't even have the decency to call me.*

His mouth felt dry and he eyed the micro beer... *Darlene's Wicked Ale.* It was a curious name and made him recall their kiss at the bar. He picked up a bottle and let out a moan realizing he did not have a bottle opener. Remembering a trick from college, he used the side of his desk and popped the cap off.

The contents smelled sweet and he took a small sip. The ale had a fruity taste with a hint of apple. He disliked harvest brews and never understood why people messed around adding foreign stuff. If he wanted apples, cranberries, or pumpkin he would buy a fruit salad for a few hundred bucks. What's next? Chocolate beer for Valentine's Day?

Experience taught him that after chugging the contents sometimes the odd flavor would recede. After draining the entire bottle, he thought about trashing the remainder. "Well sweetie, you better come up with a more creative way to show your appreciation than this swamp water from the orchard," he said between burps.

He surveyed the waiting stack of paperwork and reasoned it would still be there in the morning. He began tidying up his desk while deciding what type of street food to grab before meeting up with Loretta. Before he left, however, he planned on reviewing the paperwork on Todd's sell order. What stocks did he sell?

The sound of the vacuum cleaner made him pause. Retrieving the five remaining bottles of beer, he hurried into the hallway.

"How are you doing Al?" he asked with practiced concern.

"Fine Mr. Ponzell," the bent old man replied. He smiled broadly, even without the benefit of front teeth.

"Glad to hear. You know Al, I was just thinking how dependable you've been and want to share a special beer from one of my new clients."

The old man's gray eyes glistened. "That's so kind of you, Mr. Ponzell. I'll save it for a special occasion."

"No, you don't want to do that," he said quickly. "Who know how long these home brews last? Enjoy it as soon as you can."

The janitor winked. "Then tonight will be special, indeed."

He turned to leave. "By the way, I noticed my rug is looking a little dingy. Any chance you could shampoo it before you leave?"

"Certainly, Mr. Ponzell. My pleasure."

"And oh, one other little thing," he said looking past him. "I was auditing the processing floor tonight and noticed the cubicle belonging to Loretta Wells is below company standards."

The janitor raked his thick white hair with arthritic fingers. "I apologize! I will clean it right away."

Brad waved his hand. "No, that's not what I meant. I noticed she has animal posters on her cubicle walls. I don't think it's appropriate given the image we want to promote. Do you?"

The old man looked puzzled by the question. "What would you like me to do?"

"Please discard all the posters. If she asks tomorrow what happened, let's play it cool and shrug. I'll wait a few days and issue a memo reminding everyone about cubicle standards." He slapped him on the back. "Our little secret, okay?"

The janitor nodded in respectful agreement.

"Business is business," he said and turned away

Al turned the vacuum back on. "What a putz," he whispered. At least Darlene pays in cash.

CHAPTER TEN

They sat against a gigantic black and white speckled boulder watching the water lap the shore and slowly spit out pine needles. Small clumps of orange dotted the shoreline.

Cotton used the head of a ten-penny nail to pry open a bottle of the home brew he took as payment for changing the water pump on a '65 Chevy Impala. "The other night we were talking about growing up and I was pretty vague about things—especially my uncles."

"No worries. I could tell you didn't want to talk about it." Jennifer touched his arm. "We all have relatives that require too much explaining."

He handed her the bottle. "Well, tonight we have some liquid sedative to help with the painful tale. You see, none of my uncles were actually related to me, but they were all brothers in what they wanted from Momma. I was about nine years old when I figured out the birds and bees. After that I nicknamed all of them Uncle. Looking back, I should have called them either Tom, Dick, or Harry. They might have laughed too but Momma brought me up to respect my elders, especially the ones that kept a roof over our heads. So, she had me address all of them as sir, probably to keep me from mistakenly referring to her previous beau. When things fell apart as they always did and she was in the market for a new squeeze, the hopefuls would buy me a cherry-dipped cone so they could have some alone time with Momma. But she wasn't easy like that, and most were gone before the ice cream melted. Lucky for us the walk home was never far.

She gave him the bottle back and he started peeling the silver foil label with a thumbnail that could use a date with some clippers. "Momma went through a baker's-dozen of tutti-frutti live-ins looking for love and security. She found neither but sure put in the effort. If anything, it felt like the sequel to *Groundhog Day.* The opening scene always opened with Mr. Hopeful stopping by the house for a drink. Then the wooing would commence with roses for her and bags of candy for me. Occasionally, the uncle-to-be would let me tag along. He'd smile a lot and pretend he cared for a couple hours."

Jennifer took the bottle from his hand for another sip. Usually when beer is lousy, you suffer until the alcohol kicks in. This stuff, however, tasted like carbonated water dispensed from a urinal.

"Then I'd wake up one morning," Cotton continued, "and my new uncle would be alone in the kitchen. He'd look down at me kind of embarrassed and just grunt. The worse one's would hog all the milk I saved for my Frosted Flakes."

"I'll save my comments about all the uncles until later, but cereal deprivation too?" She handed the bottle back. "Why the horror!"

Cotton shot her a sideways look and grinned. "Think I'm kidding? That meant toast for breakfast which in my book is nothing more than accelerated stale bread made edible by a thick layer of peanut butter and jelly—a pair which rarely visited my house." He took a deep breath reliving the moment. "The lust-fest was always the high point. Fast forward a few months and Uncle would be yelling a lot and Momma would be telling me how she fell down the back stairs again. I never knew stairs could be serial abusers and gift such nasty shiners."

They listened to an owl hoot from a nearby pine tree. "I learned early on the worst dragons don't breathe fire but disarm you with a smile." He held the bottle in front of his face before taking another slug. "I can't explain why she always gravitated toward the same type. Maybe they reminded her of my father—but unlike him, she made the abusive one's pay."

"How? Did she call the police?" she asked, uncertain if she really wanted to know.

Cotton squirmed a bit against the rock before running his hand through his hair. "Let's just say some of them developed a dislike for toast too."

"Hmm, that sure sounds like a blurb for one of those true crime shows."

He brushed the shredded bits of paper off his lap and began scraping the residue glue on the bottle. "I try my best not to think about the particulars. Back when I was really young, I hoped my real father would appear and throw the imposter out. Then he'd go to the grocery store and buy me some real Frosted Flakes, instead of the generic crap Momma got from the food pantry. That's one confession I never made to anyone until now."

Jennifer thought of the quarry she and her friends swam in as kids. They would climb the branches of a birch tree worn smooth by generations of hands and feet. One by one they would put on a brave face and jump. Sometimes she would break the surface of the water so cleanly she would rocket down a good ten feet. Then courage would turn itself inside-out and she feared not being able to hold her breath long enough to make it back to the surface. Their first few dates had been enjoyable and light, but tonight Cotton jumped into water much deeper than he probably intended.

She rubbed his arm. "You never thought of contacting your dad and hearing his side of the story?"

"No," he snapped, "and if I ever ran into him and he flashed a smile, I'd push his front teeth down his throat for abandoning us. My momma blames him for twenty-five years of misery including Sun-Kissed, which is a cosmic comedy. Given that, I can't fathom why she worked so hard cursing his memory only to chain herself to other losers like him."

She pointed at the bottle. "Aren't you afraid all this talk will skunk your beer?"

He laughed. "Actually, that might be an improvement for this swill. I'm seriously considering removing the water pump from the Chevy as payback. In terms of my family life, I know how Prometheus must feel being chained to a mountain with an eagle pecking every day at his liver. Whenever I give Momma any lip, she reminds me of the plans she had—how she wanted to be a scientist working on breakthrough vaccines but gave it all up because of me. She constantly flaunts how she worked lousy jobs to make ends meet. Now she's trying to help Nana with waitressing gigs and cleaning homes for the Tanned. You hear people talk all the time about how great their lives were before Sun-Kissed. Well, for Momma, her storm came much earlier but fried her soul just the same."

She touched his arm. "I feel sorry for her. She sacrificed a lot for you and your grandmother."

"Sacrifice is the right word. She not only gave me life but went through some horrible stuff to support me. I'm grateful for everything, and just wish she could reclaim some of her dreams. Every now and then, she will see something on tv about cancer drug research and it will get her thinking about starting over. Last year she even enrolled at a community college under that special government program they keep advertising. But after a few weeks she became discouraged juggling everything and dropped out."

"I read how the intentions of the program were good, but the details were sorely lacking. Without financial assistance and job placement after the training, who wouldn't get discouraged?"

"We all handle things differently but she lets her scars define her. I got tired of being an enabler. I'd go hunting for her when she didn't come home and would find her at some godforsaken watering hole with another uncle-to-be."

He took another gulp before pouring the rest of the beer in the sand. "What a fitting way to end this ugly story."

Jennifer gave him a slight shove hoping to rescue the evening. "Next time, I'll bring the beer."

They sat for a while listening to the cricket's chirping, enjoying the warm night and the gift of fall—no mosquitoes. "My father took me fishing here," she said breaking the silence. "Besides teaching me how to bait a hook, he'd weave in key lessons like how the good book should be read every day instead of just sampling it on Sunday's. I can still hear him saying," as she looked up at the sky, "how Abraham descendants would be as numerous as the stars in the sky."

"Now there's a contrast," Cotton quipped. "Momma would point her cigarette at the tobacco-stained ceiling in our apartment and ask God to smite her enemies."

Inside she winced thinking she should have kept the memory to herself.

Cotton sighed. "Sometimes, I can rival a lemon in terms of being sour. Sorry about that." He put his arm around her and looked up at the sky brimming with celestial bodies. "It's fascinating how people see different things when they look at the same object. Take the stars. The first challenge is getting people to raise their heads and notice more than the weather. That's a bit easier now as people aren't married to cell phones anymore. Some keep looking up expecting an asteroid to finish what Sun-Kissed started. Then there's the crazies that watch for a comet that will transport them back to the mother ship if they're wearing the right brand of sneakers." He pointed at a section of the sky where a group of stars congregated. "They look so close to one another, but there's a terrific sea of space between each."

She gave him a stronger shove this time and he almost fell over. "Boy, aren't we the romantic tonight. I can't wait for the bowling lanes to reopen." She coughed and deepened her voice. "Aim carefully, Jenny! There's a terrific sea of space between the pins."

"Well, I do like bowling except for the community shoes."

"What are you talking about? They sanitize them."

"You think one little spritz from a can erases the sweaty residue from dozens of backwoodsmen with gaping holes in their socks come league night? And don't get me started about the other six days of the week. Before you write me off, though, let's see if I can redeem myself."

"I'm still working on getting the image of sweaty feet out of my head."

"Stay with me. I flew into Boston one night a few months before Sun-Kissed hit. On the approach into Logan, I looked out the window and the traffic below resembled long strands of Christmas lights. As the plane descended, I began thinking how each car had a different destination with no idea of who was in front or behind. Each represented its own world; its passengers caught up in their own stories."

She nodded as his gaze transferred from the sky to her face. The frustrated expression was gone. "I also realized the night sky is mostly black because you only see color up close," he continued. "My life has been mostly filled with people that possess the warmth of a fluorescent bulb." He caressed her cheek. "Your beauty and warmth are changing my perspective and coloring my world."

"Nice recovery, but don't forget about gravitational pull too." She leaned in and gave him a tender kiss. "I'm finding you're a cowboy philosopher packaged with an interesting nickname. Do the guys at the ranch see that too?"

He laughed. "Since you grew up here, you know the answer. Yeah, it's been an adventure of sorts. When I first started my nickname was "green broke" and I thought they pegged my situation perfectly. A few days later I learned it described a horse trained just enough to be manageable, but not necessarily reliable. I put in the hours and even learned how to chew tobacco and spit a fair share."

"Well, that's what the Tanned folks expect when you take them out riding. They want the full experience."

"It starts when you first meet a family. They're nervous about getting some crazy horse and we go through this big rigmarole matching a horse to a person's personality. I never thought I would play matchmaker." He leaned the naked beer bottle against the rock and gave her a side glance. "Enough about me. What makes you stay here?"

"It's a pretty short story. I spent my whole life here in the pines. Like I mentioned, I lost my mom when I was ten. My father passed last year."

"That's a long time. Did your dad…ah, ever…"

"No string of aunts if that's what you're asking," she said with a quick laugh. "The only things in my dad's life were church, family and the store. I remember seeing a few baited hooks disguised as blueberry pie or a loaf of pumpkin bread, but Dad fished a lot and knew the art of nibbling. He would graciously accept the goodies and when the follow-up dinner invitation came, he would apologize and say he was in the middle of taking inventory. Can you imagine a woman's reaction at being rejected in favor of counting cans?" She clapped her hands. "I take after him, because I like my freedom too and can be as subtle as a two by four across the head sometimes. My parents had something special. Sorry to wreck your theory, but their stars revolved around each other with little space in between."

He laughed. "Why do you remember that instead of my poetry about you?"

She smiled. "My guess is they're having a heck of a time up there. My father is probably finagling a way to open a small tackle shop. Saint Peter may have the keys to heaven, but when my dad has a plan, he's a force to be reckoned with."

"Are you happy with the store?"

"Yes, but I get restless every now and then. Sometimes I think if I don't start exploring soon, I'll be a miserable senior citizen." She flexed her right hand and looked at her fingers. The nails were long and she couldn't remember the last time they had any polish on them.

"There are worse places outside this protected area. At least here some things feel almost normal," Cotton said watching her.

"Yeah, nothing like faking things so the Tanned stay super happy. This will always be my home. It's in my DNA, but I'd like to travel a bit. Maybe drive across the country so I have something to tell my kids about.

"What's holding you back?"

"For a while it was my father. He leaned on me quite a bit after he got sick. The last couple of years were a sad blessing. So many lose the one's they love suddenly. We had time for puzzles, *Monopoly*, and some great dinners. The memories will keep me warm until I see him again."

"That's wonderful, but you didn't venture out after he passed? I know there's always a bunch of troublemakers outside the designated area protesting. Is that why?"

She shook her head. "I made plans, but they went nowhere. A few months back, I even closed the store for the weekend to check out Manhattan. I loaded up the car and made it fifty miles before I had a panic attack and turned around. It came as a complete surprise and reminded me of the sheltie we adopted when I was young. My father installed an invisible fence and outfitted Max with a special collar so if he tried leaving the yard, he would get zapped with a small electrical shock. After a few weeks, we didn't need the collar anymore because Max knew the consequences. When I took him out for a walk, he would begin shaking near the boundary line and I'd have to carry him across. In some ways, I felt like I had a collar on when Dad was alive, content with my surroundings. Now he's gone and I'm learning what that means. I guess in a sense, I'm waiting to be carried across too."

Cotton put his arm around her, and she buried her face in his shirt. She was surprised by the sudden emotion that welled up and could not blame it on the awful beer. She hated women that cried easily and did not plan on showing any vulnerability this early.

She coughed and decided a change in scenery was needed. "I'm guessing no matter how bad the brew; you still want the empties?"

He started gathering them. "Yeah, you know me well."

"When are you going to let me in on your secret?"

"What secret?"

"This mission of yours. You're making me think your new nickname should be Bottle Bill."

Cotton laughed as he put the empties in a brown bag. "That's a good one. I'll tell you soon enough about the fishing."

They held hands and walked the short trail leading back. Halfway there, an acrid smell filled the air.

"That smells like a strange bonfire," Cotton said.

Jennifer quickened her pace while scanning the tree line.

They broke into a run at the same time and rounding a bend saw flames engulfing the Adirondack General Store.

The Oslo Volunteer Fire Department was already on the scene and directing multiple hoses at the flames.

Jennifer tried running toward the store, but Cotton held her back. A stocky fireman approached and removed his helmet. She recognized him as the gym teacher at the high school.

"We're doing pretty good knocking the fire down, even though it got a jump on us."

She was too shell shocked to comment. No matter the cause, she let her father down.

Cotton ran over to a fireman on the east side of the building to assist.

Jennifer remained frozen in place. Her eyes locked on the rising smoke and noticed how it obscured the sky.

CHAPTER ELEVEN

Brad flushed the toilet and stumbled back to the bedroom.

Marcy greeted him by pointing at the digital clock on the nightstand. The bold red numerals matched his wife's mood. "What's the matter with you?" She asked and punched her pillow like she wished it were his head. "It's the middle of the night and you've driving me nuts!"

"Thanks for your concern," he mumbled and collapsed into their king-sized bed.

"Don't give me that attitude. You know I have trouble sleeping. Every time you get up, you rip the blanket off me like an insensitive jerk." She let out a growl to finish the indictment. "Now you have me all worked up. I may as well get up for the day."

The complaint barely reached his ears when he heard the plumbing in his stomach gurgle again. "I must have a stomach bug."

She slapped his arm. "Did you hear one word I said? Why is everything always about you?" When he responded by rubbing his stomach, she turned over. "Where did you eat dinner?"

Her compassion underwhelmed him. "I'll lose it right here, if you make me talk about food."

"Well, I've told you a million times I put a good meal on the table every night and use real ingredients. Do you need an invitation to join your wife and son once in a while for dinner?"

She went silent and he counted to ten.

"I can't imagine the tainted garbage you're eating," she continued right on cue, "and who knows where it comes from? It's no wonder you have trouble with your stomach given all the street food you inhale. Do you really believe all those vendors use leftovers from the fancy places you never take me to? If Upton Sinclair returned from the grave, he'd write a sequel to the *Jungle* about how even the flies get sick from the places you frequent.

Upton Sinclair? Seriously? How she loves touting that literature degree of hers, he thought. *Doesn't she understand that I have to meet clients whenever and wherever they want which usually means nights? Sure, I could be home pushing some overcooked slop around a sterile plate while listening to endless minutiae, but that wouldn't pay for the high-end lifestyle she demands. I should play along and let business slow. Then she'd demand I work every night and I could explore the limits of naughtiness.*

She rolled over and faced him. "Don't tell me you were out roaming the streets again because of Todd?"

"Yeah," he whispered. *That chump is my favorite alibi.*

"What did he do now?"

"He suspended deposits and is pulling out a hunk of money. The coward called into the main number so he wouldn't have to talk to me. The handwriting is on the wall—he's dumping us."

"Us? I told you years ago to watch your back. I knew Todd would betray you if he got an opportunity to make an extra buck. Look what he did to your sister! The first time he heard her after she said "I do" was the day she filed for divorce because it came with a price tag. Steph feels so insulted by the settlement. I don't know why you're surprised."

A sharp pain in his stomach curled his toes and he sucked in his breath.

Marcy let out another groan. "If you're going to keep fidgeting, do the courteous thing and sleep in the guest room and be careful not to wake Junior. I have my tennis lesson in the morning. Thanks to you, I'll be useless."

Brad hated being alone when he felt this ill, especially in the middle of the night. However, he did not want to admit it and attract more ridicule about his shortcomings.

He moved to the edge of the bed and thought if he could lie very still maybe his stomach would quiet along with his wife. In the momentary silence, something scratched outside the bedroom window. Opening one eye, he watched the fingers of a tree branch moving in the wind. It reminded him of Darlene and her long red nails and how he once wanted them running down his back. Yet with the mind games she was playing, they may as well be the crooked fingers of a conniving witch. "Well, the dirty deal is done," he shouted behind his eyes. "I'll take delivery on the pictures and be done with her."

The whole sorry episode underscored his careless ways. Loretta would need some counseling too on being discreet and respecting office protocol. Maybe he would buy some tasteful artwork for her cubicle and wrap it up in pretty paper. If he played it right, Loretta would be very grateful for his thoughtfulness.

The branch scratched louder as a new intense wave of nausea pushed northwards. Intense heartburn, reached the back of his throat at the same time. He felt a lot worse and watched the clock change to 3:00 a.m. Feeling this sick at the devil's hour fed on his anxiety. He pushed the thought away by recalling how the designation was related to a drop in the body's immune system at that hour and not evil spirits.

Nauseous, sweaty, and strangely claustrophobic, he slipped out of bed and tiptoed to the bathroom. If Marcy heard anything, she was out of ammunition. Opening the pewter edged medicine cabinet, he looked for anything to calm who-knows-what-this-is-but-hope-it's-not-more-than-a-twelve-hour-bug, because it would ruin the new client lunch meeting. Two boxes of upset stomach and anti-diarrhea medicine were on the center shelf and he imagined them shrugging as they were clearly outgunned. The headache continued intensifying and he popped two aspirin and took a small sip of water.

He looked in the mirror and the dark patches under his eyes startled him. In an instant, he felt extremely dizzy with some superior force behind his eyes wanting to pull the shades down. He grabbed for the sink and barely made it to the toilet before a violent launch erupted from his stomach. When the contents finally arrived, the color frightened him. It looked deep red—blood red.

Brad watched the dark liquid dissipate and slowly drift toward the bottom of the bowl. Another heave followed with even more red.

He yelled for his wife in a voice he did not recognize. She replied with a tirade until she arrived. Then she let out a high-pitched cry and he wished he could pull his head up long enough to enjoy her expression.

Collapsing on the floor next to the toilet, he tasted putrid apples. He recalled the wicked ale and realized it was not the pulled pork from Betty's food truck which betrayed him. *How could I have been so stupid?*

His cheek welcomed the coolness of the tiled floor before his eyes slammed shut.

CHAPTER TWELVE

Todd watched his father sweep a bamboo rake in a wide swath, capturing a large population of multi-colored leaves including green ones which the wind dislodged prematurely. The color combination reminded him of Starburst, the multi-colored, fruit-flavored, soft taffy he devoured as a kid. He remembered nearly choking on a strawberry piece when he laughed too hard reading *Mad* magazine.

He rubbed his hands together like two sticks hoping to start a fire. "Can I ask you a question, Dad?" The words slipped out before he could stop himself. *If I start sketching my food, I'll know its terminal.*

The rake made another pass before the reply came. "If you're asking if you can help, you know the answer. It takes a village this time of year."

Todd kept his feet stationary. Darlene might get all google-eyed about the changing leaves, but dear old Dad lived in the opposite camp. Instead of admiring the intense rainbow of colors falling from the sky, he saw the autumn equinox as the opening bell in a fight that consumed every weekend until December. And if snow popped up in the forecast, he would rake by the light of the moon.

So, on a perfect afternoon under deep blue skies with temperatures hovering near seventy degrees, Dad waltzed around the yard with a bamboo rake. The crazy part was no matter the effort expended Mother Nature would mock him by parachuting in thousands of reinforcements. Arguing the point, however, was like convincing the moon-landing hoax club to fund a testimonial for the Apollo 11 crew.

He noticed the sweat stains under the arms of his father's gray t-shirt. As much as he practiced tasting the words last night, they were bubbling up with stomach acid now.

"Tell me how you settled things with Darlene," he said in one long breath before the rake could swing for his head. He thought an open probe was the best approach and allow his father a sufficient canvas to sketch the past.

The raking continued for another long moment. Then he stopped mid-stroke and bent over and dislodged a gang of rogue maple leaves clogging the rake's bamboo teeth. "Funny you should ask. Mrs. Simms retired from the library last month and she's thinking of selling the house and moving south. She thinks the cost of living is cheaper in Florida because she won't be heating a house. Guess she plans on dying from heat stroke because all the papers say only the super Tanned can afford air conditioning." He frowned. "Go figure. A librarian that sucks at reading."

He surveyed his father's slim build for any sign of tenseness but everything appeared normal. In his mind, he began scaling a ten-foot chain link fence topped with barbed wire.

"I could care less about *that* Darlene," he replied probably too quickly. He put one hand in the back pocket of his jeans and envisioned finding a pair of pliers and cutting a hole in the sharp wire before jumping down into no-man's-land. "C'mon Dad, it's been twenty-five years. I deserve to know."

"Deserve?" He replied with a quick laugh and banged the face of the rake on the ground hard. One stubborn dimpled yellow leaf remained anchored. He flipped the rake over and tore it off.

"See this leaf, son?" He held it up so they could both study it. "Pretty little thing, isn't it?" He pointed upwards at a hundred-foot maple with a huge canopy that covered a quarter of the back yard. "It blossomed somewhere up there and I welcomed it with all the others in the spring." He twirled the leaf in his fingers. "We spent many a summer day together and I appreciated the shade it offered during those horrible dog days of August; especially when the town cut the power so they could fuel the president's visit. Without a fan, I napped here in the shade and caught a few breezes in hell's kitchen."

He placed the leaf in the palm of his hand and Todd wondered if his father picked a yellow one on purpose. Stomach acid continued burning the back of his throat, but he held back the cough.

"But seasons change and it's time for dead leaves to fall. That's what autumn is all about—getting rid of what's outlived their time. No one wants the debris littering yards, getting stuck on our shoes, hiding under the snow until spring."

"I know where you're headed in that roundabout poetic way of yours, but I need to know how—"

"You never appreciated context," he interrupted, "always skipping the details for the key takeaway. Your mother and I learned the best lessons in life are captured in the journey not the destination. That's why we went into education. Doesn't seem right we were successful in passing that outlook on to thousands of children except our own son. We couldn't agree who you took after, but I think you share some rogue genes with Uncle Ned."

"Who?"

"Your mother's late stepbrother. He ended up hiding in Iceland because of tax evasion. He was an odd duck, with an extra digit on his left hand which he used as a crutch for pity or scaring little kids. Yet, he and Mildred were together for sixty years. You sure didn't take after him in that department."

"That's not fair. Stephanie cheated on me. For someone that's keen about the details, that's a big miss."

"I won't rehash your version of reality or how you responded by drinking yourself stupid. I see why you and Stephanie never made it. She wanted an attentive husband and not someone that lives by the motto: be brief and be gone, so I can get back to Ebenezer at the counting house."

He held the maple leaf by its dark stem and examined it through thick glasses which magnified steel blue eyes. "Do leaves get caught in the rake by accident? Maybe this one didn't want to be swept away and be forgotten." He ground the leaf in his hand and let the remnants fall to the ground. "I'm being a bit melodramatic, but I'm trying to make a point. We have as much power on changing the past as we have of willing these dead leaves back on the trees. Heaven knows that would suit me just fine." He began raking again with vigor. "Until that miraculous day comes, all we can do is burn, bag or add them to the compost pile and hope in time for some nice potting soil. It's the same with that youthful indiscretion of yours. It's been all raked up and disposed of thanks to me." He directed his gaze at him with the same intensity he studied the leaf. "Sadly, you avoided both the work and the insight."

The blowback took his breath away. Todd considered taking a step back in case his father took a whack at his kneecaps as an exclamation point. He glanced at his planted feet and felt the temptation to embrace continued complacency and fetch another rake. Maybe after a penitential hour, things would turn peaceful and they could enjoy a beer. A bee landed at his feet and extended its wings in the sun. He took a couple of deep breaths.

"Dad, I hear everything you're saying, but I really can't drop this," he said in the sincerest voice he could muster.

The rake began combing the yard with aggressive short strokes which pulled out pieces of weakly rooted grass. "Why are you here?" his father's voice reverberated somewhere between anger and crying. "When your mother was dying in hospice you promised to be here for me. In the two years since she's passed, I've seen you maybe a half dozen times. When you called this morning, I assumed we could have dinner after some yardwork. However, as usual, you showed up with an agenda. Last time you had no hot water and wanted to take a shower. I pride myself on being understanding, but at this stage in my life, I don't need any of this. Since you threw everything in my lap to fix, you lost the right to second guess me after all these years."

The familiar pain stabbed at his stomach. "You don't have to tell me I was... a... coward," he stuttered. "I know there's no other word for it." He scanned the sky wanting a dark cloud to appear overhead and wash him clean.

He found his dad's eyes. "I can still hear you saying go to school...live your life...put this all behind you...but promise me you'll stay away from that girl because she wants to ruin your life. I obeyed you. Now I need to hear how you fixed the whole sorry mess."

His father ignored the question and walked ten feet away and began raking again. The uncoordinated strokes left the leaves dancing from one place to another.

Todd noticed the break in his old man's concentration and closed the gap. "I always assumed you and Darlene's mother met and agreed to put the baby up for adoption. Is that right?"

His father began another retreat, but Todd grabbed the handle of the rake and wrestled it away from him. "What happened to the baby?"

"How dare you!" he seethed. "Is this some sort of mid-life crisis? If that's it, why don't you visit the new singles bar down the street. Maybe you can meet some cold fish like yourself and stop digging up the past." He shook his head. "Scratch that. You have a tragic history with women."

Todd ignored the dig. "Just level with me! What happened?"

His father grabbed the rake back from him and started toward the house.

He hated going nuclear, but what choice did he have? "You can tell me now or if prefer, we can rehash old times later with Darlene. I certainly have."

The words found their mark and his father stopped mid-stride and turned around. "What?"

"Yeah, the sky opened up and she landed next to the payphone I was using. She's been haunting me since."

"What a manipulative devil!" He rubbed his forehead hard. "That wasn't the deal," he said to himself.

"Deal? What do you mean?"

He leaned against the rake handle for support and became lost in thought. Todd noticed how old his dad suddenly looked. "She was supposed to think of you as dead," he began in a monotone, "that was the deal."

Todd sensed he was talking to someone twenty-five years ago. "It's okay dad. Tell me what happened."

His father let out a heavy sigh like an internal dam broke. "After you dumped everything on me, I met with her mother. She was struggling financially after kicking out her alcoholic husband. We sat at her kitchen table and talked late into the night over cups of black percolated coffee that gave me heart palpitations. She had a deep faith and respect for life, but blasted me with a canon of cuss words on account of me being there instead of you. And who could blame her? I was defending how sad it would be to sacrifice your future because you couldn't keep your—"

"Okay, maybe you're right and I prefer skipping the details," he said quickly. "What happened to the baby?"

He shot him a disgusted look. "We agreed on adoption, but you were never to know and I would take care of the expenses."

"No issue there because I never asked. So, Darlene went ahead with it?"

His father sighed like he was beyond exhausted and sat down cross-legged on the lawn. Todd followed. "The best-laid plans of mice and men often go awry." He pulled out a clump of crabgrass. "Things got complicated fast because Darlene is the definition of difficult. She ran away before the due date—and her mother went crazy, but I knew she would show up like a bad penny. Sure enough, a year later, she called me in the middle of the night and told me she couldn't go through with the adoption. She said the boy looked too much like you."

My son? The yard began spinning as he concentrated on listening.

"I think she planned it that way all along—" he paused, "for the money."

The spinning accelerated. "Money? You can't be serious."

"Take your blinders off, my boy. She saw you as someone that checked all the boxes regarding the life she wanted. You came from a good family, were handsome, and had career plans. Your mother and I saw her trying to get her claws into you for years. The baby became a blank check."

Todd jumped to his feet. "You think all of this is about money? I can't believe what I'm hearing!"

"Suit yourself. All I know is your little fling cost me more than a college education and then some. First, I gave Darlene money for the medical bills until the baby was put up for adoption. Heck, I even included extra dough so she could go somewhere tropical and heal when it was over. When she ran away and didn't contact you, I realized a darker plan was brewing. Sure enough, she said if I didn't provide long term financial support, she'd make things real difficult for you. So, I paid, and paid, and then paid some more until last year when I finally said enough."

The visit at Darlene's new house came roaring back. She went to NYU and Cornell. That would have taken a boatload of money even with financial aid, never mind the cost of raising a child. "Why didn't you tell me about any of this?"

"Your mother and I were in full agreement on shielding you. We also thought your marriage was like a marshmallow at a bonfire and couldn't withstand the heat if your wife found out."

"And I've been very good about remaining silent, haven't I?" Todd pulled on his hair and it unleashed a thought. "Did it ever dawn on you that he's your grandson?"

"Of course, it did." He stood up slowly using the rake for support. "But given the circumstances and his blackmailing mother, I considered the little guy just an expensive meal ticket. I know that sounds cold, but we never met. All I can say is don't judge me until you take on Darlene for two dozen years." He looked away. "She told me in graphic terms..." his voice trailed off to a whisper, "everything."

Todd clenched his fists and had to do something with his hands. In a flash, he grabbed the rake away from his old man and beat the ground. Pieces of bamboo scattered over the grass, mingling with the orange, red and green leaves. His father's eyes became glassy watching and Todd couldn't tell if it was on account of the drama or the wrecked yard tool.

"No matter what you thought of Darlene, the baby is still my son and an extension of you. Did it ever occur to you how much it costs to raise a child? I can't believe Mom would have gone along with this. I know you ruled the house, but for her to stay silent I find beyond incredible. Imagine if you had fathered a son before you met—"

"Shame on you!" his father interrupted. "Your mother loved you more than life itself. All she wanted was seeing you established and happy despite the mess you made. I won't let you talk about her that way. God rest her soul." Tears welled up in his eyes. "How dare you lecture me about biology. All I can say is the vessel poisoned my heart regarding the boy."

Todd stared at his dad wondering how all of this could have been kept secret for so many years. Past holidays flashed in his memory—carving turkeys and hams and opening presents while his son remained exiled. He suddenly saw his eighteen-year-old self; an entitled punk wearing overpriced sneakers and stomping on a poor girl's heart. The child deserved better.

"Well, does my son have a name?" he asked knowing it would not be Todd junior.

"She named him Emmett after her father. If you want to know more, ask Darlene yourself," he said turning around. "I tried my best to take care of a mess that wasn't mine." He waved him off. "I'm through."

Todd watched him head for the bouse and shuffle through a sea of leaves which made a rustling noise as he progressed. It had been easy letting his father handle the whole sorry affair and believe everything had been resolved. Instead of following him into the house to apologize, he remained frozen in place craving a bottle of rum.

A moment later his father opened the back door and yelled that Stephanie was on the phone.

When he got inside and picked up the receiver, he heard her crying.

"Brad's gone," his ex-wife said.

"Gone where?" he asked feigning innocence. He hadn't talked with her in months and was surprised by the upset. Afterall, Brad went radio silent regularly. Sometimes he left on an expensive junket without telling anyone.

"You're so thick sometimes. He's dead."

Todd looked out the window. A strong breeze carried thousands of leaves eager to colonize. They had an innate ability to fill in the spaces just raked. All were destined to be raked up and discarded.

His father's voice rang in his ears. *Seasons change and it's time for dead leaves to fall.*

CHAPTER THIRTEEN

Todd arrived at the funeral home located adjacent to St. Joseph's Church. Since Pine Grove cemetery was only a couple miles away, townies called the interment process "*the bagged, blessed, and buried 3K.*"

The autumn evening remained unusually warm as friends, family and clients gathered to pay their final respects for Bradley J. Ponzell: successful businessman, civic leader, faithful husband, and loving father.

Todd took his place in a line which weaved down a long hall like a Disney queue, except this one did not end at *It's a Small World.* However, considering the portly man crammed into the metal box, maybe it did.

Inching forward past walls painted in earth tones and air perfumed with the aromatic smell of lilies, he debated what role he should assume when greeting the family. Ex-husband, brother-in-law, client, or just all-around troublemaker? He dreaded hugging Stephanie and feeling like the real corpse. It seemed odd considering if Brad died a couple years ago, he would be standing in the receiving line too. Now he was just a painful relic from the past and while social norms required an appearance, it did not erase the awkwardness. Family would expect a drive-by condolence with no dallying. Doing the right thing proved fickle at times. Consequently, he found himself practicing the facial mechanics of looking upset about someone he felt ambivalent about at best.

Sixty-four steps later, he turned a corner and reached the widow's threshold. Marcy stood alone next to the casket. His eyes searched the room. *Where is everyone?... Stephanie?... Brad Junior? This isn't right.*

Marcy's black cotton dress stiffened slightly along with a porcelain face that could be mistaken for a fragile doll if not for the darts emanating from those emerald eyes. The death stare exceeded expectations and he sought refuge by glancing at her stationary arms. They remained paralyzed by her side which meant she viewed him as a stranger in both family and business. Brad always relished the role of color commentator. He pictured him at the dining room table, sipping merlot and spraying the air with vulgarities about his pain-in-the-butt-ex-family-member.

He reached for Marcy's hand and it felt clammy and limp for the half second of contact. Addressing the blue spiral mosaic rug, he muttered a flat "I'm sorry," while noticing a small stain on the carpet. *Sorry? How can five letters strung together be elastic enough to convey condolences at a time like this or cover the embarrassment of spilling a cup of coffee at a restaurant? I wince whenever I hear "late" or "adopted." Maybe I should add "sorry" to the list too.*

Looking at Marcy again, he suddenly felt weak in the knees and not because of the cold reception. Stripping away the fixation on his embarrassment, he saw a woman grieving the loss of a husband and father. The widow did not notice the extraordinary epiphany taking place and simply nodded her dismissal and turned to greet the next wayfarer. It did not require extraordinary peripheral vision to see her bear-hug a younger version of himself and weep uncontrollably.

The walls in the room began moving inward like a giant vice as the scent of lilies and carnations made him nauseous. He sought escape before fainting in the high traffic area and stealing the show. Nonetheless, he could not ignore tonight's guest of honor and sought refuge on the cushioned kneeler in front of the dark walnut casket. He studied the dead man's face and thought if Brad could look in the mirror, he would haunt the person responsible for the heavy make-up. Other than that, the dark blue suit looked rather slimming and wondered if Marcy also included his signature black wingtips. *Talk about having a stiff sole!* He let out a small chirp as he swallowed a laugh. After another slow scan of the exposed upper half, he concluded Brad did not look that bad for a dead guy after all.

The kneeler began wobbling and after shifting his weight, he closed his eyes and cleared his mind of fake red cheeks and pigs-in-a-blanket-toes squished in shoe leather. "*Hail Mary full of grace,* he began...but the prayer felt like a badly constructed paper plane and nosedived, so he skipped to the end: "*Pray for us sinners now and at the hour of our death.*" His parents tried passing on their Christian faith but quickly realized the seed landed on rocky soil. When he kneeled to say his nightly prayers, his mother listened to the mechanical drone and she'd whisper a quote from *Hamlet*: "*My words fly up; my thoughts remain below. Words without thoughts never to Heaven go.*"

He opened his eyes and half-expected Brad to wake and yell "Hypocrite!" *No matter. Dead or alive Brad remained an arrogant scoundrel even if social norms required elevating the good portions of a life to makes the grief more powerful. Was the net effect a quid pro quo so everyone gets a nice send off?* He scanned the room and questioned how many others felt the same way. *Down deep they probably were rehashing all the dirty tricks regarding the lying, cheating, money hungry hedonist. Shakespeare's insight "that the evil that men do lives after them; the good is oft interred with their bones," summed things up nicely.*

He looked at Brad's fingers and tried remembering how they once caressed his son. Yet, like a sand castle battered by the incoming tide, the image crumbled and he was left with memories how those same digits flipped people off, stroked any woman within reach and cradled expensive coffee cups. Now they were wrapped permanently with black rosary beads. *How foreign they must feel to him. If they whispered salvation at all, it was in a foreign tongue and remained nothing more than cold glass nuggets pressing against flesh and someday only bone.* He bit his lip. *Marcy should have stuffed a few shares of stock certificates in his hands instead of the beads. If he had his way, they would have been XRE shares so they could burn him for eternity.*

Sudden thoughts about his own demise surprised him and he turned his head sideways to count heads. *I won't win this popularity contest.* When his time came, he envisioned a short line of family and a few associates from work. No doubt, Miller would drive the funeral director nuts with questions about the mercy meal.

And what about Darlene?... Would she make a dramatic entrance with a son that no longer needed a mother's hand?... And Emmett— would he kneel and say a prayer or whisper a curse instead?... By then it would be too late to say "I'm sorry!" He took a deep breath. *How can I make it right with my son?* A small voice in his head shot back, *"You can't."*

The top button of his shirt felt like a noose and he stood up and moved to the left, knowing a dozen people were shooting daggers into his back for hogging the kneeler. He searched for the exit and found Stephanie standing in the doorway studying him. Three months had passed since he last saw her, and he hoped she would have put on a hundred pounds by now. Instead, she looked stunning, even with the sad expression. Her dark hair was pulled back and she wore a form fitting black cocktail dress perfect for any occasion. It made him wonder if she had plans later with some other stiff.

He gave a short wave. She hurried over and led him to a large outer room with dozens of folding chairs for those pretending this was an Irish wake.

"Thank-you for coming," she said touching his arm gingerly with one finger like he was a gross stink bug seeking a winter residence.

"Are you kidding? I wouldn't have missed it," he replied much too quickly and glanced down at his feet expecting the metamorphosis to begin any second.

Intense deep-set eyes blinked back tears. "It looked like you spent some time trying to make up with my brother."

He bit his lip to suppress a smile. *Just goes to show Gustave Flaubert was right. "There is no truth. There is only perception,"* he mused.

The ridiculousness of it all made him want to ask if Brad was wearing shoes but decided against it. "Any more news on what happened?"

"The doctors are still waiting on the test results from the state lab, but they think he was exposed to some super strain of botulism."

"Botulism? From where?"

"You know how my brother deplored bland food and loved gastro exploring. Marcy and I constantly gave him grief about it, but he would laugh and say he had a cast iron stomach. The Health Department has been notified just in case it's linked to another contaminated batch of ready-to-eat meals. They have begun testing local area restaurants too as a precaution. They may be on to something as a janitor in Brad's building showed up at Holy Family Hospital last night with the same symptoms. If the food is tainted like a year ago, they'll be more riots for sure."

He waved her off. "That was fake news. The hundreds that died were tragic for sure. However, the FBI proved the contamination wasn't from rancid ingredients but from some sicko's wanting to cause panic and overthrow the government."

She shook her head in strong disagreement and he shrugged. "This isn't the time or place to argue. No matter how Brad got sick, it's terrible. Go figure, though. The guy never had a sniffle in all the years I knew him, and some bad food does him in."

"Yeah, go figure," she repeated as the lines around her puffy eyes deepened. "I think he could stomach a lot of things, except family betrayal," she said with her voice cracking.

Betrayed? He replayed the greeting from Marcy. *Were his last words about me going nutso about XRE or pulling out some of my gains so I could have available funds for the opportunity Carl was pitching?* All he could do was shrug again. "Look, I don't want to get into this tonight. We had some disagreements about business, that's all."

"Well, you should have had the decency to tell him if you were planning on leaving him." The broken voice regained its strength. "I did when it came to us."

His underarms felt wet and he noticed an elderly couple sitting in the corner of the room watching the show. He rejoined the battle. "I don't know what you want me to say. I made a few changes, but nothing drastic. We talked all the time and maybe that was the problem. He got on my nerves and the feeling was probably mutual."

"It cuts both ways. When I tell my therapist about this, she'll remind me again how you lack testicular fortitude because if you had any, you would have picked up the phone and called my brother. That's one good thing about this messed up world now. You can't hide behind emails and texts anymore. Talking is the new communication tool and you blew it. My brother sometimes came across as a cad, but it was just a front to hide his sensitivity in a dog-eat-dog industry. If you ask me what—"

"But I'm not asking you," he said cutting her off and pulled her down to sit. Mr. and Mrs. Nosey continued staring from ten feet away. He looked into the eyes he once vowed to honor for the rest of his life and felt his capitalist heart blink. "Okay, I should have called Brad and explained instead of just calling into customer service." He looked down at Stephanie's black pumps and knew they probably cost five hundred bucks.

His ex-wife let out a short sigh. "Why is making you see things properly so tough, Daffy Duck?"

He rather be punched in the gut than compared with that combative cartoon character. She did it whenever she thought his love affair with finance overshadowed their relationship, which meant he heard the horrible nickname almost every day of their marriage. He wanted to tell her where to go knowing her brother might already be there but kept the warm wishes silent.

They both watched Marcy walk across the front of the room and head toward the restroom.

"How is she holding up?" he asked.

Stephanie continued looking in the direction of her sister-in-law. "Devastated of course. She thought Brad had some sort of stomach flu when he came home from work. Between the bouts of sickness, she gave him aspirin and put cold facecloths on his forehead. She called 911 when he took a sudden turn for the worse."

He looked around. "Did Loretta stop by and pay her respects?"

Stephanie returned an icy stare, and he noticed the muscles in her jaw flinch.

He covered up the gaffe by shaking his head. "Well, even a broken clock is right twice a day. I'm glad she did the right thing. It would have been awkward for Marcy," he said quickly. "How are you holding up?" he asked knowing Stephanie liked talking about Stephanie.

She dabbed one eye with a tissue she kept in a tight ball in her right hand. "Well, you know how close we were. Being the big sister, I always watched out for him." She paused and caught another tear with the paper ball. "He really stepped up after we separated. Now he's gone."

Anyone else would have immediately responded by providing comfort—a pat on the shoulder or a hug. Given their circumstances, however, he did not want to make a spectacle of himself and risk rejection. Instead, he reached for a box of tissues on a side table and offered her one. Surprisingly, she shook her head no and continued using the spent one.

"Can I get you a glass of water?" he asked gently.

She closed her eyes and ignored the offer.

Her tears always softened his stone exterior. "Look, I'm really sorry about Brad," he offered. "We had our ups and downs, but hey, what family doesn't? Remember that vacation in Maine we took with Brad and Marcy? We rented all those *Three Stooges* videos and you laughed so hard you wet your pants. Now those were good times." He reached over and grabbed her hand and a thousand memories flashed in his mind. *How did I let it go wrong?* He shook the thought off with a forced smile. "If you think about it, Brad and I outlasted our marriage."

She let out a small chuckle.

The ice continued melting as he held her hand. "Would things have turned out differently if we had succeeded in having a baby?" The thought tortured him since the divorce and more so since speaking with his father.

She let go of his hand. "Why would you ask that?"

He was good masking his intentions and hesitated for a second. "Well, I saw little Brad in the other room. It got me thinking, I guess."

"Wow! Thinking of something other than numbers? Now that's a surprise." She reached for a new tissue and blew her nose. "On our first date you said you had a twenty-year plan with nothing written in pencil. Kids were in the margin with a question mark. How did that work out for you? For us?"

The back of his throat began hurting and he felt like reaching for a tissue too. *Big boys don't cry. Dad drilled that into me. I didn't when Mom died or signing the divorce papers.*

"You said you knew the way but were too pigheaded like most men to stop and ask for directions when we got lost. Heaven knows I wasted years telling you we needed assistance especially when my tests came back fine. Why you were ashamed of looking into something beyond your control I could never understand … well, until recently.

"Not shame, just regret." *What happened recently that made her change her perspective?*

She dropped the spent tissues in a wastebasket next to him. He noticed they were the first in the bucket. "Not a dry eye in the place" would never define this wake.

"Funny you should autopsy our marriage at a funeral home," she continued. "A fitting venue perhaps, but as you ponder life, be honest for once and remember how you considered children a complication especially as time went on and nothing came to be. If there were a crystal ball for an alternate reality, you would see our child sitting here with me and you still tethered to a spreadsheet back at the office." She gave him an odd look. "Did you ever want a son?"

The question made him clear his throat in an attempt to block the image of Darlene laughing. "That's not fair. You're twisting my words into a pretzel. I distinctly remember saying yes, children required a huge time investment, but we wanted to start a family. In the meantime, we had our careers and plenty of time."

"Funny, how you mention time. I guess funeral homes make you think about that too." She looked around the room. "Losing my brother puts everything in perspective. It makes me realize I should have a wake and bury all my regrets, but then I recall the little consideration I got in the settlement and it makes me furious. Pitiful pennies on the dollar."

"C'mon! You're really going there tonight?"

She stood up. "I'll be fine. My little brother will be watching out for me up in heaven. I have to get back with Marcy."

He watched her disappear in the crowd and he headed in the opposite direction. On the way out, he ran into the ancient looking funeral director. The shriveled prune of a man wore a bad white toupee and looked so gaunt he might have already died, but no one had the heart to tell him.

"Will you be attending the funeral tomorrow?" he inquired in a deep voice.

Todd hoped no one was eavesdropping. "It's a shame I can't," he replied sounding contrite while picturing the sea of spreadsheets he would be swimming in and remembering Stephanie's prophetic words.

He had his tie off before he got to the car and wanted to forget this emotional hit-and-run disaster. However, he didn't make it out of the parking space before his ex-wife appeared out of nowhere and banged on his window. She was smoking one of those new thin hand-rolled cigarettes.

He rolled down the window. "When did you start with the underground cancer sticks?"

"When did you become my father?" came the curt reply.

She leaned in the window and Todd smelled her perfume. It reminded him of the romantic getaway on the Cape when they were first married. A nor'easter whipped up the waves and they laughed watching overly confident surfers get walloped. She thought it was a metaphor for them: crazy but committed no matter what nature threw at them. They had no need for cellphones or tv that weekend—they had each other and that was enough. Well, at least until they checked out and he got into an argument with the front desk about the mini-bar charges. He complained about it for most of the ride home and by the time he turned into the driveway, an uneasy silence settled in like the front of a slow-moving storm.

The memory broke when Stephanie exhaled. The smoke drifted in and he waved it away.

"Did you notice the sympathy bouquet I ordered for you?" she asked.

"Were they yellow?" He wished they were dandelions.

She rolled her eyes. "No."

"Haven't I apologized enough for one evening? There were so many flowers. Did you expect me to read all the tags to locate mine?"

"They were beautiful carnations and nearly impossible to get. They cost you a hundred dollars," she added with the countenance of a loan officer.

"Okay. I'll send you a check."

She reached in and touched his shoulder quickly. "Things have been a bit tight for me lately. Can you pay me tonight?"

He almost asked if the treasure she received in the settlement was housed in Fort Knox for safekeeping. That she continued complaining about the amount, made his cheeks hot. The request was also sort of crass—the dead guy's sister chasing him at the wake for flower money. He bit his tongue and squirmed reaching for his wallet.

"Well, I got forty bucks, will that do for tonight?" he asked quickly. "I can send you the balance tomorrow." He hoped the lunacy of the situation would hit her.

Instead, she just pouted more. "Marcy's had a tough day, and I thought a nice glass of cabernet would help her unwind. Tomorrow is going to be surreal with the funeral and burial. I was planning on taking her to Stowell's as they just reopened. Forty bucks will hardly cover a mouthful of two buck chuck. Can you give me a check? After all the dinners we've had down there, I'm sure they'll cash it."

If he wanted a laugh, he would shadow her for the next couple hours. Knowing Stephanie, she would comfort the widow by finding some unlicensed food truck that served peanut butter gelatin squares. Any extra compassion would equate to slowing down in front of Marcy's house long enough so she could jump out. The truth was his ex-wife probably had a late dinner date with some muscle man with no wallet.

Todd found the spare check he kept hidden in his wallet and quickly scribbled the draft and handed it to her.

She examined it for a second making sure all was in order. "Okay, I'll see you tomorrow at the funeral."

He was lost for words and just nodded. Miller was being a taskmaster about the budget and Carl wanted a commitment about investing in the Bad Creek plant. There would be blowback from Stephanie for sure, but begging for forgiveness was easier than asking permission. Unfortunately, that list was growing.

CHAPTER FOURTEEN

Todd located *Big Bertha* on a shelf in his father's garage. The 10 x 12 forest green tarpaulin was the type every retail store sold—and this one's sole mission was transporting leaves and pine needles. While Tanned folks used lawnmowers and blowers for the fall clean-up, his dad preferred the manual method used since the Pilgrims arrived. Todd carried the neatly folded tarp into the back yard and began the painful process of unfolding it on the lawn. Bertha cooperated until a puff of wind came along and she instantly fashioned a sail hoping to escape the tedious assignment.

Todd jumped on the tarp trying to keep it earthbound and half expected a wrestling referee to appear from behind a tree and judge the meet. The combat sport also defined the father-son relationship for the past week. As penance, his father asked him to move a dozen piles of leaves strategically located around the yard. Anchoring Bertha down with rocks in each corner, he began the laborious task of moving the first monstrous pile onto the tarp. As the transfer progressed, he discovered lime green grass underneath, indicating the fall castoffs were suffocating the lawn. It made him think how Emmett was buried under everything too.

With the gluttonous tarp fully loaded, Todd bent down and discovered the rope handles missing. Whether this represented added punishment by his old man, he couldn't say.

After letting out a low groan, he grabbed one corner of the beast and began walking backwards. After a few feet, he was out of breath and stopped. The journey's end remained a good hundred feet away and required navigation around a large pine stump. Only then could he empty the contents onto the official Dolan leaf pile, which now stood four feet high by ten foot deep.

While he respected tradition, exhaustion convinced him to seek an alternate home for this load. Looking around, he spotted the compost pile half the distance away on the edge of the woods. His dad discarded all sorts of miscellaneous things there: coffee grinds, grass clippings, annual flowers after a killer frost and a few buckets of rogue leaves. A rusted pitchfork leaned against a nearby birch to turn the refuse over. "Garbage to gold," the suburban alchemist would brag.

He started diagonally across the lawn while keeping a watchful eye on the house. Thankfully, the house stared back in silence. He could envision the old man banging on the glass, and pointing toward the official leaf cemetery. "Because in the Dolan family everything is disposed of properly, including a grandson," he whispered.

When he reached the destination, he aggressively attacked the area with the pitchfork. As he turned over one clump after another and moved congealed chunks aside, puffs of white smoke rose, and a pungent smell of decay filled the air. After moving enough material, he emptied the illegal shipment in the hole. Then he picked up the pitchfork, intent on scattering the displaced compost on top of the leaves. If he could fake being a landscape artist for a few more minutes, the transgression would be hidden.

Looking again at the pile, he froze.

Laying on top of the leaves was a white sheet covering a small form. Using the end of the pitchfork, he carefully peeled back the linen and discovered a naked baby boy about a year old. He had dark hair and a cowlick in the middle of his forehead. Studying his gray face, he noticed the nostrils were plugged with leaves.

He lost his balance and fell backwards. Struggling to get up, he saw his father running across the lawn toward him. His white hair stood on end as if electrified.

"I warned you about digging up the past!" he yelled.

Turning back around, Brad was sitting where the dead baby had been seconds ago. He was jaundiced and his hands were wrapped with black rosary beads which made deep indentations in the rotting fingers.

The dead man leered at him. "What are you trying to hide? We have a glass ceiling down there and see everything!" He tilted his head and smiled. "You'll see for yourself soon enough. For the damned, it's like winter without the hope of spring."

Todd sucked in his breath…and heard a loud pounding on the front door. He bolted upright and wondered if he was still dreaming while struggling to free himself from the bedding.

"Who is it?" he yelled, before reaching the front door and expecting to hear a ghoulish laugh from Brad.

"You sound like a scaredy-cat that lost his night-light," a familiar voice answered.

Todd winced and glanced at the miniature grandfather clock in the corner of the hall. Even in the dim light, he could see it was 1:30 a.m.

His fingers fumbled with the lock. When he finally succeeded in opening the door, the porch light illuminated Darlene's red satin blouse.

She rolled her eyes like she had been waiting for an hour. "And I thought I slept like a rock. Tell me, did you sleep through the riots too?"

He blinked hard still questioning whether this was a dream. "Why are you here so late?"

"Another example of how we perceive things differently. I think it's early, and you say it's late." She looked past him. "Are you going to invite me in or wait until sunrise?"

Do I have a choice? He held the door open and scanned the empty driveway.

She moved slowly past him and he automatically held his breath to not smell her perfume. He followed her into the living room, wondering how she seemed familiar with the layout.

"Don't you ever wear a coat?" he asked, stifling a yawn. He turned on the track lighting outfitted with only two bulbs.

She spun around and approached him like he asked a very inappropriate question. The first two buttons of her shirt were now unbuttoned, and he noticed the tip of something red against her white skin. He tried diverting his eyes before she caught him, but it was too late.

Darlene smiled seductively and pulled the top of her shirt aside revealing a tattoo of a thin branch running across her chest and disappearing over the right shoulder. The bark had an alligator skin appearance and populated with a myriad of teardrop red leaves.

"There's nothing like sumac; so vibrant, so symbolic," she said softly. "Not like a rose that advertises its defenses so you can avoid the thorns. One discovers the cost of touching sumac afterwards. It's the same with me." She stopped within inches and he made the mistake of inhaling quarter-century kryptonite.

He made a half-hearted attempt to stop his hands, but they were already pulling her in. He bent over to kiss her.

She pulled back at the last moment before he found her lips. "Do you have something you want to say first?"

The question startled him out of his momentary weakness. *What am I doing?* He backed away.

She looked surprised at his retreat and folded her arms. "Why do you look like a deer in the headlights?"

What does she want me to say? That I confronted my father and he finally caved and told me the whole sorry story? The nightmare of the baby on the leaf pile with leaves stuffed up his nostrils weighed heavy. He did not need any help interpreting the dream and the mea culpa bubbled up from the deep. "*I'm sorry for being such a self-centered coward,*" he imagined saying before his father interceded. "*Given the circumstances and his blackmailing mother, I considered the little guy just an expensive meal ticket.*"

The internal struggle ended in a draw and he faked a yawn instead. "You still haven't said why you're here in the middle of the night."

"I've waited too many years to hear what you would say if given the chance and couldn't deal with another sleepless night. Not that I expected you to beg for forgiveness, but I thought with age you would at least acknowledge what you put me through." She brushed past him and stopped at the hall. "What was I thinking? You haven't changed at all. At least I have clarity moving forward."

Todd noticed her glassy eyes and thought he could smell alcohol mixed in with the floral perfume. He knew the aroma of both well.

He hesitated too long. "We'll revisit this at dinner," she said and headed for the door.

"Dinner? I'm working late all week. Let me put some coffee on and we can talk now."

"No. Just be at my house at seven." She opened the door and looked back. "Because if you don't show up, I'll bring the party here, and it will be very late indeed."

Todd watched her disappear down the driveway and debated whether to go after her. He decided against it because if he gave her a lift home, she might press him about complicated things, and he needed time to think. He shivered thinking how all he wanted in the middle of the night was simplicity which almost led him astray.

After closing the door, he realized any hope of sleep left with Darlene—and crazy as it seemed, he craved a short run to unwind. After quickly changing and lacing up his sneakers, he was on the dark sidewalk in ten minutes.

He started a slow jog and his legs felt pretty stiff. Back in college, running proved more therapeutic than a keg party in releasing tension. His roommate told a funny story about going out for a run after arguing with his girlfriend. Two miles into the run his anger subsided and after a couple more he forgot what the fight was about. After the tenth mile, he could not recall his girlfriend's name. Todd was willing to circle the globe for that type of amnesia. Successful leaders were masters at compartmentalization and until recently, he thought he could lock things away in mental boxes too. Now everything was melting into one dirty puddle.

The real motivation for the short run presented itself when he reached the antique Airstream that doubled as a mobile convenience store. Ten-feet inside the oversized aluminum can, he located a six pack of government sanctioned beer. The Oriental man behind the counter studied him for a moment before ringing up the sale. Todd knew he made a strange sight; a middle-aged jock risking bodily harm by roving gangs for a small buzz.

The journey home proved painfully long as the wet T-shirt turned cold. Approaching the house, he noticed the back porch looked especially dark. *Did the bulb burn out or did some roving derelict steal it?* He left the beer on the back stairs and at the same instant spied a broken pane of glass on the door. The adrenaline rush ignited his thoughts. *Had Darlene come back crazier than before?* He considered running next door but feared they would call the police before assisting a neighbor they never met, or pepper him with buckshot.

He decided a weapon was necessary and retrieved a garden rake from the shed. It had heavy steel teeth that would cause some real hurt if he swung it with gusto. Opening the back door, his fingers found the light switch and no one from a slasher movie pounced on him.

He held the rake in front of him like a sword and began exploring the house.

The bedroom door was strangely closed and he leaned against it and listened. Nothing was perceptible above the pounding in his ears. He half convinced himself that he scared off the intruder but nevertheless carefully opened the door and scanned the bedroom from the relative safety of his position. Everything seemed in order until he saw a small green cube placed on his king-sized pillow. He walked over to retrieve it and discovered a Rubik's cube—except all the tiles were the same color. A small sticker on the top center square read: *Not much of a puzzle when all you see is green.*

"Darlene!" he whispered. Nothing else seemed out of place. A wad of cash remained in the top drawer of his bureau. He made one more sweep through the house just to be sure.

The grandfather clock read nearly three-thirty. Exhaustion rolled in like a thick fog trapping his anxiety. He debated whether he should rest a while with one eye closed and then remembered the beer. When he went to retrieve it from the back stairs, however, it was gone. He let out a string of profanities and searched the house for the over the counter therapeutic to no avail. *Should I dial the police? And report what? One broken pane of glass, a missing six pack of beer and an adulterated Rubik's cube? The cops might keep a straight face while they took the report, but he would be marked as a nutcase.*

He retrieved Darlene's phone number from his wallet. He counted three rings before the phone clicked. "Hello?"

Her sleepy tone surprised him, although it meant nothing. He hung up without saying a word.

Todd reached for the Rubik's cube. "Color hers red," he mumbled.

CHAPTER FIFTEEN

Darlene knocked on the door and a second later it flew open and a gaudy Hawaiian shirt pulled her into the apartment.

"Talk about hitting paydirt!" Carl sang as he slammed the door shut. In one swift motion he picked her up and deposited her on the black corduroy couch. The worn springs were still squeaking when he began driving his hands into her sides. She hated the painful tickling and he rarely stopped until she cried. No matter how often she explained this weird fetish was physical abuse, he would laugh it off and say his older brother did the same to him growing up. "*Do you think it's coincidence he's doing five years for aggravated assault?*" she would remind him.

She punched him in the arm as hard as she could from the awkward position. "Knock it off!"

Carl did not acknowledge the command, but stopped. He flopped on the couch next to her and began pumping one leg like it had assumed the body's circulation duties.

"Babe, this has the makings of a masterpiece." He revved his leg into red line territory. "This operation is located somewhere between the Madoff Ponzi scheme and the Nigerian prince email scam. Dolan drooled thinking he could double his money in a year. When he heard you invested two-hundred-fifty thousand, Mr. Tanned was all in at half a million. Guess he wants to seriously outdistance you." He rubbed his hands together. "Is there another moron from your past we can swindle?"

Darlene checked the buttons on her shirt from the assault. "No, he's my perfect storm. When will you close the fool?"

"Todd says the money from his brokerage account will transfer any day. Once it hits the bogus account, Tony will immediately move it."

"So how much will we net?"

He stood up and reached in the back pocket of his tightly fitted jeans and fished out a small piece of paper. "Minus the fees and gratuities for the cast, four hundred twenty-seven thousand." Reciting the number made him jump up.

"Are you really sure no one can trace it to the Cayman Islands?" She asked for the tenth time in the past week. She memorized the bank account number and made sure her name was on the joint account.

His eyebrows dipped. "You keep acting like you have dementia. It's the same questions over and over."

"Well, I never transferred money out of the country before. With the Feds watching everything, I'm on edge."

He rolled his eyes. "Okay, I'll say it again. The channel we're using is secure. Tony made my head spin explaining how he'll move it in and out of cryptocurrency before it lands in our account. No Sherlock will be able to trace it. Even so, I plan on giving him some grief about the service charge."

Darlene studied his fake tan and how it did not penetrate some of the creases on his neck. In his defense, when this "landscaper hack" had any issues regarding Todd's endless inquiries about the hydropower fantasy, he would make a few calls and expand the cast of characters. That said, the longer she was with him, the more she likened him to oven cleaner. You needed gloves to handle his caustic nature, but with a little patience he sure could put a shine on most things."

Carl rubbed his flat stomach. "I've been thinking, we made a huge mistake in not fleecing him for everything instead of taking only a piece. You could have taken care of your mother's housing issues if she lived another twenty years."

She jumped up. "Don't give me that nonsense about looking out for my mother. You just want a bigger pie. I might be a bubble-head about some of the mechanics, but I brought you into this and defined the rules. Greed would have raised a red flag."

"With whom? The dead guy?"

She shook her head violently. "Look, we caught a break when Ponzell caught a nasty bug."

He waved her off. "Give me a break."

She felt her cheeks get hot. "You're the one with memory loss here. I'll say it again. I planned for every option, but had nothing to do with his demise. We were just lucky, that's all. I can read people pretty well and he would have blabbered something to someone."

He looked her up and down. "You'd be a real bore in Vegas. Let me explain how risk brings rewards. We have a small window of opportunity with that broker guy dead. His business must be in a state of chaos and they're processing everything. If our luck holds it will be a while before Todd realizes he's been stung. Check with your friend on the inside and see what he can do to help. We'll make it worth his efforts."

"You can't be serious! He's a janitor."

He ignored the comment. "We need to liquidate the rest of his holdings. Maybe you can draft up a sell order or something. Leave a couple bucks if you're scared of closing the account."

She studied the palm trees on his hideous shirt. *They burn quickly without giving off much heat... Just like this talking head.*

He grabbed her arm. "Did you hear one word I said?"

"For someone that's been so careful in building this house of cards, you're acting incredibly rash." She tried breaking away, but he tightened the grip.

"We have to at least try," he said in a seductive voice and pulled her in. "If something doesn't smell right, we'll blow out of town as planned. Look at it this way: besides taking care of your mother you can set up your boy, so he isn't a Burned for life. Why leave it to chance Todd moves the rest before your son ever gets a penny? With Brad's death, don't you think the beneficiary change will come to light?"

She hated using Carl in a master plan she had been formulating for decades, but sometimes the labor pool is limited. "Don't go lecturing me about my son like you care one iota. You've never asked anything about him."

"Sure, I have!"

"Like what?"

"Well...you told me he likes horses."

"Okay, what's my son's name?"

A pained look overtook his face like he stuck his finger in a light socket. "C'mon! You know I call everyone Champ."

"Says the man who majored in fake ID's. Greed is blinding you. The plan worked better than we dreamed. We made some incredible money so let's enjoy the haul. Wasn't that the goal when we started planning this whole thing?" She eyed him with as much sincerity as she could muster for the litmus test.

The results came back faster than anticipated. Carl pushed her hard and she fell backwards on the couch, hitting her head. Before she could blink, he was in her face. "You're nothing but a self-absorbed loony," he yelled and pinned her arms. "Obsessed over a teenage crush that had his fun and deserted you. That won't qualify for a yawn these days. Better blink hard honey and look around at this cruel Sun-Kissed world and understand you're no different from anyone else. We're all victims! So, throw away the crutch or you'll never learn to walk without it." He lowered his face so they were eye to eye, and she could see the squiggly red veins building bridges across the sclera. "I want to eat real food and not care what beer costs. You should too. Want a life with me? This is the price. Finish the job and I promise to be your cabana boy forever."

She tried wrestling free but he held her tight for another long moment before grunting and getting up.

He hovered over her. "I've been the brains behind this whole scam. What have you done but play make believe in that oversized doll house and blackmail a chunky broker to keep his mouth shut?" Without warning, he reached down and tickled her in the side, except this time it was more of a jab. "Why, I could have paid my ex for more creativity and she's been in a coma for the past year."

He walked into the kitchen and returned with a paper bag of government issued shelled peanuts. "We rushed through this too fast. I blame myself."

She jumped up and blocked his way to the recliner. "What are you talking about? We have almost half a million bucks! I kicked this whole thing off to save my mother."

He shrugged. "Well, she's not on the street yet and could die in her sleep tonight. We should have demanded payment for the pictures of Brad and his mistress. I'm sure he would have been good for twenty-grand. The way we played it, he got off scot-free by changing a beneficiary that Dolan can change back tomorrow, unless he catches the same timely bug as Brad." He took a handful of peanuts. "Lucky for me, I got a cherry for the top of the sundae."

"What are you talking about?"

"Remember that portfolio modeling software?" he stopped and used his finger to dislodge a peanut on a back tooth. "I quoted Dolan three hundred bucks and he gave me a check the other day." He looked in the paper bag and took out another handful of nuts. "A little acetone and three hundred became three thousand." He let out a small laugh. "Sure, hope he has overdraft protection, or he'll be bouncing checks all over town. I don't need modeling software to see a downward trend in his net worth!"

She grabbed the bag away from him and flung it on the floor. "Are you crazy?" she yelled. "What were you thinking?"

"About our future! If it weren't for me, you'd still be wearing a blue apron and shagging carts," he fired back, dwarfing her volume.

"But that wasn't the plan!" She pulled on her hair. "This has real consequences. Why didn't you check with me?"

"Because you'd give me nothing but grief and I don't need your permission. This isn't my first rodeo, you know. I wanted to do a little shopping before we head south. The check went through without a problem." He picked up the peanut bag. "No sweat."

"And you call me crazy?" Her hands went from her scalp to her hips. "We thought Todd wouldn't know he was scammed right away, so we had some time to pack up. Now that's gone. Maybe if you kept the check under a grand, he wouldn't notice right away. But three thousand? Why not thirty?"

"Because I didn't want too much attention when I deposited it."

Darlene shook her head. "You always say go big or go home. Well, you're headed to the big house for sure. Once he finds out, all he has to do is look at the check number and will know it's you."

Carl faked a yawn. "Go ahead and rant all you want. He's going to hate me more for the half million we took. At this point, three-grand is a rounding error."

"Did you consider how the police will review the bank video? She let the comment hang for a long moment. "Did you wear that ugly shirt to the bank too?"

"Why, this is my lucky shirt," Carl snickered as the edges of his lips began twitching slightly. "You're a bag of worry because you overlook one thing. We'll be long gone, or at least, I'll be!" He bent down and looked her in the eye. "I'll get your mind off this real fast. Add something to our pot, or Tony will move all the money one more time and you won't see a penny. Ignore me and I'll use a third party to turn you in too. Who knows, maybe Homeland Security will give me a reward." He looked in the peanut bag. "You're cute all right, but not as hot as you think. As a matter of fact, I'm considering other offers." He laughed. "It's crazy the women you attract as a Tanned."

Other offers? Darlene cocked her head and studied the waste of skin standing in front of her. She had all the info she needed.

Carl wiped his hands on his jeans. "I'm starving. Let's eat early since you have a lot to accomplish."

Darlene forced some tears and let them hydrate her mascara for the right effect. Nodding quickly, she reached for her purse. "Let me freshen up. I heard there's a new roving foodie bus at Tuscan Village."

He grunted and wandered into the kitchen.

She slipped into the cramped bathroom at the end of the hall and locked the door. Her reflection in the mirror showed no hint of remorse—just the usual beaten-up expression. When the water got good and hot, she cupped her hands and splashed her face. Yet, no matter how much she rinsed her eyes, all she could see was the ugly Hawaiian shirt connected to a bobbing head. *I needed him for his connections. Carl may have an inkling of what's in store for Todd but doesn't realize he's playing with fire. He's no different than the others; just another plastic Ken doll. Now he will pay too.*

Retrieving the tube of mascara from the bottom of her purse, she began applying a liberal dose. She remembered Carl's swagger as she was rounding up shopping carts on a humid summer day. He looked ruggedly handsome in a burnt orange short-sleeve shirt that accented his tan. The good-looking stranger stopped and helped her push the long train of carriages into the USDA store. She thought chivalry died long ago. Later on, he confessed eying her in a bar the night before. The offer of assistance was nothing more but a loan on sexual favors he expected repaid with interest.

Emmett badgered her for years about the string of men she dated. He called all of them Uncle which upset her—not because she loved any of them, but that her son saw her as needy. *The silly lad, didn't he understand how she lived according to the maxim of an eye for an eye?* The recipe for payback consisted of three ingredients dispensed in equal parts: patience, opportunity, and creative microbiology. Thankfully, she knew how to mix, incubate, and dispense. No matter the recipient, they were all fallen descendants of Adam and none worse than Todd. Carl would be the latest four-lettered victim.

She opened the mirrored medicine cabinet and found her boyfriend's mangled tube of government supplied toothpaste. It looked like it was run over by a Mack truck. Not surprisingly, he was one of those lazy derelicts that squeezed the tube from the top.

Her right breast began to ache, and she pressed her fingers against the sumac tattoo hoping the pain would disappear as quickly as it came. The doctor at the clinic said the prognosis looked good, but she knew the cancer cells that escaped the chemo were simply hiding and regrouping. When the ambush came—next week, month or year, she would be ready. After all, she knew what betrayal felt like. Maybe the cancer had some empathy and ached in support of the master plan.

She unzipped a small side pocket in her purse and retrieved a plastic ampoule loaded with the deadly concoction. *So tidy and convenient* she thought, as the old-style glass ampoules required a special breaker. While the screw-off top allowed for the contents to be dispensed with a single squeeze, she planned an additional step for today's application. Using a small hypodermic needle from her purse, she loaded the clostridium botulism suspension into the chamber and carefully transferred it into the head of the toothpaste tube and repeated the procedure throughout its body.

She placed the toothpaste back on the shelf and smiled. *With a good brushing, he'll be on his way in no time.*

She flushed the ampoule down the toilet and wrapped the needle in a wad of tissues and put it back in her purse.

Carl sat on the couch surfing the channels. "This is a rip off," he protested. "In the old days, I got the wrestle mania channel for free. Now all I get is the news or reruns of some ancient show called *Bonanza.*"

"Poor you," she almost sang, and checked her watch. "I'll see what I can do to add to our kitty, and talk with my son about looking after my mother. It may take a day or so and then we can head south."

Carl turned off the TV and jumped up and gave her a hug. "It's about time you came to your senses." He planted a wet kiss on her neck and then began tickling her before she grabbed his hands. "Just think how we'll be sipping Pina-coladas on a tropical beach soon. We'll be set forever."

"We just need a bit more luck."

He waved her off. "You make your own. What happened in the bathroom that made you a convert?"

"Our little spat made me see the whole situation in a new light. Maybe I'm going about this all wrong." She smiled at him again. "It'll take your breath away when you see how fast I work. Now hurry up and get ready," she said and kissed him on the lips.

Carl's eyes danced for a second before noticing the disgusted look on Darlene's face. "What's the matter?"

She pinched her nose. "All I smell are peanuts! How many did you eat?" She pointed toward the hall. "Make sure you brush your teeth extra good, or we'll both taste them all night." She grabbed him around the waist. "Let's buy a bottle of something special tonight instead of rotgut vodka. We can toast our good fortune and our future in the Caribbean."

Her boyfriend looked almost giddy at the thought of becoming an instant millionaire. Carl cupped his hand and smelled his breath. "Yuk, I see what you mean."

Darlene followed him into the bathroom and watched him reach for the toothpaste. The contents flowed out a bit watery, but her boyfriend was too blinded by visions of easy living to notice. She remained vigilant and cheered him on, cajoling him to brush good and long and not forget his tongue. He readily obeyed and in a couple minutes she felt satisfied the soil had been sufficiently hydroseeded. Now nature would do the rest.

After Carl spit out the remainder of the toothpaste into the sink, she retreated to the living room. The last thing she wanted was a contagious kiss.

He called out from the bathroom. "Should I wear my conman outfit?" he asked. "I may as well get some use out of it."

Darlene thought for a moment and almost laughed at the irony. It was the blue suit he bought to impress Todd. Soon it would impress the mourners at the funeral home. Everyone would notice how handsome he looked in the casket. She hoped he would be there by the weekend as her calendar was booking up fast.

CHAPTER SIXTEEN

The hard-shell suitcase survived a mile in the bed of the rusted Ford F-150 before nearly getting ejected. Cotton heard the telltale thud after hitting a pothole and pulled over for a pit stop. Thirty seconds later he had the jade green valise wedged between a spare tire and a milk crate filled with jugs of antifreeze.

When he climbed back into the cab of the pickup, Jennifer scooted next to him on the cracked leather bench. She fumbled with the radio knob looking for a country station.

"New Hampshire or bust!" he laughed and hit the accelerator.

Jennifer looked out the rear window at the tucked-in suitcase. "With all the antifreeze I see back there, maybe I should have brought hiking shoes."

Cotton gently stroked the dashboard. "C'mon Jenny, have a little faith in my girl Ethel. Up until a few months ago, she was sleeping under a tarp in a farmer's barn. Now she's enjoying an unexpected afterlife. That said, I should mention Ethel gets a bit temperamental about the weather."

"You mean she doesn't like rain?"

They hit another bump in the road and he grabbed Jenny's arm as she came out of her seat. "It's all a matter of degree. Sprinkles and brief showers are fine, but anything heavier and Ethel feels like she's being water boarded. I've had a few mechanics look and they can't figure out why the motor cuts out." He shot her a quick look. "I guess you could say she's a fair-weather friend."

They followed an old state road traveling northeast that weaved through a succession of small towns. Some showed more recovery than others in terms of new construction. Regardless of location, they all contained dozens of burned and boarded up buildings waiting to be razed and endless piles of stacked firewood in every nook and cranny. The outskirt of each town told a similar story with vast fields filled with cars and trucks as if some modern-day Woodstock festival were underway, except these represented the electronic-fried-casualties. Jennifer took it all in and understood why Dad thought life in the designated area might be a bit surreal but the best place for now.

Between towns, the road turned rural for long stretches and they passed farms and meadows and forests, a nice departure from the interstate that worshipped straight lines and smooth pavement. The Indian summer day felt so glorious Jennifer thought nature might skip winter altogether. In typical male fashion, Cotton joked how the sun was determined to undress the trees.

Between laughs and small-talk they enjoyed the music, comfortable enough with each other for the empty spaces in-between. This proved fortunate when the radio copped an attitude and intermittently cut out, usually in the middle of a song.

Amid this kaleidoscope of color, Jennifer thought creation never looked more alive than when pieces of it were dying. She marveled not only at the beauty, but how the leaves fell from the branches without a breath of wind. *What tells them it's time to let go?*

She glanced every now and then back at the suitcase and thought about the store. It felt odd taking a trip instead of tackling the burned-out mess. She rushed into the store at first light after the firemen left and wandered through a soggy ashtray. Some things looked salvageable, but until the insurance company completed their inspection and cut the check, there was little she could do.

So here she was with a guy that picked trash cans for some inexplicable reason and made- up lyrics when he forgot the words to a song. *Was Cotton a distraction or something more?* The next few days might provide some clarity to the question. Meeting his mother also promised to be interesting. Maybe she collected odd things too.

When they crossed into Massachusetts at Sturbridge, they jumped on the Mass Pike and as quickly as the speed limit changed, so did Cotton. The singing and happy-go-lucky demeanor disappeared. He seemed to be steeling himself for the visit home.

It was past dinner time when they pulled into the driveway of Rockingham Nursing Home in Salem, New Hampshire.

She looked at him sideways. "Interesting destination for a romantic dinner."

He laughed for the first time in fifty miles and it made her feel good. "You're like my momma, very quick on the draw." He opened his door. "C'mon. There's someone I want you to meet."

They held hands and walked through a nicely appointed and brightly lit front lobby. The long corridor ahead was lined with elderly men and women. Many were in wheelchairs. Every now and then the smell of urine permeated her nose and she instinctively held her breath. Cotton did not seem to be bothered by it at all and she figured he was conditioned to stronger smells from the ranch. As they continued on, Cotton stopped to gently pump one man's hand and hug another woman in a wheelchair. Jennifer found the contrast jarring; she focused on avoiding unpleasant smells while he worked on touching souls.

They stopped at Room 302. Even with the door half closed, the guttural snoring sounded like the F150 minus its exhaust system.

"Nana likes the door mostly closed, because the light from the hall keeps her awake," Cotton explained. "I think if the nurses had their way, they'd nail it shut and cover it with insulation." He pointed down the hall and smirked. "You may have noticed she's the only one with a private room and it's probably prevented a murder or two. I don't snore, but I'll sure learn how to fake one if I ever end up in a place like this."

Cotton slowly pushed the door open. The light from the hall illuminated a small woman with snow white hair lying on her back in a hospital bed. Even though the temperature in the room bordered on tropical, a white wool blanket reached her shoulders.

Cotton pointed at the snoring woman with her mouth open and free of dentures. "Meet my nana," he announced in a loud voice.

"Won't you wake her?" she whispered.

He smirked. "We could light off firecrackers and she wouldn't stir a muscle. I've never seen anything like it."

"Wish I could sleep like that," she replied still in a whisper.

"Unless a fire breaks out and then it could be a problem. At home, she used to set two alarm clocks to bring her back from the dead each morning." He scanned the empty dinner tray on a side table and chuckled. "I don't know how she stomachs the gruel they serve in here. You wouldn't know it by her small frame, but she can really pack it away. She loves nothing more than boiled dinners. After watching her consume a platter of corned beef, carrots, cabbage, turnip and potatoes, I thought she was in training for Nathan's Hot Dog Eating Contest—and that was before dessert. The hilarious thing is whenever Momma began clearing the table, she'd ask for a crust of bread. Some might call it gluttony, but Nana went hungry as a kid."

"Given the last few years, hunger has become a universal memory."

"She's fond of calling it the years of plenty before the tribulation. Given a tough childhood and now trying to afford this place, scarcity has been the bookends of her life. Maybe that's why she enjoyed being as full as a tick."

Cotton stroked his grandmother's white hair demonstrating a gentleness Jennifer rarely observed in a man, never mind a novice cowboy.

"She kept me sane," he continued, "and whenever I stayed at her house, she made me feel like a king. I'd wake up to the smell of bacon and would find her hand squeezing orange juice. Who else in the world gets pampered like that? She would laugh at my astonishment and say if I grew up in the 60's, I would have complained if it wasn't *Tang*, because that's what the astronauts drank."

"I haven't seen a carton of orange juice in years." Jennifer let out a sigh. "I hear they offer it now at fancy places like the Four Seasons with real eggs and bacon."

He winked. "If you like Spam, I know a guy. With Nana, it didn't stop with breakfast. After stuffing me, she'd begin baking a dessert for dinner and I'd lick the frosting bowl. It's a wonder I'm not diabetic from those days." He stopped for a moment reliving the memories. "Man, she spoiled me rotten and I had a bit of an attitude when I got home.

Then Momma would re-introduce me to the real world and sometimes a new uncle."

"I'm sure you gagged on your cold cereal the next morning."

"Or watch Uncle hog the milk."

She frowned. "Well, there's nothing like a grandmother to make you feel special."

"No disrespect," he said pointing at the bed, "but she's in a class all by herself. Whenever Uncle raised Cain or my mother went on a binge, Nana would swoop in and whisk me away. I'll never forget being nine-years old and standing day after day at recess watching the kids play baseball. I begged Momma for a glove. "Next week when I get paid," she'd promise, but payday would come and go, and she'd say things were tight. I wasn't sure if she was talking about money or the new sweater she bought."

Cotton's bottom lip quivered for a second. "I'd try to play without a glove which didn't impress my buddies none when I dropped anything that came my way. Then some smart aleck kid would suggest I jump rope with the girls. I had more than a few fights."

Nana stopped snoring and the sudden silence made them both watch her for a few seconds before a new chorus began.

"The humiliation went on for months," Cotton continued. "Then one afternoon Nana met me after school. I thought Mom went AWOL again, but she assured me everything was okay and winked. "I'm taking you downtown for a baseball glove," she said. And I remember thinking, "but it's not my birthday." Cotton took a deep breath caught up in the memory. "Nana wanted to protect Momma from being embarrassed. Instead, she blamed it on watching the Sox lose the night before. She said I'd better get learning how to catch fly balls if I was ever going to handle the Green Monster someday."

"How special."

"When we arrived at the sporting goods store, I couldn't believe how they had gloves sorted by type: catchers, first baseman, outfielder. You could smell the leather from ten feet away. I picked out a glove and all I could do was smile and begin punching the palm to break it in. Before we left, Nana bought me a bat too. Having a bat made me special at school and in the neighborhood. It not only gave me instant respectability, but a lot of invites for pick-up games. The thing is, I never told Momma anything about the humiliation at school, but somehow, she knew. She was always doing things like that for me even though she couldn't afford it."

Sleeping Beauty's eyes popped open. "Emmett?"

"Hi Nana," Cotton whispered.

"What are you doing here in the middle of the night?" she asked hoarsely.

"Watching you sleep."

"Well then, hand me my glasses so I can watch you watching me."

Cotton turned on a small lamp and found her silver wire rim glasses and handed them to her. Slipping them on, she came to life. "I baked brownies this afternoon and put in some nice fat walnuts." She began moving her fingers as if stirring the batter. "I gave a few to Helen next door but she didn't invite me in for a cup of tea. I know ungrateful when I see it. She's just an old bird that wants my recipe!"

Cotton winked at Jennifer. "No worries, Nana. You could give her the recipe and all the ingredients, and she'd still come up short."

A knowing smile rose on the old woman's face. "Who is the lovely girl with you?"

"This is Jenny," he said putting his arm around her.

She reached for Nana's hand and it felt softer than a baby's bum.

"What a beautiful smile you have," the old woman commented. "You must be someone special. My grandson never brings anyone to visit me here."

She let out a short cough and her face suddenly turned serious. "Where is your mother? I haven't seen her in a month."

"I'm sure it hasn't been that long," Cotton replied and flashed a smile camouflaging the disappointment. "She's been working extra shifts, like everyone else."

"That girl worries me so! She works so hard trying to support herself never mind helping me. I hate being a burden." She took off her glasses and her face melted into exhaustion. "This vacation has been wonderful, but think I've overstayed my welcome. I'm ready to go home."

Cotton nodded like he heard the same request a hundred times before. "Nana, remember how you fell and broke your hip and the doctor said you needed special care?"

"And who is this lovely lady?" she asked again. "Can I get you both something, maybe a nice glass of lemonade and a brownie? I just baked some this afternoon and left the walnuts out. Too many people in here with nut allergies, you know."

Cotton bent down before turning off the light. "We'll be back soon. Get some sleep."

"God bless you both," she whispered.

On the way out, a heavy-set man in a black suit appeared in the doorway of the administrator's office.

"Mr. Connolly, can we have a word? Your mother has not returned my calls and we need to make some decisions."

Cotton nodded and turned to Jennifer. "This will only take a minute."

She continued on and felt relieved when the lobby doors opened. The air was cool and the crickets continued singing. Meandering into the courtyard, she felt like running through the adjoining field because she still could, unlike the aged humanity tucked into bed behind her—their dreams frosting the windows and doors.

CHAPTER SEVENTEEN

Darlene opened the front door before he reached the stairs. *So now the chameleon is a provocative blonde?* If he had any stamina left, he might inquire about the Dolly Parton wig. Instead, he focused on her new attire of navy-blue sweater and jeans.

"You look like you went fifteen rounds with the boss and lost," she commented in a matter-of-fact tone.

He searched her face for any leftovers from their last encounter. "Yeah, I was down on the mat for the count. In desperation, I asked Miller about his favorite food and he backed off and started sketching an antipasto."

She shot him a quizzical look. "I don't understand."

"Neither do I." He followed her down a short hall and she opened a closet door and took out a hanger.

"I've had a chill all day, so will keep my blazer on," he said as part of the exit strategy.

She hesitated before returning the hanger to the closet. "Better take care of yourself and don't get too worn down. I hear there's some nasty bugs going around. How's the budget coming?"

"It's like giving birth to a twelve-pound baby," he replied before wincing inside and quickly faked a cough. "Sorry, but I'll have to eat and run. The dog and pony show begins early tomorrow so there won't be time for any last-minute tweaks."

"If you're so miserable, why do you stay? Surely, a Tanned professional wouldn't struggle finding another job. Even if you jumped

off the hamster wheel for a while, at least you could reflect on things."
She looked away. "Maybe set some things right."

Clearly his gaffe didn't get by her and she had a weird way of letting
him know. "Don't mind me, I'm always dark this time of year. After the
fire drill tomorrow, things will return to the new normal. I'm still
working on my long-range plan, despite what the sun throws at us."

"You've been working that twenty-year plan since grade school."
She led him to an adjoining room and Todd expected to find old-world
ambience complete with mahogany tables and leatherback chairs
strategically placed on an exquisite Oriental rug. Instead, he discovered
an empty dining room with a green card table centered in the middle.
A small white votive candle served as the centerpiece. He eyed a couple
white plastic lawn chairs sitting in front of a curtain-less window with
the shades drawn.

"Why Darlene, I love what you've done with the place," he said in a
haughty voice that reminded him of Brad. "Is this what they call ghetto-
chic? Since the riots, minimalism is in vogue." He worked on stifling a
laugh. *It's so much better to give then receive.*

"Touché," she said with a forced smile. "The most frustrating part
is I watched the movers load up everything in New York. They even
promised to beat me here. After a dozen calls, I found out the
dispatcher messed up and sent everything to San Diego." She looked
around the room as if the furniture might magically appear. "I'm
thinking maybe we've turned into one of those third world countries
where you have to bribe folks first. A friend of mine has a stash of
Godiva chocolate, which will move mountains. I'm calling her
tomorrow."

Todd let his eyes wander around the room and given the beautiful
woodwork didn't understand why she seemed so embarrassed by the
situation. Nevertheless, he enjoyed seeing her play defense for once.
"Well, I'll keep my voice down to reduce the echo." He noticed a gas
fireplace in the corner of the room and pointed at it. "How many do
you have in this house? I only have one and love it. So easy with no
mess. That said, I do feel a bit guilty using it given all the people still
scrounging for firewood."

Darlene walked over and flipped a switch on the wall and a blue flame popped up and embraced a fake log. "Yeah, easy with no mess. I see why that appeals to you."

"A table for two?" he asked pointing at the card table intent on moving the painful conversation along.

She retrieved a glass of red wine sitting on the mantle. "I planned on cooking you some real food, but I'm still living on paper and plastic. Hope you don't mind but I picked up some Chinese. It's warming in the oven."

"Chinese? Where did you find that around here without going into Boston?"

"Wouldn't you like to know. It's crazy the things we took for granted, isn't it?" She let the comment hang for a moment. "I assume you didn't give up Crab Rangoon along with alcohol and marriage."

He swallowed hard. "I can't believe you remembered my weakness for crab puffs. Can I give you a hand?"

"No, just relax and I'll be back in a minute."

As she headed for the kitchen, he retrieved the plastic chairs from the wall and placed them at the card table. He sat down and reaching for the votive candle, noticed how the table rocked side to side. Looking underneath, he located a slightly damaged leg. "I know how you feel," he whispered and took it as another sign he should have canceled tonight.

He felt the beginning of another headache coming on and rubbed his temples. Between the deadlines at work, the fallout from Brad's death and doing due diligence on Carl's investment pitch, he was ill-prepared for the coming battle. Frankly, until things calmed down, he knew he should delay the conversation about their son. He had already achieved what he set out to do, namely, tap into Darlene's financial network. What was another day or two after twenty-five years? Yet at the same time, he hated this perpetual game of chess. Frayed nerves or not, he wanted the whole mess out in the open.

He leaned on the table and it wobbled as Darlene rolled in the glass tea cart transporting a half dozen pint-sized boxes of Chinese food along with paper plates, utensils, napkins, and drinks. She docked the moving feast alongside the table.

She poured them both a glass of water from a crystal pitcher and then handed him the first of many boxes. *Brad would have a conniption eating off paper,* he mused. *Now the worms were enjoying Brad tartare without the need for fancy flatware.* He took a small bite of fried rice and over-chewed it looking for the right words to begin. A similar strategy with his father failed miserably. An awkward uneasiness settled in as they both played with their food. Taking a sip of water, he repeated the pep talk he gave himself on the way over. *Be contrite but don't let her back you into a corner.* It rang hollow in Darlene's presence.

He swallowed and took a deep breath. "I'm happy you're doing so well, or so I thought," he said with a smirk looking around the empty room. "I'm glad I bumped into you and apologize again for the hard landing. I also want to thank you for introducing me to Carl. We've had a number of conversations, and I really put him through the paces. He answered all my questions and even put me in touch with the project manager at the Bad Creek plant. I'm happy to announce I decided to sign on. Guess we're on the same team now."

Darlene didn't react and fiddled with the box of chicken fingers—but who knew what animal they were made from? "Guess, that explains why I haven't heard from him."

He needed to establish a beachhead and reached for her hand, surprised how rough it felt. She studied their joined fingers with a curious expression. When he finally pulled away, she went for the wine glass instead of the mystery meat.

While she imbibed, he stole a glance and marveled how attractive she looked even with the wig and questioned whether he ever appreciated her beauty. It would be so easy postponing the hazardous terrain ahead and just enjoy the marvelous Chinese food. The Lo Mein hanging over the edge of the white carton, however, reminded him of the dead baby with the leaf plugs from his nightmare. As Darlene moved food around her plate with chop sticks, he couldn't help but think this was a dinner for three.

"I... spoke...with my father," he began with hesitation. "We had a terrible argument, but he finally told me everything. I know you won't believe me, but I never knew you kept the baby until a few days ago."

ONLY DEAD LEAVES FALL

Darlene shot him a quick look and returned to her food.

He sensed the brick wall under rapid construction. "Did you hear me? I really didn't know."

Her expression remained blank and she picked up another carton. "Have a Crab Rangoon. Their big and juicy and to die for." She deposited one on his plate.

This is pure Darlene! She knows I'm ready to throw up and she ups her game. The table wobbled badly as he squirmed.

She sat back in her chair. "C'mon Todd, I got them just for you."

He played along and bit into the deep-fried dumpling. The remainder he left on his plate. Thirty years ago, he loved the mysterious seafood entombed in cream cheese, but he wasn't a kid anymore. It grossed him out thinking what the current offering contained.

Darlene watched him intently until he finished chewing.

"Can you acknowledge what I said?"

She closed her eyes and took a deep breath as if meditating. There is power in silence and as much as he hated a vacuum, he waited. After a long minute, Darlene reached for her purse on the lower shelf of the tea cart and pulled out a pack of generic cigarettes. She lit one up and took a long toke. Exhaling smoke high into the air, she reminded him of Stephanie at Brad's wake.

"Yeah, your daddy's a real stickler about the rules," she offered in a flat voice. "Not that you're worthy of any leniency considering what happened, but after dealing with him all these years, I understand why you're wired like you are." She searched his face. "Let me guess. He's on his deathbed and has regrets. How touching, but pitiful." She sucked again on the cigarette, birthing a long tail of ash.

He didn't recognize the woman addressing him. "No, my father is doing fine. The way he takes care of himself, he'll probably bury me. Like I said, things got pretty hot."

She examined the end of her cigarette.

"What I don't understand is why you followed his demands? You were never a rule follower. Why didn't you contact me?" He asked the questions using a non-combative tone, hoping empathy would pry open the topic.

She took another deep drag and blew the smoke at the votive candle extinguishing the flame. "Convictions cower quickly when you have another mouth to feed. What would you know about that? You moved on with your life and swept the problem away with your father's checkbook. What I'd like to know is why you never called *me*? You were the one that got me pregnant and moved on. Why didn't you reach out to see how I was doing? Too scared of Daddy?"

Todd wished she would take off the blonde wig so he could argue with the woman he recognized. "Okay, I deserve that and more. I should have handled the whole thing differently, but cut me some slack, we were both young."

"Gee Todd, you disappoint me. After all these years all you have is another cheap cliché? A puddle of spit is deeper than your conscience."

He pushed his plate away. "Sorry, but it fits. I was stupid about sowing my wild oats."

She stuck out her tongue and used the nail of her index finger to capture a renegade piece of tobacco. "Wow! I haven't heard that one in twenty years. Have any others lined up? How about boys will be boys?" She leaned across the table not waiting for a reply. "Before you make a bigger fool of yourself, how about we try a little improv and I'll play you. She grabbed his hand and took a deep breath.

"Darlene, I have to be honest. I was just messing around with you. It was kind of like signing up for little league to learn the fundamentals. Then you went and ruined my fun by getting pregnant and expected me to step up and marry you. Maybe if I loved you, I would have considered it for thirty seconds, but you were just a play thing." She sat back and crushed the cigarette on the paper plate. "How's that for starters?"

Todd stared at the mutilated cigarette and noticed how the tobacco burst out of its protective paper jacket. It reminded him of the leaf his father crushed in his hand talking about the past.

Darlene looked like she was searching for his soul. "I hoped to silence the echo of abandonment. That's why I showed up at your house early this morning. Give you one last chance to say a couple one-syllable words, but you couldn't and still haven't."

He pushed back from the table. "C'mon Darlene! Of course, I'm sorry. If anything, I struggle to say it because it feels too small regarding what happened and how I handled it." The words reverberated around the room. He knew the apology sounded patronizing yet at the same time he couldn't contain something else bubbling up. "It's not an excuse, but it takes two to get into that kind of trouble."

"Except?"

"Except what?"

"The first time. I said no over and over, but you were too revved up." She caught her breath. "I cried all the way home."

The memory came back and there was nowhere to hide. He looked at the cart and the open bottle of red wine. He imagined his right hand reaching for it.

"After that night, you beat a well-worn path to my garden. I let you in because I loved you." She stopped and the vulnerable teenager reappeared as her eyes filled. "Last night, I saw you calculating whether it was worth the risk to make one more visit, but it's a barren place now." She tucked the fake blonde hair behind her ears and sniffed. "I know you had the hots for another girl and just used me." She touched the back of her wig. "Come to think of it, didn't she have blonde hair too?" She let out a short laugh. "I'm sure she hasn't aged as well as me, though. Just a bag of dusty bones by now."

Todd worked on keeping a poker face as she clearly wanted to light him up as the new centerpiece. "I want to know more about the baby. Why did you change your mind about the adoption?"

Darlene looked surprised at his focus and stood up. "I need some of my reserve stock." She headed for the kitchen.

Todd's hands were shaking, and as he grabbed the table, it wobbled again. He looked around for something to use as a shim and spied a wastebasket in the corner. Digging through the refuse of various cleaning agents and rags, he came across a crumpled strip of photo booth pictures capturing Darlene and Carl in various poses. The last picture showed them locked in a passionate kiss. He hid the strip in his back pocket and continued pawing through the garbage until he came across a cardboard carrier from a six pack of generic beer. He froze before picking it out of the trash. Darlene was probably enjoying one of the stolen beers when he called. The green Rubik's cube came to mind, and he rummaged a bit more looking for clues.

The sound of footsteps made him retreat. Darlene appeared with a bottle of wine and headed straightaway for the plastic chair.

He tore off a piece of cardboard from the six-pack and folded it before placing it under the troublesome leg. It solved the problem.

"Where do you get beer around here?" he asked.

The question didn't register so he dropped it for the moment. "I heard you went to New York. What happened up there that made you change your mind about the baby?"

Darlene poured herself a glass of red wine. "The Sisters at the home tried preparing me mentally," she started, but I couldn't go through with it and ran away."

"Where is he living now?"

She took a sip and Todd sensed she had no intention of answering. "This is like pulling teeth."

She shot him a look like she considered him a snake shedding its skin. "Why? Are you planning to parachute in after all these years and play daddy?" She let out a snicker. "It was more than poetic justice that you and the wife couldn't have kids. More like Divine retribution if you ask me."

How does she know that? He thought back on all their conversations searching for a clue and came up empty. She read his puzzled expression. "Did I hit a nerve, sweetie? You and Stephanie had careers, right?" She took a small bite of Chow Mein. "You should try this stuff before it gets cold. It's worth the crazy price."

He wondered if he should call her Sybil. "You didn't answer me. Where is Emmett living?" *I can't call him my son,* he thought. *She'll flip.*

Darlene stared at the containers of food. "I always order too much and after a few bites I'm stuffed. But tonight, feels different. I'm sitting here pigging out and drinking while you play detective. It feels like a mystery dinner show." She looked at his half-eaten plate and put down her chop sticks. "Okay, it's my turn to watch you eat."

He didn't know whether to throw up or wing the rest of it at her head. Maybe both.

"You haven't finished your Crab Rangoon," she added.

It was his turn to embrace silence.

Suddenly, her hand bolted across the table and stole the half-eaten Crab Rangoon off his plate. She inspected it carefully and Todd expected her to eat it, but she jumped up and flipped the table over. The air became a maelstrom of food, dishes and glasses and simultaneously, instinct took over and he pushed back from the table trying to escape the flying debris. The terrible noise of everything hitting the hardwood floor was still echoing when she tackled him chest high.

The plastic chair collapsed and they went surfing a few feet on the waxed floor.

Before he could react, Darlene was on top of him and stuffing the half-eaten crab puff in his mouth. He tried pushing her hands away while she let out a high squeal and continued smearing his mouth. He rolled hard and she fell sideways off him.

Todd sat upright gagging. A good-sized piece was in the back of his throat and he swallowed to keep from choking. It got stuck in his esophagus and he coughed a few times before it finally went down.

"What's wrong with you? Have you lost your mind?" he yelled in a hoarse voice.

Sitting cross legged on the floor, Darlene retrieved a cigarette lighter from her pocket and relit the votive candle to further illuminate the disaster. "I always loved candles," she began. "Before electricity they were the only means of lighting the night. They enjoyed quite a renaissance with Sun-Kissed. Now they're on their way back to being superfluous, just pretty decorations or to carry prayers heavenwards." She held the small votive candle up and the flame flickered. "I bought this little gem at one of those little shops in the depot years ago. The clerk claimed after a few hours it would burn itself out—just like me." Darlene stared at the small flame before placing it carefully on the floor. "Don't be upset with me. I asked you for dinner and you came with an agenda."

"You're unhinged just like your father," he said hoping it would sting but not expecting her to come at him again. This time he caught her by the wrists.

"Take that back!" she yelled. "He had a bad temper and drank too much, but never touched that scheming girl. She was helping him clean out a closet and saw an opportunity to get rich."

Todd let her go and she slumped back on the floor. The scandal from high school flashed in his memory. The papers were filled with the girl's accusations of being molested by the teacher and the police rushed to believe her, especially after Darlene's mother divorced him. Although there were many holes in the girl's statement, the town settled instead of defending the teacher with an unblemished record. Her father ended up working at a run-down factory pouring cement into clay molds for tacky garden ornaments. A co-worker found him floating in the river a year later. The town was divided whether he committed suicide out of guilt or from being wrongly accused.

It was a tactical mistake involving her father. "I'm sorry. I shouldn't include him in this."

"So, now sorry comes easily?" She began to tear up.

The next question tasted as sour as the Crab Rangoon in the back of his throat. "Does he know who his father is?"

"Yeah, but I didn't outline the family tree," she said sarcastically, "since you amputated that limb before he was born. He knows the type of man you were."

"Why are you referring to me in the past tense? I'm not dead yet, unless you're going to tackle me with a knife next. If you're so bitter, why do you keep inviting me here?"

"Hoping you recovered your sight. If anything, the last few days proved you've been blind since birth. I can't imagine what you told Stephanie when you were courting her, and she asked about your first love." She caught herself. *What am I saying? That would have been the dead blonde. Did you mention me when describing your first real kiss? Something tells me no.*

Stay focused. He picked up the chair and sat down. "Tell me about Emmett."

"Well, you're a day late and a dollar short," she said with a laugh. "See how you're infecting me? I'm sputtering clichés now." She looked at the food spread all over the floor. "I hate to see waste." Even though it's beyond the three second rule, I think it will be fine if I box it up. I washed the floors myself so it should be okay."

Has she lost her mind? She intends on sweeping up the rice and Lo Mein and making doggie bags?

"Well, I've gagged enough for one night, thank-you." He stood up. "We still have a lot to talk about."

She blew out the candle. "And not much time."

CHAPTER EIGHTEEN

The battle gray colonial sat behind a massive white birch with its
yellow leaves back lit by the full moon. Jennifer got out of the truck
and began massaging her lower back which recorded every bump in
the two-hundred-and-fifty-mile journey.

She surveyed the house beginning with the field stone foundation
that looked naked without any shrubs. Even in the moonlight, she
could tell the house had seen better days. Half the shutters were
missing, and one window on the second floor wore a piece of dark
plywood like an eye patch. If grass existed, it hid under a thick mat of
leaves.

"What do you think of the house?" Cotton asked after retrieving her
suitcase.

Be polite, she warned herself. "I'm guessing it was built in the early
twentieth century?"

He nodded. "Built right before the Depression. When Papa came
home from Vietnam, he no sooner married Nana when this place came
on the market."

The growl of a motorcycle erased the silence and grew in intensity
until it raced past the house. Cotton let out a groan as the echo waned.
"Nana tells me when they first moved in, she could sit on the front
stairs and sometimes wait a good minute before a car passed by. No
matter the day, she would also hear carpenters pounding nails as
people discovered affordable suburban living here with no income or
sales taxes—not to mention the folks that came up from Massachusetts
to shop and go to Canobie Lake Amusement Park or bet on the horses

at Rockingham. I admit enjoying the silence for a while after the cars got fried. Every time I come back to visit there's more volume.

He cupped his hand to his ear and listened. "How much you want to bet if we wait another minute, we'll see a cruiser chasing whatever contraband was on that motorcycle?"

Jennifer waved him off. "I know a losing bet when I hear one. Makes me realize how protected we are back home." The grumble of another vehicle without a muffler approached. "Must be hard getting a good night's sleep in the summer with the windows open."

"Momma constantly moans about it. I never appreciated what she meant until a dozen years ago when the town relocated a house and shut down Main street for a few hours. It reminded me how new life springs up after a forest fire. People came out of their houses with their kids in tow and meandered down the middle of the street. Some met their neighbors for the first time. Instead of a speedway, you could see a neighborhood taking shape. When the house finally came by on a huge trailer, it resembled a parade." He looked towards the road reliving the moment. "Then the DPW came by and took down all the detour signs and everyone retreated back to their yards. I watched two guys yell back and forth on opposite sides of the street as cars raced between them. What a shame."

"Until Sun-Kissed shut down everything."

He nodded. "At first, everyone looked out for one another—shared generators, split and stacked firewood, had pot-luck dinners so no one went hungry. As the months dragged on though, and the hoarding intensified, some homes became armed camps. Alliances were made between families, but it's not much of a neighborhood anymore."

"It was the same back home in Oslo."

He picked up her suitcase. "I see a light on upstairs, which is always a good sign."

When they reached the front door, Cotton bent down and found the key under the mat.

"What an original hiding place," she said with a laugh.

Cotton smirked. "Back in the day, my computer password was 12345." He unlocked the door. "Anybody home?" he called out.

Jennifer followed and immediately noticed a cuckoo clock hanging prominently on the living room wall. The bird remained silent while Cotton yelled "hello" a few more times.

"Maybe she thought we were coming tomorrow?" she offered.

"No, she knew," Cotton replied with a hint of irritation and stopped at a small table in the narrow hall. A red light on the answering machine blinked with one new message.

"Did she know we were stopping to visit your grandmother first? Maybe she thought she had time to run an errand."

Cotton did not reply and continued staring at the obsolete machine enjoying a second act in the twenty-first century. She expected him to hit play and took a step closer so she could hear the message. Instead, he backed away from the machine like it was a rabid animal. He walked into the adjoining room and turned on a floor lamp. The forty-watt bulb unveiled a sad looking living room featuring a couple of tweed recliners heavily bandaged with white duct tape. A large television sat in the corner but given the layers of bath towels draped over the unit, it apparently remained blindfolded during the country's adventures in martial law.

"I bet she ran out to trade one of her ration tickets for something special to impress the company."

"Why, is someone else coming?"

"No silly! You're the company." The comment broke the somber mood. Cotton grabbed her by the waist and dipped her backwards before planting a kiss on her neck. "I haven't brought a girl home before and Momma is probably nervous. It'll be interesting to watch how she deals with the likes of you."

She rolled her eyes. "Should I take that as a compliment?"

He smiled. "Of course. Are you hungry?"

"Yeah, for your grandmother's brownies."

"Tell me about it. I'd sell my truck for some. The guys at the ranch tell me we may see chocolate back in the stores by Easter. I mean the real stuff and not the powdery imitation junk the USDA raffles off."

He led her into a tired looking kitchen with yellow linoleum flooring and harvest gold appliances. She did not consider herself materialistic but mused how the house straddled the Elvis and *Saturday Night Fever* eras.

Cotton attacked the cupboards. "Let's see what we can rustle up from the rations, shall we?" He shot her a wide smile. "Go ahead and search the fridge for something edible. But beware! Momma saves everything until it's rancid. I can only imagine the number of ready-to-eat tubes you will find foaming."

She hesitated. "This feels a little weird. Growing up, I never went into anyone's fridge. It was considered rude."

"Imagine that. Five minutes here and I already have you breaking out of your comfort zone."

She swung the refrigerator door open and immediately faced a tall stack of polystyrene dishes on the first shelf. "Does your mother collect weird looking Tupperware?"

"What do you mean?"

"Well, there are stacks of plastic dishes in here and by the color of the contents I'm guessing it's not Jell-O."

He came up behind her and looked over her shoulder. "Momma has a thing for microbiology. Since I was a kid, she's been fooling around with mold, fungus, and bacteria. Like I mentioned, when she's in a good place, she'll take a college course and learn more about her favorite critters. I can judge her mood by how high the dishes are stacked in the fridge. By the looks of it, she's bordering on manic." He opened a nearby cabinet and frowned at a jumble of plates and cups.

Jennifer searched the other shelves in the fridge. Except for an open container of brown rice that looked so congealed it could be mistaken for a misplaced brick from the pyramids, the petri dishes ruled the cold landscape. Eyeing the rice again, she wondered if it should be categorized as an experiment too. *I don't know if this is sad or simply weird.*

"Did it ever bother you sharing the fridge with your mother's microbe pets?" she asked her headless boyfriend as he searched a deep cabinet.

He fell back a few steps and pulled on his eyelids and stuck out his tongue. "Why do you ask?" he replied before laughing. "I think you've seen too many horror movies. When you meet my mother, she'll explain we live in a sea of bacteria and viruses and the vast majority are harmless. She thinks you can learn a lot about life from studying them."

"Well, the only biology I remember is you don't mess with pathogens." She shut the refrigerator. "I have no idea what they are, so I'm playing it safe."

"You're imagining an army of flesh-eating monsters where there aren't any. Just respect their territory, and they'll leave you alone." He reached deep into the cabinet. "You're not going to believe this, but I found a couple cans of real chicken soup." He pulled them out and studied the label. "These date back to when the sun only gave us sunburns and skin cancer."

"Ah, the good 'ole days." She inspected a can. "You think they're still good?"

"Says the woman who eats whatever the government provides."

She handed the can to him. "I love men that can cook."

"Nowadays that means opening a can or squirting ready-to-eat grub on a plate like fine cat food. I found if you cut the tube a certain way, you can write in cursive."

"Your range of talent is apparently limit-less."

He wrapped her in his arms. "Yes, and Momma will share all my other shortcomings." He glanced toward the front door. "Before she shows up and roars like an angry grizzly from her hike downtown, why don't you go upstairs and unpack. In the meantime, I'll heat up the soup. You can have the bedroom in the back. It's the second door on the right. That way the traffic won't keep you awake. If you hear any chirping up there, you haven't lost your mind. Momma keeps a few parakeets in her bedroom."

"Parakeets? Don't they keep her awake?"

Cotton shrugged. "She sleeps a lot like Nana." He started for the hall. "I'll get your suitcase."

She stopped him. "After stocking the store shelves for so many years, I can probably bench press more than you."

He was still laughing when she reached the top of the stairs. She headed down a short hall and passing a closed door heard a lonely chirp. She stopped and cracking the door open, turned on the overhead light. Immediately, a choir of chirping birds filled the air.

She inched her way across the bedroom. In front of a boarded-up window, she found four green parakeets housed in their own cages. She admired the colorful birds and noted Cotton's mother was very attentive. All the birdfeeders were full, as well as their water bottles, though the fluid had a yellowish tinge. Lining the bottom of each cage were obituaries from the *Eagle-Tribune*. She scanned the rest of the room, and a portrait on the opposite wall caught her attention. It was a young woman in a sleeveless white wedding dress with a delicate lace bodice that complimented her long neck. The soft smile made her think it must be Nana.

The white crocheted bedspread looked inviting and she sat down gingerly on the queen-sized bed. The pillow top mattress felt so soft she could not resist the urge to lie down for a minute. Goldilocks came to mind but the stronger image was the store engulfed in flames. She chased the troubling image away by recalling the landscape art on the drive from New York.

A muscle spasm in her lower back woke her up. The unfamiliar surroundings made her bolt upright before remembering where she was. She glanced at her watch and calculated a good half-hour had passed. Then she noticed the bedroom door shut and surmised Cotton must have checked in on her. She gritted her teeth. If his mother came home, he was probably trying to explain.

Jennifer tiptoed down the staircase listening for voices but heard none. The answering machine was not blinking anymore and when she entered the kitchen, the table was set for one.

She spied Cotton through a window over the farmhouse sink, sitting in a white plastic Adirondack chair and strumming a guitar. The light from a small lantern at his feet cast an eerie glow. Cotton's sweatshirt was hanging on the kitchen chair and she threw it around her shoulders and headed out the back door. She had to sidestep a number of green trash bags tightly knotted before joining him.

Clouds hid the moon, and she could smell rain in the air. Cotton glanced up and kept on picking at the strings.

She grabbed a plastic chair nearby and brushed pine needles off the seat. "I didn't know you played."

"Just a few chords." He stopped and stood the guitar against a railing with half the balusters missing.

"Don't stop on account of me. Sorry I fell asleep. I couldn't resist checking out the birds and made the mistake of sitting down on your mother's bed."

"You're tired."

"I haven't been sleeping great since the fire," she replied quickly. "Are you joining me for dinner, or did you already eat?"

"No, I'm not hungry. I have your soup warming on the stove." He picked up the guitar again. "If you prefer my mother's room, you can have it tonight. It's more comfortable than the cot in the back room. I can move the birds."

"Why? Is everything okay?"

He did not look at her and began tuning the instrument. "It's nine o'clock. Do you know where your mother is? I sure don't."

She thought of telling him she knew exactly where her mother was: right next to her dad at St. Joseph's Cemetery on the outskirts of Oslo. She took a breath. A flip remark would not help matters. "Maybe something happened."

"Something happened all right." He slapped the body of the guitar underscoring the point. "She didn't miss the bus or get mugged or go out begging for a cup of sugar so Nana can make another batch of pretend brownies." He cradled the guitar. "I've seen this movie too many times and know the ending. She's chugging bathtub gin with some loser she met that has a few coins."

The words were hotter than the chicken soup could ever be. She stood up thinking maybe she was still dreaming.

Cotton grabbed her hand. "I'm terribly sorry Jenny. Please forgive me. Momma puts me on edge sometimes." He kissed her fingers. "You don't deserve hearing me whine." He looked at the guitar. "Maybe I should write a country song about tears and broken hearts and dead—" He stopped and bit his lip. "See? There I go again. Sometimes I think you'd be better off not knowing me."

She sat back down. "I don't scare that easily." She rubbed his bare arm and it felt cold. "What makes a gentle cowboy feel this way? I sensed a change the closer we got to Salem. I figured there's more than what you told me at the lake."

Cotton hesitated for a long moment. She hoped he would come clean on what was eating at him.

"When I was ten, I wanted to be a fighter pilot," he began. "Momma just patted me on the head, but Nana arranged it so Santa brought me a classic aircraft carrier she must have found on eBay. You should have seen this thing! It took eight fat batteries and came with working elevators and even had a catapult for the planes. I spent hours working my way across the living room and dive bombing my uncles."

She noticed how his eyes were brighter than the gas lantern. "A cowboy-fighter pilot?"

"Something like that. You have to understand, as a kid life seemed as black and white as the television set Nana used to watch. I wanted to join the Navy and live on a floating fortress and drop big bombs on the bad guys responsible for 911. I imagined they all looked like my father. Then in high school, I came home one night and found Momma pinned up against a wall with a bloody nose because she smoked all of Uncle's menthol cigarettes. I might have been a hundred fifty pounds wet then, but I could swing a frying pan like Babe Ruth. I caught Uncle upside the head. He went to the hospital and I ended up in jail."

"For rescuing your mother?"

"The way Uncle told the story I was a jealous brat. It didn't help matters that his cousin was the chief of police. Then Momma started acting weird because there were few jobs at the time and we needed a place to stay. Long story short, she put up with a little bruising now and then until she didn't. That's when the reckoning took place."

"That's terrible, but I still don't get it. Your mother sold you out for a roof over her head?" She hated being blunt, but the words tumbled out unchecked.

Cotton shrugged. "Sometimes people do what they think is necessary, even if it hurts those closest to them. Self-preservation I guess you'd call it. I was hauled into court and sentenced to sixty days. I caught a break on the timing and spent the summer at a juvenile farm. It was a strange summer raising vegetables like a migrant worker with ten other delinquents. At night, one of the guards would march a few of us into the woods and familiarize us with a different type of crop he needed help with and we'd get high. By the end of August, I headed home and discovered Uncle had passed." He rubbed his forehead. "Thankfully, he got sick from some bad stomach bug, and not from the concussion, or I might still be farming. Momma apologized for the mess. It was the only time I ever heard her say sorry without blaming my old man." He hesitated again. "I went back for my senior year, but my heart wasn't in it and I copped an attitude."

"That's awful, but you could have still joined the Navy."

Cotton didn't answer and lowered his head.

She tapped him on the arm. "Okay, so you were unfairly treated for protecting your mother. I bet you had the most interesting senior essay on how you spent the summer. Right?"

The air remained quiet.

"Look, if you want to drop it, that's okay. I'm just trying here."

"I have no trouble sleeping. Given how he treated Momma, I'd do it again."

"Okay, then what's the big deal?"

He began to fidget like he wished he never started, but it was like a pull on the sleeve of a sweater waiting to unravel. "It opened up a gulf between us that only got worse because of my stupidity."

"Such as?"

"Well for starters I never graduated," he said in almost a whisper, "because of the Honda 350 I bought in the spring. I loved that black pocket rocket and watching the tachometer red line. It felt like flying, but without the wings. My good buddy Griffin had a bike too and we horsed around a lot."

"Okay?"

Cotton sighed. "We were playing hide and seek on some back roads. I was going way too fast and looked in my side mirror for maybe half a second thinking I lost him. Suddenly Grif came flying out of a trail and stopped in front of me. We weren't wearing helmets and I remember seeing his wise guy smile thinking he outsmarted me, until he realized I couldn't stop. When we collided, I flew over the handlebars, but my bike drove Griffin into a pine tree." Cotton closed his eyes. "Pine is supposedly soft wood. Believe me it ain't."

Jennifer rubbed his back. "You're sitting here so I know you survived. How about your friend?"

"Depends how you define it. He lost one of his nine lives that day for sure. Two years later, he lost the use of his legs. That's on me too, but I can't go there tonight."

"I won't pretend and say I know how you feel because I don't. Accidents prove how fragile life is."

"The thing is Momma doesn't believe accidents are unfortunate mishaps. The second she saw me in the emergency room, instead of asking about my broken ribs or Grif's internal injuries, she launched into how the sins of the father are visited upon their sons down to the seventh generation."

"Are you serious?"

"I can't make this stuff up. Nana thinks Momma only sampled portions of the Old Testament because forgiveness is such a foreign concept to her. I know she loves me because I'm her son and all, but the scars run so deep I'm surprised she didn't have a hysterectomy to erase any remnant of him."

"That's a horrible thought. Did you ever think she lost her sense of worth and that's the reason for all the uncles?"

He nodded.

She looked down at the guitar piecing together everything she heard. "What happened after the accident?"

"I went out on my own." He rubbed his forehead. "After Sun-Kissed turned the world on its head, I moved to New York. I come back every few months and visit Momma, Nana—and try to reconnect with Grif."

Jennifer felt the tears welling up. "So that's why you go fishing?" she asked. "You help your buddy?"

Cotton didn't answer. The look on his face said enough. If only she could wipe away the guilt he felt and replace it with the good she saw.

He took a deep breath and shook his head hard. "Don't go putting a halo on me, because you don't understand. The reason—"

She heard enough and pressed her lips against his to dam the words.

CHAPTER NINETEEN

The bold white numbers on the digital clock were in a font large enough for the visually impaired. Todd shut off the alarm before it made the day any more stressful. Nausea and sharp pains in his abdomen jolted him awake hours ago and he spent the remainder of the night searching for a comfortable position. More than once he relived the terror of Darlene jamming the Crab Rangoon down his throat and he could still taste sour cream cheese. Making the discomfort all the more concerning was knowing he should be at the top of his game for the budget presentation in a few hours. Miller embraced an all-hands-on-deck approach for the annual dog and pony show. Absences were only approved if your current address was a drawer in the morgue.

A disciple of routine, when the clock flashed 6:00 a.m. Todd rolled out of bed slowly as both stomach and head protested. He stumbled into the bathroom and popped more ibuprofen and washed it down with a generous swig of Pepto-Bismol.

After a hot shower during which he leaned against the tiled wall for support, he got half-dressed before doubling over with knife-like stomach cramps. "Please, not today," he whispered hoping his immune system would rally. On the way to the kitchen, he hoped a light breakfast of dry toast and a mouthful of tea might quiet his gut. Reaching for the kettle, the phone rang. Why Miller called him before every big meeting tested the limits of his endurance. *Is he afraid I forgot and slept-in?*

Picking up the receiver, he braced for Miller's heavy breathing. Instead, he was greeted by loud crackling. Spotty phone reception was a constant nuisance.

"Stop ignoring me. The…is no good!" a high-pitched woman cried.

Even with the missing words, he recognized Stephanie's theatrics. "You're breaking up. What's no good?" he asked.

"Besides you, the check that bounced. How will I ever show my face again at Stowell's?"

Her angry words beat against his eardrums and made his temples throb. *Stephanie and this stomach bug must be first cousins. If only ibuprofen could relieve both.*

"Did you hear what I said?" she yelled so loud no phone was needed.

"Yeah. Something about feeling bouncy?"

"Stop mocking me! I asked for a little help after losing my brother and you had the gall of writing me a bum check? I went there last night and Billy wouldn't even talk to me. Even though it was *your* check, he blamed me because I cashed it there. This is so like you, looking for any occasion to embarrass me." She paused to reload. "I've seen pet rocks get better settlements than me. Brad agreed too."

"Funny, I thought Brad was dead." He closed his eyes as the virus was infecting his mood too. Things seemed frighteningly out of sync this morning. "Look. There must have been some sort of mistake at the bank. I just wish you waited until your morning happy pills kicked in before calling me."

"There you go again with the insults. I'm not arguing about this. You're going to stop by Stowell's today and apologize to Billy and make it right."

Stephanie reminded him of the alarm clock he used since the death of cell phones: a colorful device that demands attention every morning and buzzes nonstop until you push the right buttons. He knew he could have put the receiver down, taken another shot of Pepto and come back in time to hear the second half of the monologue. If stock investing did not work out, he thought he could pitch her as Kramer's sister in a *Seinfeld* spinoff.

"Okay, let me look into it."

"Call me back after you settle it with Billy. Then we can talk about how you lied and disrespected the memory of my brother by blowing off his funeral." She hung up.

He let out a loud sigh. "Good talking to you too." Sick as he felt, he still managed half a grin imagining how her jaw must have bounced off the floor when Bill Stowell gave her the stink eye. Maybe if he let the bad check dangle for a while, she would have to wash dishes.

He leaned against the wall and dialed the bank. Although the mechanical voice sounded strange after recently coming back-on line, he still winced hearing his current balance was negative four thousand two hundred dollars. A new stomach cramp doubled him over after he hit zero and he reassured himself some teller with a lazy index finger keyed in an extra digit and caused this havoc.

A sleepy attendant answered the red-carpet service line reserved for preferred customers.

He no sooner began explaining the issue when the customer service rep interrupted. "Sorry sir, the bank doesn't open until nine o'clock. You'll have to call back then."

"What good is preferred service when things go bump in the night?" He slammed the phone down quicker than Stephanie ever could. In the old days, you could use a computer and monitor the account or examine pictures of cleared checks. *Pictures!* The thought made him remember the snapshots he confiscated from the trash last night at Darlene's and he beat a slow path back to the bedroom. They were still tucked in the back pocket of his food-stained suit pants and he sat on the bed to study them. In the photo series, Darlene wore a yellow tank top with her red hair pulled back highlighting her high cheekbones. She looked not only amazing but happy too. Carl on the other hand, had a ripped beige t-shirt and besides being unshaven looked pretty buzzed. In three of the photos they flashed silly smiles, but he was mesmerized by the final shot of them embracing in a deep kiss. None of this jived. He closed his eyes and remembered meeting Carl for the first time—the white socks and beat-up brown shoes, the gaudy business card, mispronouncing Canseco, fumbling with the car keys. In subsequent meetings, Carl seemed at ease and a cool pro, and thought maybe he got a little flustered in Darlene's presence. *Even so, he only provided the information I requested or put me in touch with contacts that could answer my technical questions regarding Bad Creek. He never offered any personal perspectives or any interest in talking shop. Odd.*

Fighting hyperventilation, he started dialing Brad's number before remembering the dead guy was not taking calls. Although still early, he took a chance and dialed another number.

The phone rang twice before connecting. "Good morning, Loretta Wells." The strong voice sounded like it was lunchtime instead of breakfast.

"Loretta it's Todd," he fired off in shorthand.

"Who?" she asked in a sharp tone.

"Loretta, it's me." He held his breath.

"Yes, Mr. Dolan," she acknowledged coldly. "Our Customer Service Department is currently closed, but I will have someone return your call."

"Hold on!" he pleaded. "I'm afraid something is wrong."

"I agree. You didn't show up for his funeral. You're spineless. I went, knowing things would be tense."

He tried a different tact. "You're right, Loretta. I should have been there, and regret it. We had our issues, but we were brothers. What no one knows," he hesitated thinking through the alibi, "is the argument I had with Stephanie at the wake. She didn't want me adding to Marcy's grief."

He waited until he detected a sniffle before continuing. "You make me see things differently. If I could do it over, I would have snuck in and sat in the last pew with you. Now everyone thinks I stiffed him." Todd beat his forehead at the poor choice of words. "I know how much you loved him and planned on explaining all of this once the anger died down." He pulled on his chin, not believing his mouth could have the runs too.

"Okay, I'll give you a pass on the funeral, but not the rest."

"Thanks." He hesitated and waited for additional blowback, but the line remained silent. "Look, let me explain why I called. While it's not the good the old days where everyone risked getting hacked, bad things still happen. Can you please call up my account?" A long pause followed and he feared she had her finger on the disconnect button. "Please," he begged. "This is really urgent."

The woman let out a long sigh and he heard some typing. "Okay, I have it. What's the huge emergency?"

"The half million I liquidated."

"That's an emergency? Looking at the profit, you made a killing, but may feel differently after paying the taxes."

"It's not that. Did the money get wired yet to the account I authorized?

"I'll have to check with the Processing Department.

"Can you possibly try while I stay on hold?' he asked so sweetly Loretta should have seen through it.

Another long sigh. "It's still early. I'll see if anyone has arrived yet."

The phone clicked into some terrible elevator music and Todd rubbed his stomach. Minutes passed and he feared she abandoned him. He considered hanging up when the music suddenly cut out like musical chairs.

"Okay, let's take a look." He could hear her shuffling the paperwork. "Everything looks in order and the funds have transferred out." She began to cry.

"What is it?"

"Brad made some marks in the corner of the sell order like he was playing hangman." She sniffled a few times. "Under the noose, he wrote "traitor" and underlined it a few times. That was the night he got sick."

Dropping the phone, he wished he could start the day over. He sensed no amount of ritual could repair the alternate universe he now inhabited.

CHAPTER TWENTY

With the defroster not functioning, Cotton drove with the truck windows cracked open and kept his back pressed firmly against the cloth seat hoping to trap a little warmth. The temperature this morning flirted just above the freezing mark and he envied the birds that flew south for the winter. Another month or so, the remaining feathered creatures would be huddled around neighborhood chimneys like all the Burned folks fighting hypothermia.

Glancing out the passenger window, he noticed how the frost crystallized a large field framed by a rambling stone wall. It reminded him of Nana looking out her kitchen window and saying how the white crystals resembled the manna God provided the starving Israelites. His five-year old self became so excited he ran out the back door with a jar of peanut butter intent on making a manna sandwich. Nana had a good belly laugh when he discovered just cold wet grass. She infused his life with benevolence, the Bible and baseball. Sadly, he couldn't remember the last time he graced St. Joseph's church or Fenway Park.

The morning star rising in the east framed the pastoral road ahead. As it did, the frost slowly softened and rose like smoke around an outcrop of fiery match-stick maples. He fought the urge to pull over and wander through Eden's landscape and watch squirrels gather acorns for the winter. Maybe he would help them gather a few as payback. He knew a few families after Sun-Kissed that were so hungry they competed for the oval nuts and boiled them to remove the tannins before eating.

Jenny filled his thoughts. He intended on waking her with a kiss, but she looked so peaceful he hesitated after tiptoeing into her room. Instead, he watched her full lips caress each breath and followed a line of freckles running over the bridge of her nose. He also considered what he'd do if she suddenly opened her eyes and found him gawking like some love-struck fool or a creepy stalker. *I'd kiss her and apologize about last night. Promise I'd explain everything about Griffin over coffee.*

However, the longer he stared at that lovely face, the more his courage waned. Jenny didn't suffer fools gladly and he questioned whether their budding relationship could handle the sordid details. He had not forgiven himself, so why should she understand? Even so, she needed to hear the whole story and he would tell it straight. Spooked by the thought, he rationalized she needed more rest given how poorly she slept since the fire. So, he retreated and jotted a quick note explaining he had to see Griffin right away. He left it on the stove and felt as empty as the cans he collected.

The country road meandered for another mile before splitting in two and Cotton instinctively leaned with the truck as it ventured left. The destination appeared over the next rise in the road and it would have been so easy blasting right on past. Instead, he gritted his teeth, and turned into a short gravel driveway leading up to a boxy looking yellow ranch.

He parked behind the badly rusting powder-blue '72 Dodge Dart Swinger. The vehicle sat so long in its current position that it doubled as an ornament among the weeds for three seasons and a pain-in-the-butt-to-shovel-around come winter.

The coffee from breakfast began making its way north from his stomach. "C'mon man, what are you doing? You promised to call and take advantage of that state program paying cash for junks." He rapped the steering wheel hard and gave the front yard a glance. The matted grass looked like it had given up any hope of being mowed and the evergreen bushes were in the process of being strangled by Oriental bittersweet.

The serenity of the open road evaporated. He jumped out of the truck and slammed the door so hard it rattled the frame.

"Is that you, boy?" a high-pitched voice called out.

He glanced at the front door expecting Gracie to be waiting with that perpetual sour look she reserved especially for him. Thankfully, the door remained closed. He promised himself he'd bring her some sweet tea next time as a peace offering.

Cotton walked across the wet lawn and up a set of crumbling red brick stairs that were in the process of divorcing a rod iron railing. The living room window was open a good six inches with the shade drawn. The sorry welcome wagon made him realize the state of their friendship.

"Tell me Grif, are you aiming for the white trash look?" He glanced at the window. "If so, you nailed it."

"Go to blazes buddy," came the hoarse reply. "If you're riding that high-horse of yours like always, you can gallop right on by." A hacking cough interrupted the insult. "Riddle me this about obsessing over broken promises. Why didn't you buy the Pinto I found? Like I told you on the phone, fix that pony up and you'll be turning heads from here to New York."

"Not to mention the jerks wanting to rear end me to see if those gas tanks really do explode." This back and forth through a shaded window made him realize he should have postponed the visit. If another hour-long monologue about the benefits of restoring the Pinto lay ahead, he would need some of Griffin's pain medication.

"Speaking of commitments, I thought you were getting rid of that Dodge loitering in the driveway?" he asked hoping to change the subject.

"Where did you ever get that idea?" the open window answered. "She's a classic. Those idiots in Detroit should never have abandoned slant six motors. Plus, they'd have the market cornered if they ignored all the fancy electronics the solar storm fried."

"Yeah, and maybe they should develop an armored station wagon for the zombie apocalypse some folks are betting on next. Just remember that Mona Lisa of yours has a blown head gasket. I keep telling you the government is buying up all the rusting hulks and melting them down for new projects. That puts money in your pocket," he said slowly like he was lecturing a watermelon. "You won't fix that old hemi, so make the call."

"Go to blazes!"

Cotton looked up and down the street. "This is getting ridiculous. Anybody walking past here would think I'm arguing with myself or had a fight with my girlfriend. I'm coming in."

"Use the back door."

"Why, is the front door still barricaded? I can think of a million other houses that would be invaded first." He walked quickly around the back of the house, afraid if he slowed his pace, the F150 would beckon like an irresistible siren. Gingerly opening the warped screen door, the sight of flies colonizing a plate of kidney beans on the kitchen table presented another unforgettable image.

"What a pig," he mouthed and stomped loudly toward the dark living room. The hulk sat hunched in the far corner of the room, punching away on a keyboard. Cotton debated saying something but decided to play it stubborn like his old friend.

The typing continued for another minute before stopping. "Are you going to stand there like the bogeyman? If so, go and hide in Gracie's closet. She could use a good scare when she comes home."

He walked to the window and raised the shade. "Says the vampire missing his eye teeth."

Daylight streamed in and highlighted the stainless-steel wheelchair Griffin occupied. His friend's gray hair remained shoulder length and he had not shaved in a few days. Specks of blue paint on a threadbare sweatshirt barely covered a thick mid-section. *What a mess,"* Cotton thought. The remnants of the high school jock were long gone. That familiar heavy feeling began tugging at his chest.

His friend scowled at the window. "What are you doing? This ain't your house and I like it dark in here. So does my computer."

"Why because it's in a coma? Trying to coax it awake makes as much sense as sitting in that junk of a car outside waiting for a new motor to drop from the sky."

Griffin slapped the side of the wheelchair. "Can you stop nagging me about the Dart? Regarding the computer, I'm part of a beta group testing the internet. It's dial-up like the AOL days, but it's the first step in connecting the world again. Soon, the crazies will be back online arguing about everything and nothing." He shot him a sly smile. "Tell me you can't believe I scored this gig!"

Cotton glanced at the computer screen and some gobbledygook programming. "Go to blazes!" he snapped back.

"You first!" his friend replied.

They both stared at each other for a long moment before Griffin's tough guy mug broke first. They howled in laughter. Cotton thought about punching him in the arm or shaking his hand, but his feet remained fixed in place. He took out a small wad of ten-dollar bills from his pocket and threw it on the keyboard.

"More than last time and hopefully less than next," he added quickly, recalling all the sticky cans he collected and the mountains of metal and plastic waiting in the years to come.

His buddy eyed the money hungrily for a second before looking away. "I keep telling you, money changes nothing." He pushed the wheelchair back from the desk and faced him. "The last time you stood there and emptied your pockets, I told you I'd shove the money down your throat if you did it again. Now I'm wondering if you have some sort of mental deficiency or just like insulting me. Either way, I'll whip your butt like I used to."

Cotton knelt down so they were eye to eye. "You know I hate reruns so imagine how much I look forward driving up here every few months so you can repeat the courageous cripple routine. I told you since the day they grafted that chair to your bottom, I'd help you until they plant me six feet under. So, save your drool and get over it. And while I'm on a soapbox, instead of blowing my meager contribution on beer and grass, hire that punk paper boy you always whine about. Let him take a sickle and cut your front lawn."

Griffin grabbed a wooden ruler off the computer desk and beat the metal legs of the wheelchair making a loud clanging noise. "You don't know squat about my sit-u-a-tion," he quipped, with the emphasis on sit. "How dare you saunter in here like you're doing penance and then give directives on what to do. Who died and made you king?"

"King?" he repeated, feeling the root ball growing in his throat. He lifted one foot and caressed the worn leather boot. "I'm just a would-be cowboy."

Griffin huffed a few times and rolled the wheelchair back to the computer and began pecking at the keys again.

He stood there watching his friend's profile wondering how long before the cloud lifted.

Thankfully, it lasted less than a minute. "I forgot you're a modern-day Johnny West. Tell me, have you found Mae West yet?"

"Maybe."

The typing stopped. "Okay, let's sweep the first part of your visit under the Dodge. Tell me more. I don't get out much and can't afford cable even if they offered it. Who is the flavor of the month?"

"You know I'm not that type of guy," he replied, wishing he were back at the house watching Jenny sleep. "I brought her with me so she could meet Momma and Nana," he said and hesitated, "and of course you. To be honest, I'm struggling how to…ah… explain things."

"So now I'm classified as a thing?" He scratched his cheek. "I remember learning in grammar school a noun is a person, place or thing. So, I've moved down two pegs? Did you tell her my name or just refer to me as Cousin Itt?"

Cotton felt his cheeks grow hot and wished the shades were back down. "You have it wrong. I'll tell Jenny the whole filthy story. Just didn't want to scare her away before she knew me better."

Griffin chuckled. "You think knowing you is to love you? Now that's funny."

He felt the ends of his fingers begin to tingle. "I know it sounds arrogant and don't mean it that way. I'm going to tell her everything, just thinking through how to say it."

"That sounds mighty lawyerly for a country boy. More like yellow-bellied if you ask me. He picked up the ruler again and shook it at him. "What are those cowboys teaching you around the campfire? Not much memorization is required for a story that can be summed up in a few sentences? Harris wanted more money for the weed, and we didn't have it. You took off with the grass and I got shot. Instead of stopping, you kept running. The end."

Memories from those frantic first months after the solar storm came roaring back....*Initial solidarity dissolving into hoarding and violence... Demand for liquor and marijuana skyrocketing... Momma scrounging for brown rice and beans...Nana with no heart meds... Survival requires bartering for the basics.*

"Let's not rehash it, but that's pretty one-sided, don't you think?" He shook his head so the reel playing in his thoughts would stop. "We both knew the risks going in. You ran too."

Griffin rubbed his face. "Yeah, but when Harris started shooting you morphed into a roadrunner and never looked back. Don't worry. I have no desire revisiting that sorry day either—like your money, it won't change a thing." He leaned over and studied the side of his wheelchair. "So, what did you tell your girl about me besides being amazingly handsome? Knowing how much you like drama, you probably told her I'm into racing this contraption." He patted his thick middle, "I'd sink mighty fast in Canobie Lake."

Todd lowered his eyes. "A couple of our war stories, like the motorcycle accident back in the day."

"I bet you embellished it so much I wouldn't recognize it."

"No fish story this time. I explained how you hit the pine tree."

Griffin laughed. "Imagine me a tree hugger? Let me guess, she was so moved she gave you a kiss and said she's been looking for a sensitive guy like you her whole life."

He bit his lip recalling the tender kiss that ended the conversation. "I'll come clean soon. She's got a lot of spunk and I'm afraid she'll tell me where to go, which is the same place you keep trying to send me."

"And one of these days, I'll succeed." He began fidgeting in the chair. "I wish I could get my hands on some popcorn and watch you squirm retelling that dark tale. In the meantime, I have something to show you."

Cotton followed him down the hall and into the rear bedroom. The bedroom walls were painted a light blue which complimented the glossy hardwood floor. In one corner, he noticed a dark oak rocking chair. *Am I in the same house?*

"What do ya think?' Griffin surveyed the walls. "Sanding, priming, and painting from a wheelchair took some patience, but I persevered.

Gracie helped me with the trim." He reached down and touched the refinished floor. "I applied four coats of poly so the wheels on my chariot will glide."

Cotton nodded as the movie-for-one resumed: *The back alley is dimly lit and smells of mold and piss. Long-haired, stick-skinny Harris waves his green and red tattooed arm in the air, demanding another hundred for the brick. I glance over at Grif and his eyes say this is a big mistake.*

I look back at Harris. He's laughing because he knows we're scared. I don't know whether to try reasoning with him or just cold cock the creep. One thing is certain, we don't have the extra scratch..... Momma's hungry...Nana's short of breath.

I grab the brown paper package off the trunk of his car and take off toward the corner of the building. At most, it's a fifty-yard dash. Man, I can run that in seven seconds. Grif is two steps behind me. We're three seconds away from food and meds when a large boom fills the alley... Grif lets out a hideous scream...By the time I convince my legs to do a one-eighty, three MP's have Harris on the ground.

If I go back, there's no food or meds...

"Don't lean and get the wall dirty." his friend snaps.

Cotton moved and the internal movie paused.

"You look as surprised as Gracie did. I know she drives you nuts sometimes, but she's been my rock."

"Where is the little woman?"

"You can delete the word little."

"From what? Tubes of ready to eat mush or deep-fried-who-knows-what from the foodie trucks? Given what I read, everyone is courting dysentery these days, not high cholesterol. I know she's a health nut, so I gotta see what these times have wrought." He suppressed a smirk. "Sorry man, I'm just razzing you."

Griffin eyed him for a long moment and then had a good laugh.

"What's so funny?"

"You're so clueless sometimes, I don't know how you make it through the day." He pointed at the highly-glossed floor and the satin finished walls and the rocking chair in the corner. "Take a good look around Sherlock. Can't you see you're standing in a nursery? Gracie is three months pregnant," he announced with a gopher-like smile. "I'm not spending money on beer and grass, but have been remodeling the house."

Pregnant! How are they going to support a baby? The news confirmed he should have blown off this visit and stayed with Jenny. Maybe forget about the brokenness surrounding him for a bit.

"Who's the lucky guy?" he asked needing a laugh.

"Go to blazes! I may not have my legs, but the rest of the equipment is working fine, thank you very much."

Griffin sniffed the air before wheeling over and opening the window. "I can't have Gracie breathing in all these fumes. I started the renovations in this room as the baby will be sleeping in here. I plan on taking it slow and easy and go room by room," he explained before his face brightened. "If I can steal you for an hour, maybe you can help me with a couple things. That way I can check it off my honey-do list."

He was speechless and just nodded.

"I know what you're thinking but stop worrying. Gracie does okay with her part-time job and with my SS disability. I also have a ton of beta testing with the internet gig."

"You know I've always been a worry-wart." He punctuated it with a shrug and tried keeping his eyes from looking at the wheelchair. The territory for redeemable bottles and cans would need immediate expansion.

His friend looked out the window. "I haven't sold the Dart because a friend of mine is a magician and located a motor. Maybe I'll even get one of those "Baby on Board" magnets so we can tick off people. Then I can tell them all to go to blazes! Okay, one more test."

"Shoot."

"Any idea if we're expecting a boy or a girl?"

"He didn't answer because he realized who the cripple in the room really was.

CHAPTER TWENTY-ONE

The first thing Jennifer saw upon waking was a ceramic angel marooned on a pine nightstand. She thought the six-inch statue would be better suited protecting a rock garden rather than an overnight squatter. Multiple nicks and scratches lashed its ivory shoulders and wings, tell-tale signs that celestial life can sometimes be rough. The angel's head tilted downward either depressed from being grounded or embarrassed by its appearance. Maybe both. She reached over and felt the jagged edge of one wing.

She rolled on her back and surveyed the yellowing ceiling. No blemished spirits hovered overhead but a large cobweb in the corner did. Thankfully, the web looked abandoned and strangely made her think of the good home her parents provided. Now they were both gone, and her father's legacy badly damaged. *If I kept his strict hours, I would have been there when the fire started. Instead, I was drinking horrible beer on the beach. Now I'm hundreds of miles away sleeping in a stranger's bed. What am I doing?* She wished she could have coffee with her dad and talk over the long list of repairs needed before the store could reopen. He drank his java black so he would not "dilute the flavor none." Even now, the reality of him being gone seemed temporary if not for the background silence only she could hear. She knew if her parents could spring back to life this morning, it would make for good reality tv. Mom would shadow her all day repeating horrible tales about big, bad insurance companies and rip-off contractors multiplying in the new normal. Dad would take it all in and ask a few questions meant to clarify what was needed and then assure her everything would turn out okay.

She pulled the sheet over her head and smelled citrus which reminded her of dandelions. The spring weed made her think of Cotton's troubled past. *What else wouldn't he tell me about Griffin?* Her father would have been beside himself watching Cotton fish outside the store. *"Growing up, your grandmother thought I attracted every nut out there,"* he would say. *"Can't deny she was right about some of my acquaintances."* Then he would point at the headless man searching through the barrel for cans and bottles. *"That boy seems nice enough. Just hope he doesn't turn out to be a wooden nickel."*

Jennifer heard someone coming down the hall and hoped Cotton would appear with a cup of coffee and dispel her dad's fears from the great beyond.

She tucked the sheet under her chin and pretended to be asleep. *I'm no sleeping beauty, but let's see how romantic this cowboy can be.*

The heavy wooden door creaked open followed by a prolonged silence. She tried not to laugh.

"Who are you?" a high-pitched woman suddenly barked.

The voice catapulted her into a sitting position and face to face with a middle-aged woman standing in the doorway. The angry expression was unencumbered by any of her red hair which was pulled back in a tight ponytail.

Jennifer hesitated replying and looked past the sudden tempest hoping Cotton would rescue her. The hall remained empty, so she went on the defensive and flashed the biggest smile she could muster given the circumstances.

"You must be Cotton's mom!" she said loudly still hoping for a reprieve.

The intense blue eyes narrowed. "Cotton comes from a plant. If you're referring to Emmett, yes, I'm his mother. I can also assure you I'm not deaf." The angry woman's right hand remained hidden behind her back. "For the second time, who are you? Trust me, I won't ask again."

"I'm Jennifer Pearson, Cotton's—I mean Emmett's, friend," she stammered. "He said you were expecting us?" *Does she have a gun stuffed in the back of her jeans?*

The scowl remained, but the hidden hand suddenly appeared and pointed at her. "Putting aside the awkward introduction, what are you doing in *my* bed?"

She thought of saying something funny about Goldilocks but changed course because she resented the insinuation. She pointed at her pillow. "Just sleeping," she replied and mirrored the mother's glare.

"Where is my gentleman of a son then?" She quickly eyed the open closet and then moved on to the space behind the kitty-cornered bureau before settling her gaze at the foot of the bed.

When a half-naked Cottom didn't slither out, Jennifer smiled like she did when a rude customer irked her. It either disarmed or made them furious. "Did you check his room, or out back?" she asked with a sweet voice. "He likes to play his guitar out there."

Darlene replied by pursing her lips.

She tried another tact. "We're going to see Griffin this morning. Maybe Emmett went to get some gas? He told me townsfolk line up pretty early around here."

The stern face melted into a "poor you" look. "Well honey, that explains it. You misjudged my son by oversleeping," she said with a dramatic flair, and let the accusation hang in the air for a moment. "Looks like he went without you. Better hope he remembers you on his way back because it's a long walk to the bus station. And then you'll find yourself in limbo since the buses run pretty sporadic these days."

Wow! This lady is a trip and a nasty one at that, she thought. "Well, I'm usually up before dawn, but haven't been sleeping well. I'm sure he ran out for something and will be right back."

"What time did you say you were visiting Griffin?"

"We didn't set a specific time. Just agreed to go early."

"Well, early is certainly before eight o'clock. Why, that's halfway to lunch for my son! How long have you known Emmett?"

"A few months."

"Well, I've known him a tad longer and mark my words he's gone to see his buddy without you." She eyed the bed, clearly not happy of conducting this interrogation from its current location.

"I have some coffee on, or you can go back playing Miss Rip Van Winkle. Suit yourself, but please strip the bed before you come down." She turned to leave.

The woman's hospitality underwhelmed her. Ignoring the order, she jumped up and threw on a white cotton robe and followed her down the creaking stairs while searching for a pistol in the dungaree back pocket of those swaying hips.

When they reached the kitchen, Jennifer stood off to the side and watched Darlene fill a mug and take a seat at a retro table with a white Formica laminate top. After taking a sip, she lit up a hand rolled cigarette and sucked on the tobacco stick until her cheeks grew hollow. Jennifer lost count before the woman exhaled. When she did, smoke drifted out of her nostrils like the dragon she didn't have to work hard to imitate.

"Cups are in the cabinet above the stove," she said not hiding any disdain. "Hope you like it black sweetie, because milk and sugar are reserved for royalty these days."

Cotton's story about the uncles hogging all the milk came to mind. She selected a chipped ceramic mug that would have paired nicely with the angel, and poured some of the brew. It wasn't a difficult decision to choose a seat at the opposite end of the human chimney.

The coffee was the definition of bitter, but she did not let it show.

"So how did you meet my Emmett?" Darlene asked.

She took another sip while considering her response. "I own a convenience store in Oslo and he was a regular customer." She had no intention of sharing anything about Cotton fishing for bottles and cans.

"Your store?" She rubbed her eyes.

"Yes, it was my late father's."

"Let me get this straight." she said with a smirk. "Your old man is dead and you're here because playing store is boring?"

Cotton liked to crush the non-redeemable cans he found with the heel of his boot before launching them from three-point range into a bucket. She began flexing her right foot. "I've worked in the store since

I was old enough to walk. Business is fine, but there was a fire and it did some damage." She felt a lump in her throat.

Darlene failed to notice her drill hit water.

"Nice house you have here," Jennifer half whispered while working on regaining her composure.

Cotton's mother ignored the compliment and closed her eyes.

"I noticed all the funny plates in the fridge last night."

Darlene jumped up like she touched a live wire. "Did *you* touch any?"

"No!"

"How about my Emmett?"

She shrugged. "I don't think so, but I went upstairs and fell asleep. *Good grief! She's going to think I sleep for a living,* she thought.

The woman's shoulders relaxed a bit and she sat back down. "My son knows about respecting my experiments." The first hint of a smile made a brief appearance, but it set as quickly as the December sun in New England. "I get a bit crazy about my plates. Emmett knows."

An opening! "Yeah, he told me how much you love microbiology. That's really cool." She knew it sounded patronizing.

"I find bacteria and viruses such little engines of efficiency with so many uses; some good and ..." her voice trailed off. "Are you a history buff?"

She ignored her internal compass and nodded. At this point, she would endure a lecture in Latin for a little acceptance.

The half-smile reappeared from behind the clouds and this time her eyes got big too. "Did you know more soldiers died in the Civil War from water borne pathogens than bullets?"

Okay, that's a rather bizarre factoid, she thought, but grew up playing poker. "That's really interesting," she replied with enthusiasm.

"If you don't believe me, look it up," she boasted before returning to her coffee.

"No, I believe you."

"Good, because it's true. Microbes are incredibly clever. Take President Taylor. When he died in 1850, doctors thought the cause was gastroenteritis. Conspiracy rumors circulated for years about arsenic poisoning. The debate grew so intense a judge finally ordered Taylor dug up. And guess what they found?" she asked, pointing at her.

Jennifer could only shrug.

"Acute gastroenteritis," she explained with a wink. "And why wouldn't they? He consumed raw vegetables, cherries, and iced milk at a July 4th celebration. Sometimes the best conspiracies are in plain sight. If someone plotted to infect Taylor and make it look like a gastro bug, all they had to do was…" She bit her lip.

"Do what?" This sounded like one of those investigative shows she liked.

Darlene shook her head. "I'm just getting carried away like a science geek," and retreated to her coffee.

Jennifer wondered whether the woman was eccentric or an egomaniac. Either way, she hated leaving the mysteries of the nineteenth century given the warmth it exuded. "So, you haven't spoken with Emmett?"

"I think the conversation upstairs confirmed that."

"Well, he was pretty worried about you last night."

"I never thought pretty and worried went together. Seems like an odd couple." She shot her a look like she considered her and Cotton a mismatch too.

"I see what you mean. Guess it's like being an awfully kind host." She sat up straight and gave the woman a big smile hoping it provided more of a kick than the caffeine. "It must be really hard on Emmett when he visits Griffin."

Darlene cocked her head. "Really hard on my son?" She studied her for an uncomfortable moment. "You're a perfect example of the pyramid model which talk radio rants about. Familiar with it?"

"No, enlighten me." Her heart quickened.

She traced a large triangle on the tabletop. "There is a vast multitude of Burned folks suffering at the base and a tiny number of rich Tanned at the peak. These extremes live in different worlds and define the difference between feast and famine. What's most concerning these days is the growing sliver of people in the middle that have more than enough but feel entitled to more." She gave her a hard look. "They warp the meaning of right versus wrong."

They sized each other up for an uncomfortable moment.

"Emmett and Grif fight like dogs in heat when they get together," Darlene continued pushing the mug away. "Eventually, they calm down and begin reminiscing and end up inviting Jimmie to help them forget what they remember too intensely. So, yeah it's hard on my son as it should be."

"Jimmie? Is he another friend?"

Darlene laughed and fingered a button on the sleeve of her red plaid shirt. "Hasn't Emmett introduced you to Mister Walker yet? He runs mostly with the Tanned crowd, but in a pinch his poor cousin Moonshine Hank will suffice. How long did you say you've known him?"

She ignored the dig. "Guess you lean on whatever it takes so you can face seeing your friend that way."

Darlene's shrugged. "If you ask me, it would take a morphine drip to keep him from feeling like a coward."

"A coward?"

Darlene eyed her with a new suspicion. "See what I'm talking about? You're one of those pity types that rationalizes everything away like a wannabee Tanned. No one is responsible for anything since we all got singed by the sun. Everything is chalked up as a disability or lack of opportunity. What a cop-out! Emmett is making amends for his mistakes. His father will get what's coming to him on Judgment Day— though if I have it my way, he'll pay well before that."

"You misunderstand what I'm saying."

Darlene slapped the table. "Look. Life is hard and brutally random. My son got lucky because he ran faster than his buddy. If not, the bullet would have found him first and he'd be the one in the wheelchair. The whole sorry episode is on his shoulders and he has to live with the consequences. He cried a river telling me he did it for me and my mother. I told him to throw that alibi in the hopper because the road to hell is paved with good intentions."

She leaned in trying to play catch-up. "Cotton said he would tell me the story and I trust he will. He did tell me about the motorcycle accident."

Darlene sat back in her chair and let out a knowing snort. "Ah, the things boys will say when chasing a girl." She smirked. "I see why he would tell you the story of being eighteen and reckless. The consequences were ruined bikes, a trip to the ER and some fines. The real tragedy happened after that. You won't find him bragging about that dirty secret."

She felt the sting. "I don't understand."

"Let me make it short and unsweet. Not long after the solar storm hit, Emmett and Griffin went to score some grass so they could resell it. My son said he wanted to help my mother and I. That might be true, but he calculated having enough left over for some good beer too. A classic example of the ends justifies the means sort of defense. Whatever the motive, the deal went bad. In the process Griffin took a bullet and my son left his best friend bleeding and paralyzed in the alley." Darlene shook her head. "And how did Emmett respond? Instead of staying here and dealing with the mess, he runs away to Sun-Kissed-sanctioned-vacationland USA." She scanned the kitchen. "I could use some help around here. I call it like I see it and believe my son inherited those desertion genes from his father."

Jennifer felt dizzy and looked at the floor trying to process everything. *Drug deal? Deserting his friend?* The image of the broken angel filled her mind.

"Honey let me give you some advice as you seem pretty gullible." Darlene continued. "Mommy and Daddy didn't do you any favors sheltering you in the woods. I learned a long time ago, men will say almost anything to get what they're after. I don't want to make you blush, but when you get home talk to your pastor about the meaning of defile. I'm hoping my son didn't get that far with you."

Jennifer bolted out of the kitchen, ran up the stairs, and threw her things in the suitcase. Half-running out of the room, she passed the four bird cages stacked in the hall. They were oddly quiet. She looked in and found two dead birds. Apparently, the end came so abruptly one had birdseed still in its beak.

Darlene waited for her at the bottom of the stairs with a small piece of paper.

"Just found a note Emmett left you. It must have blown off the counter."

She scanned the paper before handing it back.

Darlene smiled sweetly and ignored the suitcase. "I can drop you off at the mall if you like. A few stores reopened and you can wander around until Emmett comes back."

She thought of saying something about the birds but did not want to extend the visit a moment longer. Cotton's mother would find the dead duo soon enough. Maybe she'd store them in the fridge with her experiments or next to the biography of President Taylor.

"Could you drop me off at the bus station? I'm going home."

"I'll not be accused of meddling in my son's business," she responded right on cue. "I don't have time for silliness, so I won't talk you out of it. If you're intent on leaving, I'll give you a lift."

She began walking toward the kitchen. "It's a long ride to New York, so I'll grab you a snack," she said way too cheerful.

CHAPTER TWENTY-TWO

Todd made a beeline for the men's room and threw up breakfast. Afterwards, his stomach was in knots and his sight blurry. Although incredibly thirsty, he knew if he drank anything it would boomerang, so he wet a paper towel and dabbed at his lips.

The meeting room was only a short distance away, and he began shuffling towards it. Thankfully, no one in the hall inquired if he got into a scuffle given his untucked shirt and paper towel pacifier. When he reached the destination, he hesitated at the light switch as his aching eyes pleaded for darkness. Thought processes kept slipping into neutral and he figured the best antidote might be busying himself with the meeting logistics, like firing up the projector.

The large whiteboard at the front of the room contained some random notes and he began slowly erasing them. Suddenly, a new wave of nausea hit and he sought refuge in a padded chair and let his sweaty forehead rest on the walnut table. The lacquered surface felt wonderfully cool, but at the same time a bit sticky from who knows what. He closed his eyes and felt like a kid on an elevator playing with all the buttons. The ride would only get worse when the department heads arrived for the budget review. This annual exercise was equivalent to the Hardrock Hundred Mile Endurance run, except this ultramarathon required gigabytes of brain power. It also demanded the flexibility to scale a mountain and describe the horizon of corporate strategy and in the next instant, rappel to the base and autopsy a grasshopper's esophagus regarding some operational minutiae. He learned years ago these meetings were not just about the numbers but surviving a contest of wills and personal agendas. The more memorable ones were heavy on shock and awe, but he grouped all of them under the category of "death by friendly fire."

He sat back in the chair and tried psyching himself up for the imminent ordeal by chewing another Pepto Bismol tablet. *If I can keep my stomach in check, maybe I can pull this off,* he thought. *It will require a strong opening and then embracing the rare virtue of strategic silence.* Appearing weak in front of this group would be like throwing chum in the water. Instead, he intended to mimic a puffer fish and kick off the meeting by barking he was up all-night sick, so he was short on patience but committed to seeing it through. After kicking off the PowerPoint presentation, he would let the infighting commence and remain an observer until Miller intervened. Then he would introduce the next slide and let the scene repeat itself while embracing the old adage "it is better to keep your mouth shut and appear stupid, then open it and remove all doubt"—or in his case, getting sick all over them. The biggest challenge was identifying which of the hundred slides in the deck would engender the most debate so he could take a seat and rest. Standing for two or three hours would be impossible. A sudden cramp put an exclamation point on it.

"Who am I kidding?" he mumbled rather loudly. "Everyone will see I'm not up for this and pounce."

A sudden fluorescent dawn made him squint and wilt in the same moment.

"Let me ask you a question," a voice boomed. Miller entered carrying a three-ring binder and a tall cup of coffee.

He held his remaining strength for the upcoming battle and simply nodded.

"If there's one day in the year when I'm counting on you to cast a long shadow, it's today. Doubt you can accomplish that by sitting in the dark."

"The spirit is willing, but the flesh is weak," he replied. "I ate some bad Chinese food last night and it's doing a number on me this morning."

Miller eyed him funny for a second, probably thinking he never heard him quote the Good Book before. "Like I keep telling you Dolan, the missus and I remain disciplined and only eat at restaurants that are certified by the health department." He placed the binder and coffee on the table. "I know that sounds boring, but who knows where all that free-wheeling street stuff comes from?" He gave him another once over. "You look like a poster child for what happens when roadkill is used by street-vendors selling chicken nuggets." He shook his head. "Good grief man! What were you thinking?"

When Stephanie first left him, he didn't shave or change his clothes for days and Miller never noticed. *I must look really bad.*

"I'll be fine," he replied, practicing the stoicism needed for survival today.

Miller grunted and sampled his coffee. "Don't get me wrong. I keep dreaming of the day when everything is normal again and we can enjoy the smorgasbord that is America. Sometimes I even picture what I will order first. For example, mother and I loved Potters for lunch on Saturday's because they have enormous grilled chicken Caesar salads." He walked to the freshly erased whiteboard and picked up a green and brown marker and began sketching the salad. "There's a bunch of seasoned croutons underneath the romaine lettuce and chicken," he said pointing at the brown dots. It's built like a pineapple upside down cake." He traded in the markers for a black one and drew a few more lines. "I can't forget the parmesan cheese and black pepper too."

Todd listened as Miller droned on about the fantasy salad and wished he could buy a pin up of one for his office. At the same time, he pictured Miller's Weeble-like wife Mabry, who he referred to as "mother," hovering over the trough and using her pointed nose to ferret out the hidden croutons. They were made for each other and Todd often thought Darwin overlooked something important regarding natural selection. Sure, nature embraces diversity, but the nut standing in front of him proved it has a sick sense of humor too.

His boss stood back and took in the gluttonous masterpiece, Next, he proceeded to erase and redraw a few ingredients that were not to scale. Meanwhile, Todd felt disconnected as if watching this bizarre scene from the ceiling as the president of the company mapped out the fundamental relationships between lettuce, chicken, croutons, and cheese. He eyed the Styrofoam coffee cup a few feet away and contemplated throwing it at Miller and scalding his drawing hand. *Would third-degree burns and the possible need for skin grafts stop this torture?*

The saliva in Todd's mouth began pooling. "You'll have to excuse me," he said quickly.

Miller's head spun around. For a second it looked like he might cry as Todd wasn't mesmerized by the artist's rendering which now included multiple fluid paths for the mayonnaise and sour cream dressing. Creativity like this could not be interrupted by a bathroom break!

"Todd before you go," Miller said pointing the brown marker toward the bathroom, "I don't care if you need a bib and diaper for the budget review. We're counting on you."

Todd recalled a colleague coming back from a pre-Sun-Kissed overseas trip where he contracted malaria. Miller was furious the guy was taking advantage of the company's generous sick leave policy because of a little mosquito bite.

Miller gifted a rare toothy smile. "I'm especially curious about your presentation and its entertainment value."

Todd swallowed a mouthful of saliva, willing to risk an embarrassing accident on the rug. "Entertainment value? What do you mean by that?"

Miller reached into the side pocket of his black suit coat and took out a small Rubik's cube with all the tiles colored green. "Why did you send everyone on the leadership team one of these last night? I'm assuming this is a teaser on how we will reach the profitability target next year. Otherwise, I might conclude you think we're all simpletons and dumbed down the puzzle. That would certainly trash our corporate value of respect."

Todd had more questions, but his stomach could not be ignored any longer. He bolted for the bathroom and made it to the stall just in time. There was not much of anything left in his stomach, but the dry heaves continued as his stomach muscles went into spasms. As painful as it felt, he wished he could also expel the overdrawn checking account, the anxiety about the investment in the Bad Creek plant, the insanity of Darlene, Monster Miller… not to mention the guilt about Emmett.

He made it to the sink and splashed cold water on his face. As he did, the snapshot of Carl and Darlene came to mind. There was something unholy in that kiss that made his remaining virus-free brain cells wonder if they were in cahoots and plotting against him. However, he could not mull it over until he survived the meeting. When he opened his eyes and looked in the mirror, the sickly face staring back terrified him.

The bathroom door swung open and Miller marched in. "Still not feeling well?"

Todd stood up straight. "I think I got rid of the rest of it."

"What dish made you sick?" he asked, addressing Todd's image in the mirror.

"I can't talk about it right now." He wished he could stuff some of the sour tasting Crab Rangoon down the big guy's throat.

"Maybe you should blame what you washed it down with instead."

"You have a point. You never know about water nowadays."

Miller gave a devious chuckle. "C'mon Todd, you can't kid a kidder. How long have you been drinking again?"

He made a fist and pinpointed the exact location on Miller's chin where he would target the first punch. Miller would mimic a pine tree splitting apart in the high wind. The idea of nicknaming him "pine combs," almost made him smile.

Miller hovered over him. "Did you hear my question? How long has it been?"

"I told you I ate something bad, that's all."

Miller's finger drilled into his chest. "When you came to work hammered after your wife left you, I called you a cab and gave you time to deal with the issue." He paused and let the message sink in. "I also warned if you ever showed up like that again or lied about it, I'd fire your butt." He grabbed Todd's arm. "As Roberto Duran once said, "no mas," so I'm giving you one last chance to come clean."

Todd had a hard time validating Miller's perception of empathy. Sure, he had a few liquid lunches after Stephanie moved out, but he still functioned okay. Miller came by his office one Friday afternoon and accused him of being half-lit. He made the mistake of confiding in his boss about the state of his marriage. Miller responded by telling him to leave his problems at the door. Then he called him a cab and demanded a report be finished over the weekend. As an added insult, he deducted the cab fare from his paycheck. Another wave of nausea hit and stopped the replay. "Honest, I'm not drinking, Chet. Why would you think that?"

"What do I have to do? Provide you a written report?" Miller spit back. "I went in your office last night and found beer bottles in your trash can. Now you're standing here and telling me it's food poisoning? Your eyes are drooping down to your butt and you're slurring your words." Miller waved his arms. "Food did this to you? What type of fool do you take me for?"

"Look, I can explain," he said slowly, enunciating each word. "A lot of strange things are going on. This morning I discovered someone cleaned out my checking account. The other night I had my house broken into. That's probably where the beer came from since it was stolen from my back porch." He wanted to wince hearing the lousy defense. *Why did I mention the beer?*

Miller heard enough and pushed him against the sink. "Your problems aren't my issues. You're not only sick, but pitiful liar too"

He walked to the bathroom door and held it wide open. "Get out."

CHAPTER TWENTY-THREE

Cotton frowned at multiple specks of white paint on the toes of his leather boots. Before priming a few trim boards, he carefully rolled up the sleeves of his shirt but ignored what happened south of the knees.

"Do you have any turp?" he asked, after trying unsuccessfully with his fingernail to scrape the paint off.

Griffin squirmed in his wheelchair as he applied wood filler to a nail hole. "Come again?"

"I could kick myself for being so careless. Do you have any turpentine so I can get the paint off my boots?" he repeated.

"No, but you can try a little Johnnie. I've seen it strip almost anything—or anyone for that matter," he replied with a devilish grin.

"That's all I need to do is go back smelling like whiskey. I'm late as it is and don't need Jenny thinking I left so I could spend the morning getting loaded." He walked across the hall into the bathroom and rummaged through a cabinet. A menagerie of makeup occupied every shelf. *No wonder they're broke. His wife has the strategic reserves of black-market cosmetics,*" he thought. "Does Gracie have any nail polish remover?"

"Why? Are you going to paint your nails too?"

A car horn blew loud and long and Cotton looked out the window. "You've got to be kidding me," he mumbled and raced to the front room.

"I keep telling Gracie not to lean on the horn every time she finds a ride home for lunch. It scares the blazes out of me," Griffin replied from the other room.

"Well, she's innocent because my momma's sitting out there in a black Mercedes." He rubbed his eyes. "I'm sure there's a whopper of a story on how she stole that luxury car. Probably left my new uncle marooned on some back road. By tomorrow this time she'll be calling me for bail money."

He backed away from the window as the horn beeped again. "She's unbelievable."

Griffin rolled into the room, and Cotton didn't wait for his take on the situation. He tried opening the front door but it was stuck.

"Wait!" Griffin yelled.

He ignored the warning and pulled extra hard. The door flew open, but the handle came off too.

His buddy was still cussing as he lost his balance on the way down the loose front steps.

Darlene watched the frenzied approach and waited until he was a few feet away before rolling down the window.

"Where have you been?" he demanded. "I've been calling you for the last two days and left message after message."

His mother screwed up her face. "I drive all the way up here and you can't be civil long enough to say hello?" She scanned him up and down before settling on his speckled boots. "Is that the way I brought you up? Boots that need shining and apparently too lazy to take off before painting?"

Cotton ignored the diversion. "We can talk about my boots after you tell me where you've been hiding."

"I've been working," she replied frowning now at the baggy knees of his dungarees.

"That's not what Doreen told me. I called her last night after we arrived, and you were MIA. She said you're not cleaning houses anymore and got fired from a good paying waitress job." It was his turn to study her. "What's with the blonde wig and the fancy car?" He rolled his eyes. "Let me guess, you met a swell guy. He's a real gentleman and treats you like a lady. He let you borrow his luxury car so we can talk about all the skeletons in your closet and whether there's room for one more."

She squinted at him. "No child of mine will talk to me like that!" His mother punctuated the scolding by pointing a long finger at him. "You'll never understand the sacrifices I made after laying my eyes on you, so show me some love and respect." She checked her makeup in the rear-view mirror. "I'm long overdue for a change," she said examining the top of the wig. "Once upon a time they said blondes have more fun and I'm tired of being called a mad ginger." She shot him a smile and then stroked the dashboard. "The car is a loaner from a business associate of mine."

"Business associate?" he asked sarcastically. "Is that how they define the transaction nowadays? So, you're all dolled up for some Tanned guy because he's paying for—"

The door swung open. "Swallow the rest of it before I slap you good. You know more than anyone that I never stooped that low. Even if your grandmother has to sleep on the street, I'm a lady first."

He knew it would be futile pressing any further. She could duck questions better than any politician and camouflage herself from scrutiny by pointing out his inadequacies before disappearing again. They would not talk for months until he finally caved.

She slammed the car door shut as an exclamation point to move on.

He noticed a gift basket sitting on the passenger seat filled with apples. "I see you've done some midnight picking again. I'm surprised after Warren hauled you into court last year, he didn't shoot you!"

She straightened the fat red velvet bow hanging off the side of the straw frame. "Well, the risk was worth it to repay someone that's been on my mind. I'm on my way to drop it off. now"

Repay? How many uncles are still vertical? Cotton put the ugly thought out of his mind. The woods in New York filtered most of muck from the past. He could not wait to get back.

"How did you know I was here? Did you stop by the house?"

She sported a mischievous all-knowing grin. "Yeah, your new crush told me."

His heart jumped considering the idea of Jenny meeting her without him. "It was mighty embarrassing when we arrived last night, and you weren't there."

Darlene screwed up her face. "Well, I didn't appreciate finding her in my bed either. That's why we have a guest room, you know." She hesitated for a moment, searching for the right words. "Jennifer is awfully cute," she finally said with a giggle, "and rather thin-skinned." Darlene glanced in the rear-view mirror again and fiddled with the fake bangs. "She reminds me of a cigarette lighter. One flick and she's lit."

"What do you mean by that?"

Darlene cocked her head and glanced at him. "Well, for starters she didn't like your disappearing act this morning."

He swallowed hard. "Didn't she see the note I left?"

"Yeah, I handed it to her. All I can say is she woke up in a foul mood. Apparently, she isn't a morning person. I don't have much in the house and she turned up her nose when I offered to make toast. She hogged most of the coffee and complained that I didn't have milk and sugar." His mother caressed the steering wheel. "Pretty entitled, don't you think? I'm sure you remember how I handled that type of disrespect, right?"

Cotton looked away. That was a bottomless pit where all the dragons lived. He decided long ago to escape from that underworld. None of this sounded like the girl he knew. Every time they had coffee; she drank it black with no complaints. "So why didn't Jenny drive up with you?"

"Like I said, she got real upset because you left and then acted like a spoiled brat. Single child syndrome if you ask me." Darlene nodded to put an exclamation mark on the diagnosis. "I made sure you weren't brought up that way."

Cotton sensed his mother was redirecting the questions by spinning a tale. "You didn't answer me," he said leaning into the open window. "Where is she now?"

Darlene started her car. "I explained you weren't in the habit of waiting around for anyone that slept the day away, especially when you planned on visiting a crippled friend."

He sucked in his breath and took a step back. "What did you tell her?"

"What do you think? We talked, she asked, and I told her the truth." She looked him up and down again, but this time instead of focusing on the boots, she found his eyes. "The malarkey you've been feeding this tart makes me sick—stories about your easy rider days but not man enough to recount why Griffin's in a wheelchair? Maybe, that's why you wear boots for a living—because you're always knee high in manure. Better ask Nana to pray for you because I sure won't. You're acting like the monster that got me into this terrible mess in the first place. Since Jennifer will be cursing you all the way home, maybe your grandmother's prayers will cancel them out."

He could feel his pulse throb in his neck. After years of verbal abuse, his forcefield blocked most of the hurtful words. "Home?"

Darlene put the car in reverse. "Keep your cool will ya? She didn't go overseas, just back to the woods and all those pine trees forever dripping pitch. Let me give you some motherly advice and suggest you show up with flowers. Then you can try and redeem yourself by coming clean about your sins. That said, I'm not sure she's worth the effort. You can do better."

"I can't believe any of this. You're a monster!"

She put the car back in park and leaned out the window with a flushed face. "Listen to me good! I won't put up with that tone from you. If you love your grandmother like you say you do, you'd remember how she says the truth will set you free. That's all I did. I told her the truth that you kept hidden." She gripped the shifter and put the car in reverse again but kept her foot on the brake. "Better than anyone, you know how much I despise a man who twists the truth to get a woman." She let out a sigh and shook her head. "You probably can't help it. It's in your genes. Although after spending an hour with Miss Pearson, I don't understand the attraction."

She let out a small laugh and let the car roll back a couple feet before stopping again. "Seriously, there are plenty of good-mannered girls who might be interested if you tell the truth and do something about those boots."

He started backing up and didn't turn around because he wanted to remember his mother this way. It would be the day after forever before he'd see her again.

"Listen honey," she called after him, "The reason I drove up here was to let you know I'm taking a small vacation and don't know when

I'll be back. I'm hoping you'll stay at the house and look after things. I'll send you some money for Nana's bills. And please watch the birds. They may be coming down with the flu again."

Cotton did not reply. He was already leapfrogging the risky front steps to get his keys.

CHAPTER TWENTY-FOUR

Todd carried a small box of personal effects to his car. Feeling sick and numb, he put the heat on high and moved his car to the far end of the parking lot. An hour later, he woke up drenched in sweat.

A combo gas station and convenience store were a mile away and he headed there. The pumps were closed except on Saturday's and he bought a pack of peppermint gum and a bottle of water. He fought the urge for another nap by chewing the gum at full throttle and busying his mind on what to do next. The antidote for panic was action.

"The fat lady hasn't sung yet," he whispered and patted the memory stick in his shirt pocket. It contained the only copy of next year's budget and a bridge for a truce with Miller.

A pay phone on the front of the stucco building beckoned. Getting out of the car and dialing the bank took a toll. Thankfully, he was immediately transferred to Cynthia Hatfield, Vice President of Customer Relations.

The line went silent for a minute as she reviewed his account. "I see a number of bounced checks due to insufficient funds. There's a hundred-dollar check for Stowell's and—"

"Before you go on," he said interrupting, "do you see any large checks that cleared in the last few days?"

"There's one for three-thousand payable to HML Construction."

"HML? Never heard of them. What's the check number?"

"2201."

"Hold on a second." He cradled the receiver in his ear and retrieved the checkbook from the inside pocket of his suit coat and scanned the register. It was the check he sent Carl for financial modeling.

"I must have heard you wrong. Did you say 2201?"

"Affirmative."

Todd muttered good-bye and quickly fed the phone another quarter and dialed Carl's number. The phone rang a dozen times with no answer. His fingers trembled as he dialed information and requested the main number for Toole, Cresch and Shaw in Boston.

"I'm sorry, but I have no such listing," the woman announced.

"How about the surrounding metro area?"

He heard a few clicks of a keyboard. "No sir."

The words brought him to his knees until the anger kicked in.

**

As he drove to Darlene's house, the photo of two beach bums locking lips made the scheme all the more glaring.

When he reached her address, he found the driveway blocked by a white moving van and surmised Darlene's overdue furniture had arrived. He tried running up the front walk but stopped every few steps to catch his breath. After scaling the front stairs, he rang the doorbell and leaned against the black iron railing. A line of red mums glowed fire red in the front garden.

He was about to ring the bell again when the door opened. A thin man in his sixties appeared. "Can I help you?"

The man wore black dress slacks and a button-down white shirt, so he surmised he wasn't delivering the furniture. *Another accomplice perhaps?* "Where's Darlene?" he blurted, looking past him into the hall.

The man shrugged. "Who?"

"The madwoman that's trying to destroy me." He glared at the guy. "Who are you? Her butler?"

The man's cheeks quickly matched the mums. "Excuse me? I don't know any Darlene so you must have the wrong address, buddy."

Todd stumbled backwards in his fevered state and looked at the big bronze numbers affixed to the house. *Yes, this is the right house.* He prepared to barge past the man and confront his nemesis when he noticed the "sold" sign and picture of realtor Bob Olsen leaning against a wall in the foyer.

The man continued eying him warily. "Are you looking for the prior owners?" he offered. "I'm sorry, but I don't have their new number."

Todd tasted something salty. He found a used tissue in his pocket and dabbed at his mouth. It came back pink.

The man noticed too. "Are you okay?"

He knew he must be a frightful sight; sweaty, disheveled, half-crazed. "I had dinner here last night. This makes no sense," he half mumbled before re-engaging. "You mentioned the previous owners? Did you just buy the house?"

The man's eyes narrowed, and he simply pointed at the moving van in the driveway.

Todd folded the tissue while the owner began closing the door.

"Look, I'm sorry for bothering you," he said in a soft voice. "Can you tell me whether you rented the house before moving in?"

The owner looked perplexed. "No. We bought the house a month ago and had some of the usual stuff done. You know, cleaning and landscaping."

The clue terrified him as he recalled the cleaning paraphernalia in the wastebasket when he was looking for a shim to steady the table. "Cleaning? Who did you use?"

"Micro Cleaning and I wouldn't recommend them. They left quite a mess behind: wine glasses, food all over the floor. I have a good mind to sue."

Todd tried to contain himself. "Would you have their contact information. Maybe a business card?"

The man shook his head. "Look. I don't know what's going on, but I'm in the middle of a mess here. I really don't have time for this."

Todd descended a stair to reassure the man he had no evil intentions. "I apologize for the inconvenience, but this is really important."

"Okay, let me check." The door closed and a minute later it reopened. He offered a red sheet of paper. "I found this flyer on a bulletin board downtown."

Todd scanned the advertisement for *Micro Cleaning Services, specializing in deep cleaning*. A thumbnail of a smiling Darlene framed the upper right-hand corner. He thought of filling the air with expletives, but noticed a gray-haired woman watching in the side window. She had a phone up to her ear, no doubt calling the police or the not-so-friendly neighborhood security team.

He walked down the stairs and turned around.

"Thank you for your help. The landscaper—was he a distinguished looking man?"

The homeowner looked relieved to see him leaving. "I don't know if you'd call an unshaven joker wearing a t-shirt and ripped jeans striking." He pointed at the overgrown bushes surrounding the foundation. "He didn't do much of anything either. Maybe he's in business with the cleaning lady."

"You don't say," Todd replied trying his best to hold back the tears.

CHAPTER TWENTY-FIVE

The room felt a bit warm but John felt too comfy in the leather recliner to get up and fiddle with the thermostat. Afternoon naps still felt like a new concept after nearly four decades of teaching followed by five years of providing round the clock care for Mary. He missed his wife terribly and sometimes the silence was deafening.

No one had to tell him he was luckier than most in not having any worries about making ends meet. This left him with the twin riches of relaxation and ability to fret over the little things in life. Naps did wonders in perking him up for the second half of the day. *Maybe, I'll pick up a few more leaves before the daylight peters out,* he thought. The shorter days did not bother him that much, knowing the process would soon reverse itself. "I don't know which season I love the most," he would tease whenever Mary complained about the sun setting before dinner.

He closed his eyes and recognized the sound of the security drone patrolling the neighborhood. The high-pitched sound carried him to that sweet state between wakefulness and unconsciousness. The drone climbed higher in the beginning stages of a dream and he could see the outline of a tropical island with turquoise water and white powder beaches. *The sun will feel warm on my back as the trade winds kiss my face....*

The sound of the doorbell suddenly filled the house.

"Are you kidding me?" he growled as the recliner catapulted upwards and the sun, sea and sand disappeared.

During the arthritic limp to the front door, he hoped the annoying interruption would be redeemed by finding his son ready to apologize. *Why was he so determined to dig up the past?*

But no one greeted him when he opened the door. John knew the bell was real and not part of a dream. *Is someone playing a joke on me?* He scanned the yard before looking down.

There sitting at the bottom of the stairs was a large basket covered in dark cellophane wrap and sporting a huge red bow. McIntosh apples and a generous sized jar of honey filled the basket.

"Well, what do we have here?" he asked extra-loud while retrieving it, expecting someone to come out of hiding. A blue jay squawking in the distance was the only reply. He waited another moment before rushing back into the house and setting the treasure on the kitchen table. His hands trembled fishing out the card.

Dear John-

You decide—are these the first fruits of the harvest or an early trick or treat?

Either way, this is from someone that can't stop thinking about you. From a not-so-secret acquaintance.

-XOX-

P.S. Try the honey. You'll just die!

John smiled at the mystery. No doubt, one of his lady friends at the country club decided to make a bold move. Debbie Finn came to mind as the frontrunner. She sent him a tin of peanut butter fudge on his birthday and while the confectionary had the grittiness of sandpaper, her effort impressed him. Given the stubborn government rations, he couldn't fathom how she procured enough sugar for the recipe. Now she was apparently raiding beehives for him.

He sighed, thinking his nap may have been spoiled, but the thought of a piece of toast smothered with honey and a cup of tea would surely hit the spot on a cool fall day.

"I'll have a little honey from my new honey," he sang, pulling the toaster out of a drawer. The memory of the fudge returned, and he hoped this snack would not give him heartburn too. As an insurance policy, he decided against thinking about the apology his son still owed him.

Meanwhile, the kitchen window provided the perfect location to watch a human-sized petri dish take shape.

CHAPTER TWENTY-SIX

Cotton felt like the overheating truck by the time he reached Momma's house.

He ran inside and searched for clues of what transpired. The kitchen looked tidy enough—two empty coffee mugs sat on the kitchen table backing up his mother's claim. Instinctively, he grabbed both and while transporting them to the sink, spilled a few drops on the floor. A roll of toilet paper under the sink served as paper towels these days, so he tore off a few sheets to clean up the mess. As he went to throw it away, he froze. Sitting on top of the wastebasket was a crumpled note. He retrieved it thinking maybe he had been stupid in the wording.

A foreign message spilled out.

I waited and then waited some more,
but guess you think this is Club Med.
I have things to do and will be back later.
Maybe you'll be up by then.

He held his breath and read the note again. Unlike his standard block handwriting, this one featured a sloppy cursive style which unmistakably belonged to Momma. Realizing that she decided for some sick reason to sabotage his relationship with Jenny burned his throat so badly, he turned the kitchen faucet on full blast and drank from the fire hydrant. When he finished, he took a deep breath and let out a long yell which echoed throughout the house and made his throat hurt even more. He wanted his mother to be present so he could scream about the constant parade of sketchy men with hungry eyes and fast fists—and the midnight rescues from sleazy bars where bartenders held her hostage until the tab was paid. The ricocheting thoughts ended with him being ten years old and waking up to find Momma kneeling next to his bed.

"*What's the matter?*" *he asked.*

"*Mr. Shanley won't be staying with us anymore,*" *she whispered and dabbed a tissue at her black eye.*

"*Where is he moving to?*" *he asked, hoping it was far away.*

Momma took a deep breath and stood up. "*Mr. Shanley passed away this evening, sweetie. As far as where he is moving to…if you care, say a prayer.*"

He stuffed the forged note in his back pocket and headed upstairs, apprehensive on what else he might find. Momma's room was neat and the bed stripped of sheets and blankets. A small cough emanated from a green towel covering the bird cages in the hall. Peering underneath, two parakeets were dead and the remaining two were taking turns coughing.

"What else?" he mumbled. Momma had an obsession for these lovely birds but terrible luck keeping them alive. Most expired a few weeks after bringing them home and Nana got so worked up, she begged her to get a dog instead. She would hear none of it and blamed the drafty house and the ever-changing New England weather. As a precaution last year, she moved all the cages into her bedroom and never complained about all the chirping. He thought maybe after putting up with the chatter from all the uncles, these surrogates were easy. *No demands, just feed and love them… until they die.*

"This is so like her," he said still talking to himself. "Leave me with two dead birds and two more on the way." He pulled on his unshaven jaw, knowing how it felt to be sick and alone while the caregiver gallivants around town. *And where is she now, but delivering stolen apples to some loser? Then she's taking a vacation here in purgatory, without a nickel to her name. Unbelievable!*

The coughing birds refocused his attention. If he did not get them to a vet soon, they would join their buried brethren in the backyard. He retrieved a bird carrier from the closet and gently transferred them into the canvas carrier while planning the logistics: pack, drop the birds off at the vet and leave his godforsaken past in half an hour. His wallet contained a lonely twenty-dollar bill and knew he would be stuck with another expense his mother would never repay. He did not mind picking up whatever incidental's Nana needed, but veterinarian bills were beyond his means.

Suddenly, there was a loud pounding on the front door, and he rushed downstairs with the bird carrier in hand, hoping for a silver lining. *Maybe Jenny had a change of mind? If so, I'll apologize she learned the ugly truth from Momma.*

Opening the door, Cotton found a hunched over man in a badly wrinkled blue suit minus a tie. The stranger had a wild-eyed look and his forehead glistened with sweat.

"What can I do for ya?"

The stranger stared at him almost dumbfounded, then backed down one stair and gave him another long look. It creeped him out a bit.

"Is Darlene home?" he finally asked in a hoarse voice.

Cotton knew men asking for his mother never led to anything good. Moreover, the guys she attracted always wore t-shirts or ripped jeans, so this wrinkled suit seemed out of place unless he was a bill collector figuring a drive-by might shake some coins loose. As a precaution, he began pulling up the drawbridge, wishing Nana would let him dig a moat around the place. Alligators might not survive the climate, but a rabid black bear would do the job just fine.

"Sorry, she's not here," he replied quickly.

The stranger grabbed at the closing door as crimson circles blossomed on his cheeks. "Look, I really need to see her," he said and licked his lips, as if intent on keeping them unglued.

"Get in line," is what he wanted to shout. Instead, he replied "Like, I told you buddy, she's not here."

"When will she be back?" the tone turned desperate.

Maybe when she's made the world a better place by eliminating another abusive uncle, he thought. One of the birds began thrashing about inside the carrier. He adjusted his grip and studied the sickly-looking man. "What do you want with her anyways?" he asked on autopilot, while thinking if he pushed the truck really hard, maybe he could catch the bus by the time it reached New York.

The stranger said nothing, but his face went blank as he reached for the railing.

Cotton noticed the BMW on the street and thought of the Mercedes Momma was driving.

"Let me guess. You let her take the car out on a solo test drive and she hasn't come back?"

"Huh?"

He tried another theory. "Well, if you're here to repossess one of her junk cars, I hope you brought more than a beamer because you need a tow truck. If you ask me that Chevy should never have been resurrected from the junk yard, because the transmission was junk. It's sitting out back with four flats." He gave the visitor a once over. "By the way you're sweating, it makes me think the last repo was a bit taxing on you too."

"Seems the nut hasn't fallen too far from the tree. You're a smart aleck just like your mother."

Cotton searched his memory bank. None of the uncles which survived came to mind. He refused to acknowledge the gnawing feeling in his stomach and recalled some old photo albums he found in a closet many years ago.

"Do I know you?" he finally asked. Leaving the birds on the floor, he stepped outside.

The man steadied himself. "Not in person, but I can imagine what you've heard about me over the years."

"Try me."

Sweat pooled on the man's upper lip. He extended his hand and managed a weak smile. "I'm an old friend of your mother's. My name is Todd Dolan and it's nice to finally meet—"

Instinct took over and Cotton launched a savage punch that connected squarely with the sick man's mouth, sending him sideways off the stairs. A large evergreen bush served as a gurney.

"How's that for hello?" Cotton yelled from the top landing. "You deny me my entire life and have the gall to drive your fancy car here and knock on our door? And what did you expect me to say?" he asked, cutting the air with his aching right hand. "C'mon in Dad and let's have some watered-down coffee while I catch you up on everything you've missed? Then what? Have me sit quietly while you spin tall tales of all the monsters that kept you away?" He came down a couple stairs. "You think my momma wants to see you? Why, she'll claw your eyes out if there's anything left after I'm finished!"

Todd tried rolling over, but was caught in the bush.

"Please tell me you're terminal and figured you'd stop by and tell us what plot in Pine Grove Cemetery you'll be occupying. That way, I can visit your grave and make sure the stray dogs know where to relieve themselves." His eyes narrowed. "If that's not the reason, I'd be happy making sure it is."

Todd spit out some blood. "It's a long story," he whispered, "but I thought you were given up for adoption. I didn't know your mother kept you until a few days ago. I told her that at dinner last night."

"At dinner?" he yelled. "You think she would break bread with you? Let me guess, she found you on Facebook before the internet went down and has been going house to house hoping to invite you over. The truth is she cried for years thinking you breathed the same air as us."

Todd tried again to sit up but continued flailing. "Funny, she didn't feel that way when she kissed me the other night."

"Shut-up liar!"

"Look, I get it," he said trying to rally his voice. "She's angry and wants revenge so she cooked up a master scam. Now she poisoned me with something."

Poisoned? He took a step back.

"I admit I made a terrible mistake. You have to believe I really thought you were adopted." Todd wiped his mouth. "I didn't plan on meeting you this way."

Cotton headed for the truck and then remembered the parakeets. He had to get them to the vet fast and that meant getting rid of the refuse on the front lawn first. He backtracked a few steps, and reached in the bushes and grabbed a leg.

Todd let out a moan before yelling. "Please Emmett!"

"I don't answer by that name, Daddy," he said pulling hard. "Family and friends call me Cotton, and not because I'm soft. If you ever come around here again, I'll grind you into bark mulch."

Cotton made a sideway motion like he was throwing a discus and heaved Todd on the front lawn. His absent father slowly stood up and limped toward his car.

Cotton retrieved the bird carrier and ran to his truck.

All he could smell was sickly-sweet antifreeze as he peeled out.

CHAPTER TWENTY-SEVEN

Todd let the car roll a few hundred feet before pulling over to check his injuries. He looked in the vanity mirror and inspected a bloody bottom tooth which felt loose. Given the circumstances, it was strange how his thoughts centered on whether his dental insurance would cover the repair since it originated from the ultimate preexisting condition—his son.

He didn't blame Emmet, or Cotton if that was the weird nickname he went by. Did he expect any less of a reaction after Darlene filled his head with toxic half-truths for twenty-five years? It was amazing the kid held back from hurting him more.

Todd glanced again in the mirror and did not recognize the raccoon eyes staring back. Gripping the steering wheel as an anchor, he concentrated on formulating an action plan. The logical move would be to call the police and head for the hospital. His right hand, however, remained in place instead of shifting the car into drive. The setup roared through his mind. *Darlene "bumping" into him outside the grocery store... Meeting the cool finance whiz that mispronounced a popular stock...Touring her empty house with the missing furniture... Darlene offering to put in a good word with Carl so he could invest in Bad Creek... "My only watch out is Carl hates procrastinators," she warned. "If he says it's a sure thing don't insult him by over-thinking it too much." Then the myriad of bogus calls and meetings with Carl.*

His shivering stopped the internal movie. Darlene's ruse worked because she cunningly camouflaged her intentions. With her cover blown by a stupid bounced check, the playing field was now level. While it made sense to contact the police, he feared the investigation would be relegated to the back-burner given the manpower required to keep the lid on civil unrest. Even if they stepped up and arrested the pair, how much would they recover? *Nowhere near what I can,* he told himself. *I just need a few minutes and make her realize she'll rot in prison. Maybe if I dangle some dollars for Emmett, with the amount dependent on how much I get back, she will cooperate. After I recover the money, I'll call my well-connected lawyer friend and get even. I'll hold my judgement on Emmett until I find out if he's in on it too.*

Turning the car around, he hoped the story about her being gone on vacation was a lie. A long driveway across the street from her house had a border of rhododendrons and provided the perfect hideaway for the stake out.

He rationed gas by only starting the car for heat when his teeth chattered. Watching the house, he remembered all the nights he brought Darlene home after too much of *everything*. It seemed a lifetime ago, and the passage of time only underscored his teenage selfishness.

Three hours later as dusk approached, he watched a battered looking Ford Escort slow down and stop in front of the house.

"Well, will you look at that," he mumbled, remembering the beat-up jalopy parked outside the grocery store during their first encounter.

Darlene emerged from the car, hurried up the sidewalk and bent down at the front door before disappearing into the house. *After all these years, the key is still hidden in the same place?*

Seconds later, a light in an upstairs window came on. He waited a few minutes before exiting the car and half-walked, half stumbled toward a door that once welcomed him. The worn key was under the black rubber mat and after looking up and down the street for Emmett's truck, he inserted the key in the lock.

The door made a slight squeak as he slipped into the short hallway.

The staircase lay straight ahead, illuminated by a soft light from an upstairs fixture. The beating in his ears was unnerving. A glance toward the kitchen revealed a black phone on the wall. *If things go badly, I'll dial 911.*

"Emmett, look in the kitchen for my wallet," Darlene called from upstairs. "I can't go anywhere without my stupid Homeland I.D."

He heard her rummaging around and began climbing the stairs using the railing for support. The ascent proved painfully slow and threatened the element of surprise.

His luck held as he made the landing undetected. A light from the bedroom on the right, provided the beacon for the offensive. Tiptoeing across the wooden floor, he found the fake blonde on her hands and knees looking under a queen-sized bed devoid of bedding. The mattress looked stained and yellow in the dim light.

"Did you find it?" she asked.

"I wouldn't worry about an I.D for the next twenty years. The prison will give you a new number along with the orange jumpsuit."

Darlene stretched for a moment like a cat waking up before standing. Her nonchalant expression looked like they were an old married couple and he merely wandered upstairs to help with the search.

"I called your office this afternoon and the receptionist acted weird. She wouldn't even take a message for you." Her eyes continued around the room looking for the wallet.

"Yeah, I went home with what I thought was a stomach flu. Come to find out, my banker diagnosed it as a bad case of being hoodwinked."

The accusation brought a look of surprise and she gifted him with a broad smile. "That's the first interesting word you've said since we reconnected. Hoodwinked sounds better than saying you were duped. It also sums up how I felt after you forced yourself on me. I guess you thought my saying I love you cancelled out all the other no's that followed that night. If you ask me—and you never will because you don't have the guts, that back seat was a crime scene."

He moved his feet feeling for quicksand. "What are you talking about? We were both caught up in the moment. I remember you saying you wanted—"

"Your love," she said interrupting him, "but you misinterpreted what that means like most guys."

"Because you were pure as snow, right?" he shot back. "Give me a break, Darlene. Let's call it what it was—reckless infatuation with

ONLY DEAD LEAVES FALL

consequences." He took a step toward her. "This whole elaborate scheme is what? Revenge for shattered puppy love?" He took the flyer for Micro Cleaning Services out of his back pocket and held it up. "Though it must have felt spectacular going from cleaning toilets to playing Cinderella in that mansion." He clapped his hands slowly. "The best actress award is yours hands down, but my vote for best actor in a supporting role goes to Carl Michael, if that's his real name. He demonstrated his creative range by stretching from humble landscaper boy to dashing financial wizard, not to mention the band of advisors making sure I drown in Bad Creek. Am I forgetting anyone else? Emmett perhaps?"

A single tear streamed down Darlene's cheek. "How dare you." She ripped off the blonde wig, revealing thick red hair cemented in place with countless bobby-pins.

"Look!" she yelled, bending over slightly and pointing at her white scalp. "In grammar school I won ribbons for prettiest hair. Now it's all falling out. The cancer is eating the rest of me, which is surprising since I thought you left nothing behind. I figured I would just implode one day."

Todd stared at her healthy-looking locks, wishing he had half as much hair. *Just another performance,* he thought. "I'll give you one chance to return everything before I call the police."

Darlene let out a sarcastic laugh. "That says it all, doesn't it? If this were a movie with a happy ending, you'd have a sudden epiphany about your horrible life. But here we stand between heaven and hell. I remember how you sucked climbing trees, so good luck trying to scale those pearly gates before the hellhounds find you."

"There you go again transferring the guilt."

Her hands rested on her hips. "Your face is telling me you don't get it, so let me explain. You claim you just found out about your son, but never asked anything about him other than where he lives. Lose some greenbacks, though, and you're ready to go to war. I would love a picture of you holding a hundred-dollar bill by the hand or spooning with it at night." She looked him up and down and shrugged. "Knock yourself out and call the cops, but humor me. How will you explain that a Burned housecleaner and her lawn mowing boyfriend somehow convinced a VP of Finance to invest in a bogus hydropower plant? I think they will find that not only a stretch but pretty unbelievable. I dare say after the police hear you out, they may use the same dismissive words all misers like yourself toss around describing us low life's: stupid and careless."

"You're twisted," he screamed and lunged at her, but in his weak state missed badly. Darlene jumped on the naked bed and sought safety on the other side.

"Did you really think you could get away with it?" He leaned over panting.

"That's the same question I ask about you every day of my life. I was nothing but dog mess stuck on your shoes, and you scraped me off along with our son," she said in a matter-of-fact tone like she repeated it for the millionth time. "I think it's about time you invest in his future, don't you?"

Todd put his hands to his ears. "Stop it! How can I make you understand I never knew about him? Return what you stole, and we can talk about what he needs. I'm willing to make a substantial contribution on his behalf."

She extended both hands toward him. "That's your play? Swaddle your grown son in dollar bills and hope you still qualify for a retroactive child tax credit?" She looked away. "There's nothing left to say. I gave you the chance when I came by your house in the middle of the night."

"So, being swindled is the penalty for not begging you for forgiveness?" He took a couple of deep breaths. "Why, I'd pay double to have never met you—or better yet, return to my pimply-faced youth and set you up with the class jerk. That should have been my confession when you showed up at my door." He swallowed a few times feeling like he might have another session of dry heaves. "You're too insane to reason with. I'm afraid the cancer has spread to your brain as well." He pointed at her. "You're going to call Carl right now and get my money back."

Darlene smiled. "If this were only about the money, you and your father would be huddling under the Merrimack River bridge."

Todd heard enough. In his mind he was already headed for the kitchen to dial 911.

"Don't believe me?" she asked. "It's a pity you couldn't ask poor Caroline—the hottie with the bad brakes. Unfortunate accident."

The beads of sweat on his forehead stung. "What are you talking about?"

Darlene stroked the arm of her red flannel shirt. "I fancy red because it's a primary color that's never mistaken for something it isn't," she began, "except for this one time when the brake lights on Caroline's car lit up bright and yet the car kept on moving." She looked at him and winked. "You were driving behind her, and I was following you. Such a sad little parade." Darlene felt her breastbone with the tips of her fingers. "We both saw what happened next. Everyone blamed it on the poor truck driver. It's a shame no one thought to check why the Beetle had practically no brake fluid. Since, you like clichés so much, I guess here today and gone tomorrow sums it up nicely." Darlene snapped her fingers. "That was the first day of the rest of eternity for your little Caroline."

He jumped up on the bed but lost his footing. In the next instant, Darlene grabbed an angel figurine on the nightstand. When it kissed the side of his head, he saw a bright yellow flash of light and collapsed headfirst on the bed. Before he could move, she straddled his back. The soft mattress felt like a quagmire that smelled of tobacco and perfume.

"Funny, how life repeats itself. Here we are in bed again and still so full of passion!" she sang and held the angel next to his face. "Daddy made this for me when he worked down at the mill. I loved it more than anything and can't explain why I abused it after you left me." She stared at the lacerations on the body of the angel. "Some scars you can observe while others remain hidden. Some never heal." She leaned down and whispered in his ear. "Why don't you ground this angel too?"

The angel went airborne again and came crashing down.

***

Regaining consciousness, Todd found himself on the floor a few feet away from the bed. His hands were over his head and wrapped in duct tape. Darlene had one knee pressed firmly into his chest. Blood ran down the side of his head and flooded his ear canal.

Darlene's eyes looked wild. "Welcome back, sweetie." She held up the figurine minus one wing. "The amputation was a success. Are you happy deflowering two angels?" she asked, before a look of concern took over. "My goodness, you're quiet. I think all of this has taken the life out of you. I remember you saying, "you are what you eat." Matter of fact, I just told your daddy the same thing."

"What?" The room started to spin. "My... father?"

"That's right. I hadn't talked to him in a while. While you were napping, I called him. He sounded awfully surprised when I said hello. As expected, the conversation didn't get far because he started spitting out nasty words after I told him you were sleeping next to me." She looked sideways for a second lost in thought. "The last time he acted like that was about a year ago when I came home after a long shift. At first, I thought he might be suffering from high blood pressure because his face looked fire hydrant red. Then he opened his mouth and I learned between the cuss words that he was ending our financial arrangement." She shook her head slowly. "I invited him in, and no sooner got the door open when he made a pass at me. I don't know if he felt lonely after losing your mother or just curious about what his son found so inviting."

"Liar!" He tried rolling away, but the way she had him near the wall made it a one-way route.

"Sorry to tarnish the image of your father like that. But no harm, no foul since you're the only one that ever had a Midas touch with me—well, until I learned it was fool's gold." She hesitated for a second and giggled. "I can see the torment in your eyes and it looks good on you." She leaned down and whispered in his ear. "Don't worry babe, I pushed Daddy away with a laugh and he got really embarrassed. Want to hear more?"

He struggled to move but failed again.

"By the way, Daddy wanted you to know he had a bad belly ache and called his doctor. My goodness, what did the two of you eat that could have caused such distress?"

Her words nearly scared the fever out of him. A cold shiver rocked his entire body. *She masterminded this whole scorched-earth plan. How can I stop her?*

With all his might he worked on breaking the duct tape on his hands. When that failed, he tried flipping her off but she responded by pressing harder with her knee. As the adrenaline subsided, he felt heavy and numb like his body was shot up with Novocain.

"For mercy's sake, get off me," he whispered.

"I find the word mercy so interesting coming out of you. Maybe you should pray to all the Benjamins you hoarded. After all, it's what you worshipped and counted on."

The Rubik's cubes came to mind. His fingers felt a small tear in the tape, and he worked on expanding it.

"What's your plan? Sit on me for eternity? You're sick!"

"I'm sorry you're so uncomfortable, but don't fret! It won't be too long before you see the light—or in your case, the dark abyss." Her eyes filled with tears. "While we're waiting, I will tell you about the others I let in trying to erase your memory. They followed the path you paved expecting to dance in a wild garden. Instead, they got lost in a wasteland." She stroked his forehead. "They found out lust doesn't make you invincible, only tastier for the vipers. Your brethren will be excited about meeting you tonight. However, they perished on account of you, so don't expect the welcome wagon when you see them in the flames."

He looked up at Darlene and behind the fury and crazy words saw the remnants of a scared and pregnant teenager. The transformation carried him back to their last meeting at Canobie Lake before his father intervened. *It was late…there were no moon or stars and the tall pines stood as dark sentries for the secret rendezvous. Darlene arrived carrying a small suitcase apparently thinking he came to his senses and they would run away. She looked crestfallen seeing his empty hands. He tried reasoning with her and when that failed leaned on a platitude that things would work out. Truth be told, he just wanted it to be over.*

"How can you turn your back on me now?" she cried. When he began walking away, she screamed his name. He never turned around. The last thing he and those tall trees heard was a promise.

"I'll make you pay for abandoning me."

The duct tape was giving way to his efforts. "I'm so sorry. Please believe me," he whispered.

Darlene shifted her weight and it made breathing even more difficult. "It's too late for deathbed confessions. My heart is made of stone and there's nothing left," she said with her voice breaking. She moved one hand to his throat and with the other ripped her shirt half open and the sumac tattoo pulsated in rhythm above her bra. "I'll help nature along and make sure your name is mud. When the police come, I'll tell them how you broke in and tried having your way with me. Seems you were obsessed with reconnecting. They will comfort me and agree I had to defend myself. Miller will back me up on your troubled behavior. I've found out he's a nice man after all."

He worked feverishly on the tape. Darlene had a faraway look and began drooling. The saliva fell in one long string and landed on his forehead. He thought he might be sick again.

"Please, I can't breathe."

"No worries. It's a short trip to hell," she reassured him.

"Maybe you can take the trip with him," a new voice boomed.

Darlene eased up on Todd as Carl entered the bedroom.

He was brandishing a gun.

CHAPTER TWENTY-EIGHT

Darlene tried ignoring the handgun and focused on Carl's pallid complexion which really popped against his black t-shirt. Combine that with the beads of sweat on his forehead and the heavy breathing, and she knew the toxins were winning the battle. If anything, she kicked herself for overlooking the antimicrobial properties in the toothpaste that unfortunately lengthened the incubation period. Nonetheless, all the telltale signs were present indicating death in a few hours—or if his constitution proved particularly strong, a pit stop with a ventilator first. *Just be cool and let the game clock run out,* she thought. *With a little luck, mister-gotta-steal-it-all and the selfish-sinner-with-a-twenty-year-plan would soon be morgue mates.*

"Get up," he yelled at her.

She followed his orders and Todd rolled into the corner gasping for air.

"There's no need for a gun," she said pointing back at Todd. "He's harmless and saved me a trip by stopping by." She let out a strained laugh. "He believes 'parting is such sweet sorrow,' though I'm partial to Juliet's previous line: 'Yet I should kill thee with much cherishing.' When you barged in, you caught me saying 'good night till it be morrow,' or in my interpretation—when he's below the frost line."

Carl gave a quick glance in Todd's direction. The gun jumped around in his hand like it was too heavy to hold.

She busied her racing thoughts by buttoning her shirt. "He'll be a puddle on the floor in no time. We can drop him off in the woods on the way to the airport."

Carl wiped his brow. "You've been MIA all day," he said in a flat voice.

"Aw, and you missed me?" Darlene replied with a nervous chuckle. "How sweet, but things got a bit complicated. My friend on the inside pushed back on the fee which delayed things."

"And?"

Lie with confidence. "We're going to clean him out like you wanted. It's done."

"Done pretty much describes our meal ticket, doesn't it?" He pointed the gun in Todd's direction.

"Yeah, you could stick a fork in him, or better yet, a meat thermometer." She looked at the blood running down Todd's cheek. "Actually, I think he's bordering on well done." She flashed an aggravated look and headed toward the bedroom door as a precaution. "Put the gun down, will ya? It's making me nervous," she said brushing past him.

Carl caught her by the waist and shoved the revolver into her side. "Funny, I don't feel that great either. It begins about here," he said twisting the barrel of the gun. "First, I blamed the oysters and champagne we enjoyed. When you didn't check-in with me today, it got me thinking... Maybe I'm one of her experiments?"

"What are you talking about?" she spit back disguising her growing fear with anger. His grip tightened and she concentrated on the sweat hanging from his top lip. It reminded her of meeting Brad in the underground bar and how he tasted like stale beer.

"I prefer the tickling. You're hurting me."

He pulled her over to Todd and they watched him concentrate on breathing. When he didn't look up, Carl kicked him in the side.

Todd opened one eye. "You're scum," he said barely above a whisper.

Carl laughed. "Says the Tanned guy with eyes bigger than his stomach." He kneeled down beside him. "You and your buddy thought you could handle Darlene. I can't ask Brad much these days, but you'll probably agree that was a fatal miscalculation. I mean, she can hold a grudge like no one and exact some serious payback. With her it's all about execution as you're finding out."

He stood up and looked hard at Darlene. "She's one of a kind. Cross her and she will skin you from the inside out. I know you're feeling a bit under the weather, but have you seen her birds?"

Todd ignored the question and rubbed the side of his face on the arm of his shirt.

"Why do white collar clowns have such a hard time paying attention?" He kicked him in the side again. "By now you know I play a financial advisor on unreality-tv," he said with a smirk, "but that's not the half of it." He pointed toward the bird cages in the hall. "There's always a dead bird or two around here and if you look in the trash bags out back, you'll find a feathered surrogate of yourself. See Darlene is a perfectionist and is forever tweaking the recipe so it's just right before serving. You should have been here a couple weeks ago when we discarded two other experiments. She named the pudgy little bird that never shut up, Brad, even though she maintains the game of life intervened first." He put his arm around Darlene. "The other one she called Sweetie, which I'm beginning to think was code for me."

He stared at Darlene. "Given how hard you've worked bringing all of us together, Dolan and I want to make a toast before you head south." He pulled a longneck amber bottle from the back pocket of his ripped jeans.

She gasped at the label of *Darlene's Wicked Ale.* "Where did you get that?"

Carl looked confused. "That's an odd question. I watched you make it. The first batch tasted like prison wine, but you kept working the recipe."

"And I accounted for every drop."

"Or so you thought. I don't have time waiting for the light bulb to go off over your head, so I'll clue you in. You admire germs because they're so disciplined, but we're not all built that way. I signed onto your plan, but sensed being used from the start."

Darlene stared at the floor trying to find the flaw in her plan before realizing it didn't matter. *Time to rally,* she thought and waved him off. "I don't know if you're delusional or a hypochondriac—maybe both. Stop the whining and take some aspirin."

Carl knocked the beer bottle hard against the edge of the weathered nightstand. The wood splintered, but the bottle cap came off. "You might be right darling, but I have trust issues." He offered her the bottle but she refused it. "Your old crush and I don't want to infect you with our nasty stomach bugs, so this brew is all yours." He looked over at Todd. "What do you say? Should we drink to our health or hers?"

"What's the toxin?" Todd wheezed and hid his freed hands behind his head.

Carl laughed. "Glad you've finally stopped worrying about finances and concentrated on your health instead. Like they say you never see a hearse pulling a U-Haul." He waved the bottle in front of him. "We shouldn't forget to toast all of Darlene's feathered friends too since they gave so much in the name of science gone bad. If you like, we can also whisper a quick remembrance for Brad also." Carl stopped and wiped the sweat from his brow. "Given how you're looking, maybe we should include a prayer for you too."

He grabbed Darlene by the waist, shoved the gun deep into her belly and handed her the bottle. "Now that we have that out of the way, tell me how you got the venom in me?"

"What are you talking about? I love you," she said shedding a few tears for effect while disappointed Mother Nature was taking her time. "I don't know why you're sick," she pleaded. "Believe me!"

"The only thing I believe right now is seeing you chug this hooch. Then I'll drop you and your first crush somewhere cozy where no one will bother you. That way you can stalk him forever."

The room started spinning and she thought a huge drain might appear and swallow all of them. "From the beginning this was about protecting my son and helping my mom." She glanced at Todd.

"Don't hide behind them!" Carl yelled. "This has always been about your sick fantasy of revenge."

She bit her lip and looked down at the bottle.

The gun pressed deeper. "I have to get to the ER. Hurry up or I'll pour it down your throat myself."

Darlene put the bottle to her lips.

Carl tipped the bottle upwards. "Bottoms up!"

The fluid pushed against her closed lips.

Carl rocked the bottle back and forth. "Open your mouth!" he yelled.

A flash of blue denim appeared in the doorway and in the next instant, Cotton tackled Carl.

Darlene joined in the fray and Carl viciously pistol-whipped her in the head. In the mad fight, the handgun skittered across the wooden floor.

Todd rolled over and picked it up. The instrument felt heavy and the handle sweaty. He glanced at Darlene lying unconscious on the floor; the broken angel lying beside her. She looked deflated and it reminded him of the green monster float his father bought for the pool when he was a kid. When summer ended, he'd pull out the air plug and watch the ferocious beast disappear.

A loud thud roused him from the stupor, and he saw Carl succeed in getting Cotton in a firm headlock, intent on squeezing the life out of him too. Another moment and it would be over; the ledger would be cleared with no remainder. All the leaves would be gathered, bagged and ready for the mulch pile—though he doubted any planting soil would be forthcoming.

He sat up and tried taking a deep breath, but his lungs resisted and he settled for a couple of shallow breaths. Cotton's feet were twitching, in a few seconds it would be too late to intervene. *Late—there was that dreaded word again. Darlene used the word like handcuffs, and I ran like a deserter. Now my lack of intervention will undo what I helped create. While I feel no more like his father than the guy strangling him, I can make a difference. Maybe leaves can't return to the trees, but they carry seeds and ride the wind. Some do find fertile ground.*

He raised the gun and pulled the trigger.

The gunshot threw him backwards and made him deaf in the same instant. He initially thought the terrible sound merely blew Carl off his son and he expected the muscular guy to bounce up mighty angry. Seconds passed and Carl didn't get up. Instead, a dark puddle began expanding underneath him.

Cotton remained still for a long minute before rolling on his side, grabbing at his throat, and moaning softly.

Todd did not have the strength to get up and crawled over to Darlene. She was lying on her side in a fetal position. He looked at the bloody mess on the side of her head. *So much red all around me,* he thought.

Suddenly, she grabbed his wrist. "Can you smell the anticipation now?" she whispered.

His ears were ringing, and questioned if he heard her right. "Look... what... you've done," he stuttered and watched her mouth for a reply.

Darlene moved her mouth ever so slightly. "What *I've* done?" she asked, releasing her grip.

Todd shook her. He needed the information for the paramedics. If she died, they would be left guessing. Her eyes started to roll backwards, and he shook her again. "What's... the... poison?"

She opened her eyes and looked at him as if she just solved the most interesting riddle. "It's always been you." A small smile started from the corners of her mouth. "Tell me," she began.

"What?"

"If it's easier for a camel... to pass through the eye of a needle... than for a rich man... to enter heaven." She moaned and felt the side of her head. "Caroline will have fun... watching you try." She closed her eyes.

Todd recoiled as Cotton's large hand grabbed his shoulder and pushed him away.

"You've done enough damage," he said in a hoarse whisper.

He crawled a few more feet and rolled on his back. White swirls danced on the plaster ceiling. They reminded him of the footsteps in the snow he could not erase, no matter how hard he tried. *Stephanie's face suddenly appeared and floated across the ceiling and he reached for her. They met at a dinner party, and he was immediately captivated by her beauty, vivaciousness, and easy laugh. She seemed the antidote for his conservative style and careful calculation. Her almond eyes were a well of endless possibilities until they iced over like the steel gray days of November. I should have spent time inhaling her spontaneity and humor. Instead, all I accomplished was grafting my wants onto her and making her believe happiness could be purchased. She had it right; I never stopped and asked for directions.*

Fighting for air, he lifted his head searching for oxygen. The swirls on the ceiling began melting into one another. *So little air!* The wheezing intensified and his lungs froze.

Cotton suddenly appeared over him, holding his speckled red and white throat. He knew his son could see he was in serious trouble, but did not ask what was wrong, or try and help. He looked like a young boy studying his father, measuring his worth.

It was too much to bear and he rolled onto his side. His blurry vision focused on the bottom of Darlene's big work boots. The crescent moons on each heel caught his attention.

Processing the revelation, his lungs seized.

CHAPTER TWENTY-NINE

When Cotton opened his eyes, he discovered a bald, middle-aged guy unabashedly sampling strawberry Jell-O cubes from his hospital tray. His pale and bumpy pate resembled the lunar landscape but unlike the old man in the moon, he needed a good shave. *Maybe he's one of those unlucky types with a constant five o'clock shadow*, he thought. Whatever his pedigree, the dingy white shirt and plaid sports coat sure did not help matters. Studying the thief, he thought the addition of a bow tie and top hat would complete the ringmaster costume come Halloween.

The thief glanced his way before popping another cube. Their eyes met.

The man's habit of stealing food at the hospital must have been a regular gig, because he brazenly used the napkin from the breakfast tray and wiped his hands.

"How are you feeling this morning, Emmett?" he asked in a surprising baritone voice. "I'm Detective Walton."

Cotton nodded in acknowledgement.

"I stopped by earlier but you were sleeping." Walton cooed. "Given the cocktail of drugs they gave you for the pain, I'm surprised you're awake."

Cotton had trouble believing any detective would leave because a person of interest was sleeping. Maybe he did not like the mushy who-knows-what they served last night for dinner and figured breakfast might be a better buffet to pilfer.

"Can you tell me what happened last night?" the detective continued.

His tongue still felt twice as big as normal. Even though the doctor sprayed his throat with some weird numbing agent it still hurt to swallow. "I gave my statement last night," he whispered, and then made a motion with his hand that he wrote everything down.

The detective reached in his vest pocket and took out a small black notebook and scanned the first page. "Okay, let's review the party bus that arrived last night at Holy Family Hospital. The deceased was your mother's boyfriend and the gentleman in ICU is your estranged father." He flipped a page. "And let's not forget your grandfather who was an early bird and is hanging out with Mr. Michael in the morgue." The detective closed the notebook. "All we need before taking a group photo for the family reunion is your mother and we can't locate her." He cocked his head. "Know where she is?"

He shook his head and could pass a polygraph on that question.

Ironically, his mother came to life after his deserter of a father lost consciousness.

"Emmett," she whispered between moans.

He helped her into a sitting position. She wouldn't remove her hand from the right side of her head. Blood seeped through her fingers and down her neck.

He found a pillowcase and held it against the side of her head. Momma winced, but seemed more troubled by the lacerations around his neck.

They sat in silence for a few minutes licking their wounds. She spoke first. "I'll call an ambulance on my way out." She pointed at his throat. "Make sure you get checked out."

He was sick of being nothing but a tidal flow under the gravitational pull of his mother. "What? You're leaving me with this mess!"

She adjusted the pillowcase so she could see better. "Listen to me! If you love me—or Nana more, you'll do what I say."

He pointed at Carl and Todd. "No, you have it backwards. If you truly love me, you will do the right thing for once. This all belongs to you."

She nodded and slowly staggered to her feet. "Okay, rest a bit while I clean up. Then I'll make the call."

After fifteen minutes passed, he went downstairs to check on her and saw the Escort pulling away from the curb.

The car was still in sight when he heard the first siren.

"So, your mother left without telling you where she was headed?" Walton continued.

He nodded.

"Well, that's unfortunate. In simpler times, this would easily make front page news, but these days we're working on conspiracies to blow up the statehouse and rival gangs hijacking freight-cars transporting paper towels. We planned on assigning this domestic humdinger to a rookie detective, until the FDA called. Seems they're sending up a small team, which got the Chief concerned, so here I am."

Cotton looked at the strawberry gelatin. *Throw an animal in a boiling vat and separate the body parts and you end up with dessert. It's a wonder Momma didn't explore this vocation.*

The detective let out a long sigh. "Given all the trouble after the contamination scare last year, the media shadows every hospital admission. They started getting worked up about the recent death of a local stockbroker. Now we have your merry little gang here with the same bacterial infection." He smiled revealing yellow teeth and inflamed looking gums. "Inquiring minds see a connection." He pondered the thought for a moment. "Can you imagine the conspiracy theories if the internet was up?"

I'm in no mood for chit-chat, he thought. "I explained everything last night." He waited for the pain to subside in his throat before continuing. "Go bother someone else. If you hurry, maybe you can steal some lunch."

Walton leaned over the bed rail and Cotton smelled the detective's coffee breath. "I understand you have a sore throat son, but I'm surprised you're acting like a wimp. I really expected your summer on the farm would have toughened you up more." He stepped back and rapped the railing with the notebook. "I suggest you suck on a cough drop so we can talk about what happened because I find it mighty interesting everyone connected with you is either dead or on their way."

ONLY DEAD LEAVES FALL

He pointed at his notebook. "Straight is the shortest distance between two points and what we have so far is nothing but a tangled knot of spaghetti. I can't find where it begins or ends. So why don't we just throw the whole mess on the wall and see what sticks? Shall we?"

He nodded in state of disbelief that he might get blamed for all this. *This cop has sure done his homework. I thought my record was sealed.*

"My hearing is stellar so no problem if you can only whisper. Feel free to write the answers in my notebook if you prefer."

He would let his throat become a shredded mess if necessary. No way would he give the cop anything in writing.

The detective wandered to the foot of the bed. Then, he stretched out his arms as if preparing a wise pronouncement. "What we have here is a sad soap opera. Your mother is exhausted from this burnt marshmallow world, so she and her boyfriend cooked up a grand scheme to swindle your father. How am I doing?"

Cotton looked away. "You're wrong," he whispered. "She's had it tough long before Sun-Kissed. She made a lot of sacrifices raising me. Now she's doing the same for my nana. The nursing home plans on evicting her."

The detective looked unimpressed. "If I had a buck for every Robin Hood defense I came across, I wouldn't be sampling your breakfast." He flashed a sly smile apparently pleased with his creativity. "Let's talk about your dad. Describe your relationship."

Cotton kicked at the sheet. "Relationship? I met him for the first time yesterday." He replayed how good it felt sending him airborne.

Walton nodded in agreement. "Yeah, I heard about the touching reunion." He reopened the notebook. "According to his statement, your father—"

Cotton bolted upright "Stop calling him that!" he said as loud as he could, and the pain made him clutch his throat.

The detective looked up and his face softened like it was time to play good cop. "Okay, I get it. No dad-of-the-year."

The detective paused and Cotton questioned if it was for dramatic effect or expecting him to give his version. He remained silent.

"The setup took place in an impressive house your mother was cleaning before the new owners moved in," Walton continued. "She represented it as her new home and allegedly partnered with her boyfriend Carl Michael to lure Mr. Dolan into a fake investment scheme. Yesterday, Mr. Dolan suspected something was amiss when he began bouncing checks. He subsequently discovered the check he sent Michael for some software analysis grew ten-fold. Then he found out the half million he invested in a hydroelectric station was a scam."

Cotton listened but had trouble following. "This all sounds like a bunch of hooey to me. You have to understand my momma can't even spell the word finance. Heck, she walks to the bank and cashes her checks and doesn't even have a checking account. *Who needs one when the bill collectors and the nursing home beat her up like bullies in the schoolyard taking lunch money?* "I don't know anything about that Michael character either," he continued. "The first time we met he tried to kill me. It sure sounds like he was the mastermind and used my mother to get what he was after. Dolan should have been more careful. What's that old saying? Buyer beware?" He looked away. *Dolan deserted us and now Momma's left me to fend for myself with the police. How does she expect me to handle this onslaught? And what about Nana? She'll be out on the street soon. All the empty soda cans in the country won't cover that monthly bill.*

The detective waved his hand to get his attention. "Carl Michael may have been the brains behind the flimflam, but with your mother on the lam, who knows? Regardless, what I can't figure out is why, after so much planning and execution, did they risk it all by passing a bad check? Three thousand bucks is small coin compared to a half million. The money left the country, so why not blow out of town instead of broadcasting everything with the altered check?" He bit his lip. "Either it was pure greed or they wanted to torment Mr. Dolan like a cat that plays with a mouse before biting its head off."

Cotton delayed swallowing because razor blades in his throat were waiting. He couldn't follow this wild story and felt too numb to try.

The detective checked his watch. "The lab suspects a virulent strain of botulism. The petri dishes in her refrigerator and the dead birds in the trash bags on the porch, tells us your mother took her microbiology mighty serious. A witches' brew if you ask me. Hence the FDA involvement. They don't need more riots due to food contamination. My luck, they will show up with the CDC too."

"You have it all wrong. She loved growing things for experiments and had terrible luck with birds," he said with practiced conviction. A carousel in his mind began flashing disturbing images that told otherwise.

"Her experiments seem to have expanded beyond dishes and birds. Mr. Ponzell died from botulism. He was your father's ex-brother-in-law and broker and we suspect met your mother. Then there's a janitor that worked in the same building as Ponzell. He's in intensive care with the same bacterial infection. If they can name hurricanes, your momma should be memorialized with a plague."

Cotton ignored the comment and closed his eyes. He needed time alone.

Walton walked to the window and pulled the curtain back revealing a brick wall. "Nice view," he said sarcastically. "When you're feeling better, there's another detail you can help me understand."

"What?" he asked bracing himself.

"If your mother truly loves you, why would she steal from you?"

He thought of the F150 and bag of empties back home waiting to be redeemed. "It's hard stealing something from nothing."

He flashed an all-knowing smile. "Mr. Dolan's worth a couple million, or at least he was."

"So?"

"Well, we took a look at his accounts and discovered you're the sole beneficiary on his brokerage account."

He came off the pillow. "What?"

"Yeah. So, why would your mom and boyfriend steal a quarter of it from you? Was it to help your grandmother or did you get tired of playing cowboy and conspired with them to get a piece of that sweet pie until Momma's creative microbiology finished Dad off?" He shrugged. "After all, the guy abandoned you and your mother. He owes you a lot of Happy Meals."

The word "beneficiary" stuck in his mind. *I spend my days chasing nickels. Twenty empties make a dollar, two hundred pays ten bucks, two thousand before I see a hundred. After six thousand cans, I visit Griffin.* "I'll take a lie detector test and prove I don't know anything about this," he said as loud as he could muster. "Momma warned me Dolan might show up someday and whip out his checkbook like I was an overdue library book. Maybe he felt guilty and that's why he made me the beneficiary. You'll have to ask him."

"I did while I was waiting for you to wake up. It came as quite a surprise to Mr. Dolan too. Like I said, we're looking into the connection with the dead broker."

"Look all you want, but I never wanted his money. I promised myself if he ever showed his face, I'd hurt him so bad he couldn't reach for his wallet."

The detective nodded in thought for a long moment. "Aren't you forgetting something Emmett?" he asked.

Cotton shook his head.

"Deny him all you want, but if wasn't for that ogre of a father, we wouldn't be having this conversation. He saved your life by shooting the man choking the life out of you." The detective sighed and opened the notebook again. "I need a psychology degree to unravel this dysfunctional family of yours."

Cotton had enough. "Anything else? My throat is killing me."

"There's one last thing that surprised even me."

Cotton straightened the pale blue blanket on the bed. He did not acknowledge the comment.

"As a precaution, the hospital ran a blood test in case you were infected with the superbug. Your results came back negative." The detective looked inquisitively at Cotton. "Were you aware your blood type is B positive?"

"Yeah, so what?"

The detective leaned over the bed and studied his face like a human lie detector. "Did you ever think your blood type was—shall we say, interesting?"

Cotton felt his heart beat quicken. If he could get out of the embarrassing johnnie he was wearing, he would like to roll this bald guy down the hall like a bowling ball. Then he could test how much the stubble impacted the momentum. "What are you telling me, Sherlock?"

Walton smiled wryly as if complimented. "The doctors say you'll be released tomorrow. Meet me at the station. We have a lot to discuss."

"Why? Are you charging me with something?"

"I haven't read you your rights, have I? We need to talk some more," he said reverting to the soft tone.

"Besides making me regurgitate everything I've already told you, what's the deal with my blood type?"

The detective looked too pleased with himself to keep a secret. "As you know, Homeland Security issued every citizen an identification card that includes all relevant information on a chip. The I.D tracks government benefit eligibility and contains medical profiles and criminal records. After reviewing all the data, we noticed both your mom and dad have Type A blood," he explained slowly, enjoying every syllable. "If I were a patient man, I'd wait for the light bulb to appear over your head regarding the implication."

Watson eyed the last Jell-O cube on the hospital tray and popped it in his mouth. "Spoiler alert! This scam of your mother's had a longer set up time than this gelatin." He shook his head. "Can you believe there's pieces of real strawberries in here?"

CHAPTER THIRTY

The generic looking clock on the wall read five minutes to eight but it could have been midnight given the deserted halls and the resident rooms steeped in darkness. Cotton knew from talking with Nana it was a mistake classifying the sleeping residents as dead to the world. Lifetimes filled with family and careers and a hundred other categories fueled their dreams. Nana said her nights were like taking the leftovers out of a mental fridge and reheating them in fantasy. She found some memories more flavorful after marinating for years.

The silence was broken by a high-pitched scream for help from a room he just passed. A loud moan followed the woman's plea. The combination raced past him like twin waves and crashed against the empty nurse's station. Seconds later, the pitter-patter of feet approached from an adjacent hall and he came face to face with a gray-haired nurse that looked like she could use a long sleep too. Frowning, she glanced at her watch. He immediately launched a charm offensive, assuring her the visit was an urgent one and would be brief.

She nodded a quick approval and headed in the direction of the needy resident. He nearly ran to Nana's room before tiptoeing in. His grandmother was enveloped in the glow of a soft nightlight. He watched as her mouth moved in silent petitions. Momma constantly dismissed her as "pitifully pious," but he knew down deep, she was jealous of her faith.

He approached and gently rubbed her hand. "Nana?" he whispered.

The woman's eyes popped open and immediately took in his face. "Emmett, my pride and joy!"

ONLY DEAD LEAVES FALL

"Sorry to stop by so late."

"Nonsense," she replied. "I intended on giving thanks for another wondrous day but ended up filling His ears with all my problems. As if He doesn't know them already!" She let out a short sigh. "Glad you came by early, because I'm going out dancing later," she said with a wink.

He smiled. "I remember you telling me your dance card was always full in high school. Talking with some of the gentlemen down the hall, I know they would trip over each other to dance cheek to cheek with you."

"Be careful. Trip is a four-letter word in here. Even so, a broken hip or two would certainly reduce the competition."

"Did you have a good dinner?"

The old woman thought for a long moment. "I can remember the first meal I cooked for your grandfather but can't recall what I'm still digesting." She looked past him. "Did your mother come with you? I heard the nurses talking and one said the owner will roll my bed out on the sidewalk soon if I don't pay up."

Cotton felt a stab in his throat and wished he could spill his guts like he did as a boy when things looked like they were imploding. Back then, she would simply listen without interrupting and nod her head occasionally signaling she understood. That was enough for him—being present and not passing judgment. Now looking down on his grandmother, he would rather tattoo his tongue with bite marks than trouble her about things outside these walls. *Suck it up for her,* he kept telling himself. *She will understand everything on the other side.*

Questions propelled this visit and the answers might challenge his sanity. He cleared his throat. "Nana, tell me again when you first saw me."

Her blue eyes became bright. "Oh, how I thanked the good Lord. I walked around the house for days talking to myself. All I kept saying was how grand, how special you were."

He heard the story so often it no longer made him blush. Since Griffin took a bullet, he lost any hope of ever being *special* again and only wished he could make it back to ordinary. "If I were only half the guy you think I am." He looked away.

She squeezed his hand in return. "Rubbish! You're a fine young man. As proof, I bet I'm the only one here that has her grandson visiting tonight."

He thought about the bank of dark rooms he passed by on the way in. "Guess it shows timing is everything." He squeezed her velvet hand and tried again. "I'm curious. How long after I was born did you first see me?"

Her face darkened. "Why, that's a strange question." She hesitated and her mouth made some strange movements.

Cotton nodded, pressing gently. "I know things were really tough for Momma after she got pregnant with me and moved to New York. Thinking about it all, I want to make sure I have the details right," he explained.

"My dear, I've always been honest with you no matter the question. You must understand when I was a girl, the world judged how a baby entered the world. Things have changed quite a bit since then. Even so, when your mother discovered she was carrying you at such a tender age, she feared she couldn't give you the life you deserved. It still haunts me that she planned on putting you up for adoption, even though I was against it. I was divorced by then, but assured your mother we could make it work. However, she inherited my stubborn streak and would hear none of it. She wanted privacy instead of being the talk of the town. So, Father Bernard arranged for her to move in with some wonderful Sisters in upstate New York. They had a special gift of providing emotional support."

"How far along was she when she left?"

Nana thought for a moment. "A twig had more fat than her. She felt abandoned and constantly worried one of her friends would notice the first signs of a baby bump. She was only a couple months along when we loaded up the car." The serious look turned into a smile. "See, I remember some things just fine," she said then burped. "I had turnip for supper," she laughed.

Cotton smiled. "Remember anything else?"

The old woman's bottom lip began to tremble. "That's when she started wearing red all the time. When I asked why, she said your father's betrayal turned her inside out. She felt like a modern-day

Hester Prynne in *The Scarlet Letter*. It made me incredibly sad and I stormed heaven with prayers."

The admission startled him. He thought she liked red because it represented the victories over the uncles after the brutal beatings. "Did she see a baby doctor before moving away?"

"Good grief grandson, you're acting like a reporter." She rubbed her forehead with a frail liver spotted hand. "I remember the evening she came home and broke the news to me. I cried all night. Not because I didn't want you. Don't ever think that! I knew it would be tougher on her than the boy. God forgive him."

She grabbed a tissue and held it up to her eyes. "It's not my place passing judgment, but I'd like to live long enough to see the look on that boy's face when he realizes what he missed out on."

Cotton thought back on the smile Todd flashed before he knocked him into the bushes. Nana would not condone violence, no matter how deserved. He could repeat word for word what would come next in the familiar script and sought another route. "So, did she see a doctor?"

"I wanted her to see Dr. Huntley, but she felt too embarrassed since he delivered her. She planned on seeing a doctor in New York."

"Did the Sisters help her find one?"

The old woman fiddled with her hands. "Well, nothing goes as planned with that girl. She no sooner got there when she had second thoughts and ran away."

His heart quickened. "Ran away? For how long?"

"An eternity."

Momma painted Nana as cold and distant during her pregnancy which he found unbelievable. "She said her water broke and had to thumb for a ride and almost didn't make it to the hospital in time. Some truck driver stopped and gave her a lift."

Nana ignored the comment and turned her head away from him. "For months I prayed the phone would ring and it would be her. Worry is a dark purgatory inhabited by worms that feed on your thoughts." She wiped her eyes with one hand. "My agony had the sweetest of endings a year later when your mother appeared at my door in the middle of the night holding you. Since then, September reminds me how color can rush back into your life."

"Did she fill you in on the missing time?"

The old woman ignored the question. "You were so grand, I kept saying. So special! I rocked and rocked you in the living room, determined to fatten you up. Those were such happy days. We doted on you and your mother apologized for what she put me through." She closed her eyes for a moment. "We were so content we rarely left the house. Your mother wouldn't even let me watch tv. We just talked."

Gently repeat the question, he thought. "So where did my mother go when she ran away?"

Nana smiled. "Now I think you're taking after me and forgetting yourself. The answer is on your birth certificate. Sycle, New York may only be a couple hundred miles up I-90 but for me it was on the dark side of the moon."

Cotton kissed her on the cheek and she fell asleep almost immediately. Fifteen minutes later he barreled into the driveway of his grandmother's and mother's house. The headlights bounced off the yellow police tape outlining the front porch. He parked the car behind some tall evergreen bushes in the backyard.

He decided not to turn on any lights in case the police were making rounds. The back door creaked loudly when he entered and he made his way by memory through the kitchen and into the dining room. The china cabinet sat comfortably between two windows. In the right-hand drawer, he located the oversized envelope.

***

When he reached Sycle, the clouds darkened and the first raindrops seemed as frantic as him to feel grounded. It fell fast and without any wind and quickly glued the multicolored leaves to the roadway which he followed into the center of town. As local government did not transact business before nine o'clock, he sought refuge from the weather in a Salvation Army relief center across the street. After getting a complimentary watered-down coffee, he found a stool by the window and watched municipal employees entering the building through a side door reserved for the cast.

At nine fifteen he entered the City Clerk's office and eyed a woman with silver hair and a matching suit. She sat at a metal desk piled high with manila folders. When he approached the plexiglass window, she ignored him for a long minute.

"Can I help you?" she finally asked without sounding like she meant it.

"Yes, I'd like to get a copy of my birth certificate," he replied, while mentally punching the hideous gelatin-thief detective in the mouth.

"That will be three dollars."

Three bucks? On a good day, he would collect a bag full of red, green, and orange cans along with water bottles which would pay this ransom. He was willing to pay a hundred times more, even if it were just a silly tax to find his name in the great Book of Life. Even so, he toyed with the idea of lining up rows of nickels and dimes for the miserable civil servant. He ignored the temptation and pulled three singles out of his wallet.

Before the dollars disappeared in a drawer, he noticed the clerk's name: Rhonda I. Phinney and he thought of saying something funny about her initials but needed her cooperation first.

Rhonda reached for a small scratch pad and pencil. "Name and date of birth."

"Emmett Rufus Connolly, September twenty-fifth, two-thousand-two."

The clerk sauntered back to her steel desk and plugged the data into a terminal. Cotton held his breath as she hit the return key a dozen times before frowning. Getting up from the uncomfortable looking chair, she walked to a refrigerator-sized safe and retrieved a leather book. He held his breath as she began turning the pages and then abruptly stopped. Just as he was about to exhale, she began turning the pages again.

The clerk studied the scrap piece of paper and her expression alternated between puzzled and aggravated. When she returned to the counter, he knew the verdict.

"We only had one birth that day and it was a girl named Abigail. Unless you have something else to tell me, you have either the date, state, country or planet wrong." A slight smile began escaping the corners of her mouth. Clearly, she could not believe the idiot standing in front of her.

Cotton walked slowly out of the building. The rain began falling in big drops, but he must have walked between them, because he felt nothing. After making his way to the municipal parking lot, he noticed the meter still had another forty-five minutes left in his fraudulent birth town. He wished he could use all the coins in his pocket and bribe the meter to flash his origin.

The truck sputtered and he lightly tapped on the accelerator trying to coax the motor to nurse, but it stubbornly refused and died. He took the key out of the ignition and sat back in the seat and let the frustration wash over him like a giant wave intent on knocking the wind out of him. Clenching his teeth, he leaned over and retrieved the manila envelope from the glove compartment. Inside the time capsule his momma safeguarded two relics—his birth certificate and a well-worn scrap of red plaid flannel. He fingered the remnant of the baby blanket he called "Buddy" which comforted him during sickness and loneliness and when the night terrors didn't fade with dawn. It seemed appropriate to hold it in one hand as he studied the verification of his birth. The document looked official enough. It had a big gold stamp certifying he had been born to Darlene Connolly in Sycle, New York. Todd Dolan was listed as the father, although he kept his mother's last name. He studied the certificate's font and the paper grade looking for clues. *Why go to such lengths?*

Needing certainty, he opened the door of the truck. He would make nice with Ms. R.I.P and have her search the entire month before and after his fake birthday.

CHAPTER THIRTY-ONE

A very pregnant Gracie was waiting outside the front door. Cotton had not seen her in a year and thought even if it sounded like an overused expression, she did have a certain glow about her. He was also surprised how happy she looked which was highly unusual in his presence.

It came as a disappointment when her smile saw its shadow and her ebony eyes narrowed. "He's been up all night on the blasted computer. I tried asking him what's up and he won't answer me, except to bark that he needs more coffee which we don't have." She ran a hand through her dark wavy bob cut. "My father called in all his favors for the IT testing gig, knowing it could provide something stable once the internet returns. Before you called yesterday, it also kept him from overthinking things. So, can you enlighten me what's going on?" She placed her right hand on her extended belly. "He gets crotchety when he feels useless. He won't admit it, but you still rock his world. If I find out you're getting him mixed up in some sort of trouble again, I'll dropkick you into another zip code."

Cotton held up his hand as a stop sign. "It's not anything like that. Grif is doing some research for me, that's all. I'll explain everything later."

The look on her face showed she didn't like the answer but let him in.

He found his buddy typing furiously on the keyboard. Griffin motioned with his head toward a fugitive kitchen chair beside the desk, which Cotton ignored.

"You know, Gracie has enough reasons for hating me without running up my tab," he whispered. "The last thing she needs is me messing with your head right now." He watched his friend's fingers fly over the keys. "Really Grif, when I asked for help, I didn't expect you obsessing over it. I rather you save that for the baby. I wish you just called and told me what you found."

The big man grunted in reply and began searching through a thick pile of printouts on the desk. "Sit down will ya?" he ordered. "You're making me nervous."

Cotton obeyed. "I thought you were cutting back on caffeine? If not, you should be hoarding the coffee rations for when the baby is up all night with colic."

His friend did not hear him; clearly agitated as he hunted through the papers for something misplaced.

"Don't tell me I drove all the way up here and now you can't find it?" He laughed so he wouldn't attack the pile himself.

"You're the one giving me colic," came the quick reply. The madman started throwing printed pages on the floor and then abruptly stopped. "Ah, here it is!" He shoved a printed page in his hand. "I accessed some archive files under the beta testing protocol for the revamped Web. Read this at your peril."

The paper was a scanned copy of the front page of the York Herald from August 21st, 2002. The headline read: *Bush Signs Anti-Crime Bill.* "I don't understand what the President has to do with any of this."

"Are you an idiot? Read the story underneath, moron."

"Wow! Watching you explain fractions to little Jake will be a real treat," he teased and scanned the paper. "*Tragic Fire Claims Family*," he read out loud and looked up. "And?"

"Look at the third paragraph."

His eyes followed the command. *Firefighters found Jonathan and Marie Picard in the upstairs bathroom. The couple were evidently attempting to rescue their infant son when overcome by smoke. Mrs. Picard was pronounced dead at the scene. Her husband suffered extensive burns and is in intensive care. Their ten-month old son, Raymond is also presumed dead. The grim task of searching the charred nursery for the baby's body is underway.* He put the paper down. "Look, I'm too tired for this detective game. Can we just cut to the end? What does all this mean?"

His friend grabbed the paper out of his hand. "Our goldfish has more of an attention span than you do, and it died last week." He reached behind him and grabbed another sheet of paper and handed it to him.

Cotton rolled his eyes. It was another article from the same paper dated August 23rd. He wasn't in the mood for a scavenger hunt, but the headline caught his attention: *Mystery Deepens Over Missing Baby.*

He looked up and Griffin's dark eyes were studying him. He held his breath and read on.

Authorities remain perplexed as to the whereabouts of the little baby boy, who allegedly perished in the fire last Thursday. Firemen continue searching the house for the infant's body. The father remains in intensive care battling extensive burns and smoke inhalation. The police report includes a statement from Mr. Picard in which he recounts how his wife woke him up after smelling smoke and he discovered fire in the hallway. They tried making their way to their baby son's room but were repeatedly beaten back by the flames. Mr. Picard also stated he tried escaping through the bathroom window but failed."

He looked up for guidance.

Griffin leaned forward. "Okay, skip to the last paragraph," he whispered.

Todd obeyed. *Next door neighbor, Darlene Connolly spotted the flames from her bedroom window and called 911 before running over to warn the family. A friend of the deceased couple, she was inconsolable after the tragedy and recounted how she often visited the ten-month-old baby. "He was such an adorable towhead, I nicknamed him Cotton," she recounted through tears.*

The room started spinning and Cotton located a wastebasket by the desk just in time. When he finished getting sick, Griffin handed him a used napkin. He wiped his mouth and reread the articles while searching his memory as far back as he could remember. The deep dive ended in shallow water.

"How long did they look for me?" he asked.

Griffin cleared his throat. "We are a long way from the days where everything is catalogued and easily accessed. I searched and found a few articles speculating the fire might have been deliberately set to hide your murder. At first, the police suspected the father since he had a life insurance policy on the wife. The fire's origin also looked suspicious as it started in the hall between the bedrooms. Unfortunately, like many of these cases, the mystery remained, and media attention fades with time. Of course, Sun-Kissed torched any interest in cold cases."

"What happened with Jonathan? Does it say how hard he looked for me?" Cotton whispered because his voice began breaking. "Did he put up posters in store windows and on telephone poles? Did my mug grace a milk carton?"

Griffin shrugged. "I don't know. He was in pretty tough shape given the injuries. Then he had to defend himself from the accusations."

Cotton closed his eyes. He thought of a family tree floating in the air with no roots. *Nothing in my life makes any sense now.* He opened his eyes and caught a strange look on his friend's face. It looked like pity. Now he realized how he looked when he came bearing the meager offering.

"Let me...get this straight," he stuttered. "She might have lost the baby after she reached New York?"

"Or, was never pregnant," Griffin added.

Nana's words echoed in his ears. *"A twig had more fat than her."* He took a deep breath. "She abducted me to get back at Dolan? That's beyond sick."

Griffin nodded. "Yeah, that's a monster's-monster if you ask me." He bit his lip. "Though I must say, I never liked your mom much. She creeped me out and I could never put a finger on why."

His mind raced with the mad logic. "I've been thinking a lot about Momma—or rather this woman, and how she tried grafting her twisted ways onto me." He looked at Griffin and shrugged. "How should I confront her when she comes out of the hole she's hiding in? Ask her why she killed my mother, maimed my father, ruined my life? And what about the man I blamed my entire life for betraying me? Dolan thought he abandoned his pregnant girlfriend, but was that an illusion too?" He thought for a moment. "Do you think he goes to blazes when the Last Judgement takes place because he lived his life under a false assumption?"

"Given everything you've told me, guilty as charged based on intent." He touched his shoulder. "How about I get us some Johnnie? Maybe a few shots would help."

He waved him off. "Momma told me I was always at her feet. She said one time she was cooking dinner and tripped over my toys and a spilled a pan of hot water." He rolled up his right sleeve and inspected a long purplish scar running down his forearm. "I always thought it lucky how the water missed my face, shoulder and back." He raised his arm and shielded his face which highlighted the scar. "I wasn't on the floor playing but probably protecting myself from the flames."

Cotton watched his friend's eyes bulge which was the second new look today. He must have looked something like that after the bullet found him. He looked away.

"I wonder if she set the fire or took advantage of the situation."

Cotton weighed the probability of each scenario. So many lies and he missed small hints. Whenever they argued she would say, "*You'll never understand all the sacrifices I made after laying my eyes on you.*" He thought he might be sick again.

Griffin folded his hands. "A simple test will confirm everything."

"I don't need the test."

"Okay. What are you going to do?"

Cotton stood up and reached in his pocket for his keys. "I'm moving far enough south where everything is green, instead of this godforsaken place where nature can't stand still and moves from one season to the next. Maybe the people will be real there too."

He picked up the highlighted newspaper article and read it again. "What should I do with all of this?" he said, grabbing the wastebasket again. "I have a fake Momma bent on revenge and a fake Dad that spent his life running away from a lie." He felt like punching a wall but couldn't scare Gracie. "How can I make sense of this without spending the rest of my life on some therapist couch?"

He stood up. "All I have left is what they did to each other and I'm left in no man's land. He looked at the burn on his arm. "The real scars are the ones you never see."

CHAPTER THIRTY-TWO

Breakfast in the nursing home dining room was wrapping up and the residents began drifting toward the recreation room. Delores believed good nutrition and slow eating went hand in hand and consequently, she always lagged behind the others. She no sooner stood up and released the brake on her walker when a pretty young aide approached and escorted her down an unfamiliar hall.

Delores feared the eviction process might be underway until they stopped at the doorway of a darkened sitting room. The aide flicked on a light switch and revealed Darlene sitting in a green wingback chair. She wore her usual attire—an oversized red sweater and black jeans, but strangely accented it today with a knit jersey turban.

The mother abandoned her walker and rushed forward a few steps. "Is everything okay, sweetheart?"

I don't know what okay feels like anymore, Darlene thought. She stood up and gave her mother a peck on the cheek. "You used to tell stories about the good, the bad and the ugly. I'm still waiting for the good to show up."

The old woman sighed and sat down in the matching armchair. "Good is always present, you just have to recognize it. Like the night you showed up at my door cradling Emmett. Appreciate memories like that instead of constantly gulping from the canteen of hurt you carry around."

Darlene ignored the advice and handed the aide a white envelope. "Thanks for your help, Tina. This won't take long and I will leave through the side door, so no one is the wiser."

The girl nodded and left, closing the door behind her.

"What's with the new headdress?" her mother asked. "You have gorgeous hair and used to take such pride in it. Have you given up on that too?"

"No, just thought I'd try a different look." Darlene looked away. *It's not easy hiding the bandages after Carl cracked my skull open.*

Her mother sat back in the chair and moved her mouth as if still chewing the stale crust of bread they passed off as breakfast. "Well, I'm glad you finally stopped by. I can't remember the last time you did, though my grandson hasn't forgotten me."

The bandages amplified the words and made her head throb.

"Matter of fact, Emmett was here the other night," she hesitated as if making sure she was confident of the fact. "He must be going through a tough patch as he caught me in the middle of my prayers. Asked me a bunch of odd questions."

"Such as?"

Delores looked away rewinding the memory and pulled on her lower lip for a few seconds. "He asked about your pregnancy. Naturally, he's knows a piece of the story, but wanted the whole timeline. Questions like, when did you move to New York? When did I first see him?"

"So how did you handle it?"

"Truthfully of course."

She leaned forward. "Are you sure you didn't dream this up? Last time I was here you thought Dad was still working at the mill."

Her mother pointed a bony finger at her. "I may have some mental hiccups now and then, but I remember the good, bad and ugly when it comes to family."

Darlene sat back too fast and banged her head against the chair. She winced in pain. "Well, that wasn't your story to tell."

"You've had over nine thousand days to come clean with your son. I told you I wouldn't lie if he asked me about any of it. Emmett understood the agony we went through when I explained your decision about the adoption. However, he kept pressing on the span of time after you disappeared."

She tried taking a deep breath but could not fill her lungs. "I don't have time to fight with you today. It wasn't your story to tell. Now I'll have to deal with the fallout."

Her mother's eyes welled up. "When will you have time for me? Even when I have the nurses call and leave you a message, you ignore them all. Case in point: did you get my message yesterday about how they started putting my personal stuff in boxes? Pretty soon I'll be sleeping in some vagrant dormitory in Concord."

Darlene grabbed her hand. "That's why I'm here. I'm going away for a while but worked out everything regarding your expenses. I just gave Tina a partial payment that will settle things down for a bit. I'll work with Emmett on paying the balance."

"That's quite a mouthful. Even this old bird knows there's a lot more to this story. So why are you leaving and where are you going?"

She glanced at the door. "Like I said, I don't have time to explain much today. I found an overdue opportunity to make real money. The only downside is it requires some travel." *With Carl gone, she and Tony came to an understanding. They would meet on a sandy beach to discuss the happy details over cocktails.*

"Your father talked in circles like that when he was full of whiskey. When will you be back?"

Unexpected tears welled up. "Soon as I can," knowing it would require a fake identity. She sniffed and rolled out her best smile. "You're safe and cared for here and that makes me happy." She took a deep breath. "The police may come see you."

"Why? Did you have a fight with another loser boyfriend?"

"No! Just a few guys bellyaching about me. Just tell the cops I run with the wind. I wasn't here today and you don't know when I'll blow in again."

Her mother caressed her hand. "It would take another lifetime to figure you out. At my age, however, you don't miss the opportunity to say I love you in case the Lord calls me home before you return."

The pain on the side of her head spiked. "You may outlive me yet," she replied thinking some days she felt older and more broken.

"Maybe, but that's not the natural order of things." She squeezed her hand. "Anything else I need to know?"

She had a flashback of the night she gave Todd the same opportunity and he blew it. After looking at the floor for a long moment she found her mother's eyes. "I'm sorry for being such a handful. You taught me right from wrong, but I went ahead and made a lot of bad decisions anyways. I own all of them."

"You think your mistakes make you special?"

"Not with you. You love me warts and all."

The old woman reached in her shirt and fished out a silver crucifix. "Believe me, He does too. So, take a deep breath my child and do something to begin reversing those regrets. It doesn't require a big splash. A small ripple will make a difference."

Darlene closed her eyes and let the words roll around in her head. *Maybe she's right, but there's no small ripples in the tidal wave I'm riding.*

CHAPTER THIRTY-THREE

Three colossal oak trees behind the store released their brown leaves which the wind deposited everywhere. For two weeks, Jennifer began each day brushing away the huddled masses from the store's temporary plywood door. More than once, she marveled how some leaves delicately balanced themselves from touching the ground with their curled edges.

However, no philosophical musings clung to her pink fleece pullover this late autumn day which were notorious for bright beginnings and cloudy afternoons.

She was sweeping sawdust by the walk-in cooler when there was a knock at the door.

"Anybody home?" a muffled voice called.

"Well, it's about time," she whispered. Peter had been late all week and didn't show up at all yesterday. He always had some cockamamie excuse too, but she held her tongue because he was her dad's best friend and signed onto the store's rehab out of obligation. Last night she called and invited him for breakfast and now it was pushing nine o'clock. *Either he's figured out my ploy for an early start or he's tweaking my nose because I'm taking his goodwill for granted*, she thought. Frowning at both possibilities, she stared at the small pine table which held a coffee pot, toaster and a small package of nearly stale English muffins that cost her ten bucks. At first, she planned to eat while they worked, but after Dad whispered "*really?*" a few times in her ear, she added two plastic chairs. Between bites, she planned on reminding Peter they were pushing their luck on buttoning up the store before the snow arrived. Any remaining exterior work would be scheduled for the spring, which in these parts could run between March and May. In the meantime, she planned on reopening and selling the essentials: coffee, cigarettes, beer, and government squirt-meals.

When the veteran carpenter did not come shuffling in, she feared he got sidetracked again and headed outside to corral him. Opening the makeshift door, she discovered an old Ford Pinto parked a couple feet away. A large man in his late twenties with dark shoulder length hair more than filled the driver's seat. She almost laughed thinking it was a clown car until she noticed the handicapped placard hanging from the rear-view mirror.

"Good morning. Can I help you?" she asked from the doorway.

"I hope so." He gave her a quick once over before eyeing the building. "Had a fire?"

His power of deduction underwhelmed her. She nodded while scanning the parking lot for no-show Peter. "Sorry, we're not open."

The man's gaze remained fixed on the building. "What caused it?"

"Faulty wiring." She bit her lip. *Ruined by a stupid ice machine and a cute salesman.*

The driver shot her a glance and she read a certain sadness in his eyes. "When bad stuff happens, the pain can feel like spontaneous human combustion. I've been badly burned myself. Sorry."

She did not need a drive by pep talk from a stranger but returned a polite smile. "Well, Rome wasn't built in a day and they had their share of fires too."

"Atta girl. If the insurance company gives you any grief about settling for the damage, you hang tough. Just tell them to go to blazes!"

She gifted him with a short laugh and wondered if this guy was a creep or someone too genuine for her stressed-out mood this morning. Either way, if he wasn't Peter, she didn't care. "If you're looking for the nearest store, you can try Bill's Market five miles up the road. They have coffee and a good variety of ready-to-eat meals." She rolled her eyes. "Nothing like sucking beef stroganoff through a straw to make boiled acorns look tasty."

"That's a gross visual to meditate on while you chat with my buddy. I just hope you're as nice to him as you've been to me. I know he can be a real jerk sometimes, but if I can forgive him, so can you."

She screwed up her face and looked in the empty passenger seat. "Huh?"

The man started his car. "Between us, he's hoping you don't follow the news much." He hesitated for a moment like he was crossing items off a grocery list. Satisfied, he flashed a toothy smile. "I know you aren't fond of his mother and neither am I. A real imposter if there ever was one. Nice to meet you, Jenny."

"Wait, how do you know—"

The vehicle pulled away and revealed Cotton walking across the parking lot toward her. He traded in his cowboy outfit for khaki jeans, a white sweater and black leather jacket. Besides the new clothes, he must have changed his definition of treasure as he walked by a dozen soda cans sitting next to the dumpster.

She considered retreating into the store and locking the door, but practiced a hundred times for this possible encounter.

Taking a deep breath, she speed-walked toward him, primed for launch.

Cotton stopped and braced for impact. "I know you're upset and I deserve it. Believe me, I've picked up the phone a hundred times but knew the apology should be in person." He kicked at an embedded stone in the parking lot with the toe of his leather shoe.

She ignored the apology and went off script. "I read how they're looking for your mother. Is she really responsible for those deaths?"

He nodded with a pained look which made her wish she hadn't brought it up.

"I can't imagine what you're going through. Are you back at the ranch?"

"No, I'm staying at Nana's house for now. After that, I don't know." He scanned her face. "Look. I'm incredibly sorry. I planned on telling you the whole ugly story, but held off until you knew me a little better. I should have known Momma would jump at the chance to enlighten you first."

The words began tamping down the fire, but still required a lot of water. She pointed at the Pinto sitting at the far end of the parking lot. "So, you set up this big scene with your buddy. What am I supposed to do now? Melt and say all is forgiven? Then the camera will fade as we kiss?"

Cotton's eyes got big from the blowback and he extended both arms. "How can I make it right? All I can say is I'm sorry."

"Sorry is too easy a word sometimes." She put her hands on her hips, a trait she picked up from her mother when she got worked up. "You're like an éclair with extra special filling but afraid what might ooze out. You have to make peace with your past because whether you like it or not, you own it. And anyone that loves you has to know and accept it too."

Cotton listened and kicked at the ground again.

She took a deep breath. "Maybe the éclair is a silly comparison, but we can't build on what's possible until you do."

She turned and studied the store with its checkered patchwork of old and new plywood. A few blackened boards along the roof line caught her attention and she made a mental note of adding it to the ever-growing list. *Dad would cry seeing his pride and joy in such sorry shape, but he's here with me and we'll make it whole again....It will be better than before...* The comforting words rolled around her head and she shot a side glance at Cotton.

She reached for his hand. "I know it's been rough for you." She pointed at a large pile of scorched shingles by the road. "My pastor says we all have a cross to bear and some give off more splinters than others. The way I see it, you can either moan about it, or get a good grip and start walking." She eyed him. "Radiate a pure heart with courage and humility and a Simon will step forward to help shoulder the load whenever it gets too heavy."

He squeezed her hand and she saw a little boy that had to deal with some dark stuff. She had a similar temperament as her father, slow to anger but when provoked, the rage was intense and short-lived. If her father were alive, she would cherish his opinion. *No doubt, he would kiss me on the forehead and counsel: "Don't let him off easy, but love him through his faults. After all, "every saint has a past and every sinner has a future."*

She motioned towards the van. "So that's Griffin in the car?"

Cotton nodded and cleared his throat. "The exhaust on my truck let go and Grif saw an opportunity for a field trip in his vintage wheels. Speaking of which, could I get a glass of water? It's almost time for his meds. If my buddy misses a dose, he gets all worked up and will talk non-stop all the way home about classic cars, aliens and conspiracy theories. Sometimes he mixes everything up into one confusing stew. I can usually handle him, but I'm skating on thin ice with his wife. If I drop him off manic, she will send him home with me."

She led him into the store and past the breakfast table without any small talk on the way. She handed him a paper cup with spring water.

"Thanks," he said eyeing the two cups and plates.

She noticed and tried her best not to laugh as he scanned the store.

He motioned toward the table. "I should go."

She nodded and continued the tease. "Yeah, I don't know what's keeping him," she said looking at her watch.

Cotton reached down and picked up a jar of honey sitting beside the toaster and read the label. "Where did you get this?" he asked frantically.

"Good eye! When I left your mother's—" she paused, as her cheeks blushed, "she offered me some crackers for the bus ride home. When she went to get them, I noticed a few jars of honey stacked in the corner of the living room. I'll plead guilty to shoplifting a jar. I met a dear old lady on the bus, and she shared her lunch with me. I forgot all about the honey until the other day."

"Have you had any?" He asked holding it up to the light.

"No, but I thought it would taste good on the gold-plated English muffins I purchased.

Cotton opened the jar and smelled the contents. "Did she give you anything else? Any micro brewed beer?"

"No, but why are you asking? The news said they were investigating the link between her and some super bug. They didn't say how she transferred it." She stopped and remembered the petri dishes in the fridge. "Are you saying the honey is spiked?"

"Of course not," he replied quickly.

A man's voice suddenly called out from behind them. "Jennifer?"

"I'm back here," she answered.

Cotton looked uncomfortable. "Thanks for the water. Griffin will start blowing the horn if I take much longer." He stuffed the jar of honey in his jacket.

"Don't you want to meet my friend?"

A thin elderly man with snow-white hair entered. "Sorry I'm late, dear." He eyed Cotton and winked at her. "Don't tell me you went and hired someone else? I'm a little late as my hot water heater suddenly went on the fritz."

"Well, I don't like being stood up for breakfast," she teased. "Cotton, I'd like you to meet Peter, my father's best friend and carpenter extraordinaire."

The two shook hands. "Hope you're here to help? Peter asked. "There's plenty to do."

"Not today," Jenny answered for him, "but hopefully he'll be back for the grand re-opening in the spring. We'll have a cookout and serve hot dogs, whatever that means." She touched Peter's arm. "Hurry up and have something to eat. We have a lot on the schedule today."

She walked Cotton to the makeshift door. He looked uncomfortable but she remained silent. He needed to get a good grip on his cross.

Cotton wrapped her in his arms. "I heard what you said and not just with my ears. Give me a little time to sort things out." He gave her a tender kiss. "We'll talk more when I get back."

She backed away and noticed how troubled he looked. "I'm heading out myself. The fire made me realize how much I love this place, but I need to put my own stamp on the rebuild. I'm taking a cue from the shorter days and will follow the sun south. I have a good friend in Sedona that gifted me her gas allotment so I can drive out and visit." She pointed toward Peter. "My dad's best buddy will watch the store while I'm away."

"Promise me you'll be careful and stick to the main roads. Don't drive after dark."

"Will do." She held up her hand. "Before you go. I have something for you." She went behind the counter and retrieved a scorched aluminum can. She handed the burnt relic to him. "I found this when we were cleaning up after the fire."

Cotton looked unimpressed. "Still worth a nickel."

"More than that. It's the orange soda can you tossed me the first time we went out." She rolled her eyes. "That's the night you explained about the day of reckoning."

Cotton flashed the same timid smile she recalled when he first came into the store and asked permission to fish in the trash. "I'm rethinking all the fire and brimstone I was force fed growing up. Seems like it doesn't leave much room for trying to change or seek forgiveness." He studied the burnt can and placed the memento on top of a sawhorse. "I'll share my conversion story with you someday."

She handed the can back to him and reached up and kissed him lightly on the lips. "This one is no deposit and no return, because it's a keeper." She opened the wood door. "Now get going before Griffin catches a cold."

"No worries. He'd relish every sneeze so he could tell me to go to blazes."

CHAPTER THIRTY-FOUR

Todd heard footsteps approaching and expected the upbeat nurse on the second shift to breeze in and check his vitals. He planned on pleading again with his eyes, even though she would repeat in a sugary voice the restraints were for safety given his panic attacks following the intubation. Instead of the nurse, however, Stephanie floated in like an apparition and he wondered if the meds were to blame.

Happily, his ex-wife did not dissolve but hovered over him and scrutinized the myriad of tubes crisscrossing his body as the beat of the ventilator kept time.

A slight smile emerged on the soft pink lips before she leaned over and kissed him quickly on the forehead.

"We meet again, sweetie," she said like it was her only line in a movie, and with so much emphasis it sounded downright patronizing.

Yet, the tone did not matter because she was here to visit! He pulled hard on the hand restraints wishing he could breathe in her exotic perfume and run his fingers through those long luxurious dark locks. Even under the fluorescent lights, her hair shimmered with strategically placed red highlights. The new hairdo could easily make the cover of any fashion magazine if they still existed. He longed for her to lie beside him and did not know whether the intense desire was turbocharged by loneliness, the meds or both.

His ex-wife never could read him and left his side and toured the room with the countenance of a nursing professional inspecting all the medical paraphernalia. The juxtaposition of beauty and grace in motion made him long to roll back the clock and repair his stupidity in their marriage.

Stephanie stopped at the half empty intravenous bag and intensely scrutinized the drip rate of the high-powered antibiotic fighting aspiration pneumonia.

He rapped the bed with his fists and when she glanced at him, he pointed in the direction of the mobile stainless-steel tray containing a small pad of paper and pen.

She understood the sign language and flashed a pained smile. "Even though the nurse says you're medicated enough to make an elephant high; the doctors are afraid you'll try and remove the tube again." She shot him a pitiful look like he was restrained in medieval stocks for public humiliation. "I received strict orders not to mess with your restraints." She laughed. "It also makes this visit easier on me."

When did she become such a rule follower? He shook his head as violently as he could and kicked his legs, which in his weakened state was pretty pathetic. At least the hospital bed seemed sympathetic with his plea and added an annoying squeak to accompany the thrashing.

"Shhh! All right, I hear you," she whispered and looked toward the door.

He remained hungry for her touch as old feelings returned. Her fingers brushed up against his wrist as she untied the heavy cord from the bed railing. He desired nothing more than holding her hand for the remainder of the visit, but first had to clear up something gagging him more than the tube in his throat.

She studied the pad of paper and laughed before holding it in front of his face. *Sorry* was written in a shaky hand. "I see you've been practicing a lost word," she remarked and placed the ballpoint pen in his right hand and held the small pad of paper firm. It took a painful minute for him to scrawl *love u* in kindergarten type lettering.

When he finished, he checked her reaction.

She stifled a yawn. "Okay, let's tie you back up so I can take care of business."

Todd resisted and held the pen tighter until she offered the paper again. This time, he carefully formed each letter.

Did... u... leave... with... Darlene... in... the... snow?

His ex-wife waited until he finished writing to read the note and then dropped the pad of paper on the floor. The panic lasted but a moment and in quick succession, she retightened the restraint and picked up the paper and put it in her purse. Then she bolted across the room and looked up and down the hall before closing the door.

When she returned, he recognized it was not his ex-wife at all, but Darlene wearing a dark wig with red stripes. He blinked hard. *Are the drugs making me imagine Stephanie or Darlene?* His fingers searched for the call button to let the nurse be the judge.

The star of his nightmares filled his field of vision. "No need for a jury, sweetie." She moved the lifeline away. "You've already been found guilty. We sure had some fun last time we were together, didn't we?" She touched the side of her head. "Until Carl cracked me open like an egg."

He closed his eyes hoping the meds would transport him to a better dream until Darlene touched his cheek. "Seems you want to hear the backstory about your ex. Well, for starters, the setting was a piss-poor winter day where you dissed your wife before leaving for the office. You hadn't backed out of the garage yet before Stephanie began packing her suitcase. When she finished, she sat down at the dining room table and wrote you a Dear John letter. She thought of attaching it to the bank statement as an example of what you treasured most, but decided against it, afraid you would only read the account balance."

Darlene listened as the wheels of a cart passed by the room before proceeding. "She heard the doorbell ring and figured you took the wrong set of keys again, like you do when you want to check up on her. However, when she opened the door, she found this bag of bones standing there. The wild wind whipped my hair into a tangled mess and mascara streaked my cheeks. I told her I was supposed to visit one of her neighbors, but they must have been delayed in the rationing line and weren't home. I asked if I could use the phone and arrange a ride since I took the bus. She invited me in and made tea. As I began to thaw, I asked when her husband would be coming home. She laughed and I pointed out the window at the falling snow. Then she explained how you had things backwards: work was where you lived and you stopped home to merely punch the clock."

Tears welled up in Darlene's eyes and he pulled on the restraints.

"That's the last laugh she enjoyed as your wife because I dropped the pretense and carpet bombed her ears with your sins. I remember how the wind howled outside and ice crystals pelted the windows. She heard in graphic detail how you forced yourself on me and then balked at your responsibility and let Daddy buy my silence. Through it all, I kept stopping and checking in to make sure she could withstand more. In the end, she thought your difficulties in starting a family was poetic justice. Almost as deep as that anguish, was realizing you kept all of this from your wife." Tears rolled down both cheeks. "We spoke tenderly and considered ourselves sisters in surviving you."

He kicked his legs and pointed at the notebook, but she ignored the request. "To answer your question—yes, I led her out of your house and your life. I also counseled her on how a little forward planning can present unique opportunities. The key elements are discipline and patience. We vowed to keep our conversations confidential. I also explained my belief in divine retribution and recommended she continue paying your life insurance. We spoke after you fell ill and I learned she took my advice and your forensic lawyer overlooked the policy. I think it would be a white-lie to say she is rooting for your return to good health."

Todd hoped she would go on pontificating long enough for a nurse to come to his rescue.

Darlene read his thoughts. I know you're dying for relief, and so aren't I. No one will be the wiser if you suddenly lose the courageous fight today. Everyone will dismiss your death as the last sad chapter of a crazy saga."

She produced a syringe from her purse. "Wish I could stay until your sorry end, but I'm leaving soon for an exotic beach and need to buy some new clothes. I hear they serve champagne to the Tanned when you shop at the right stores. So, let's finish what Carl so rudely interrupted."

Darlene removed the protective cap from the syringe and placed the needle against his upper arm. Before depressing the plunger, she suddenly hesitated. "Reverse those regrets…. A small ripple will make a difference," she whispered.

She backed away with the syringe. "Ripples of choice...Do I have faith in reaping what I already sowed, or pursue instant satisfaction right now?" She turned around and began playing with the IV bag. He tried seeing what she was up to but failed.

She giggled when she faced him again. "I know days in here are boring, so I'll leave you with a guessing game. Did I spike the IV bag or not? It's a shame you're all tied up, or I'd leave you with something to keep your hands busy while you wait for the answer." She put the syringe in her purse and brought out a small Rubik's cube, each side covered in green. "Then again, you've already solved this one." She put it away and stroked his forehead. "My mother raised me like a lady, so I won't lower myself and use profanity to say goodbye. However, Emmett's best friend is fond of saying, "go to blazes," she whispered, "so I'll leave it at that."

He thought his only play at this point was pretending to pass out. After a long moment, he heard the door swing open. Opening one eye, he scanned the room to make sure she was gone.

Todd shook his head and pulled hard on the restraints to make the bed squeak while watching the IV drip. Incredibly, the door unexpectedly opened and an unfamiliar young nurse entered. He tugged on the restraints and pointed urgently toward the writing tablet.

"Calm down," the nurse said in an exhausted tone. "I know you don't like it, but it's for your own good."

He felt the cord loosen a bit on his right hand and tugged more. The nurse noticed and came alongside to adjust the restraint. She stopped when he opened his hand and showed her the yellow protective cap from the syringe.

"What's this?" she asked looking curiously at him.

An alarm overhead suddenly rang and Todd watched her look of concern grow exponentially as she read the monitor. "Your blood pressure is sky high. What's going on here?"

Todd's eyelashes bounced repeatedly off his lower lids, like heavy iron bars intent on sealing off the premises. Additional white coats rushed in. *Is my pressure up because of the upset with Darlene or from what she added to the IV bag?*

His heart continued in overdrive as the mechanical ventilator kept time. He closed his eyes realizing the next face he saw would be most revealing. If it weren't a concerned doctor welcoming him back, he hoped Caroline would meet and accompany him on his way to judgement. Her beautiful blue eyes melting into a spring of forgiveness.

That is, unless Darlene managed to booby-trap that too.

CHAPTER THIRTY-FIVE

Cotton stopped the tired truck in front of 27 Cardinal Lane in North Conway, a quaint village in the Mount Washington Valley. He rolled down the window hoping the smell of antifreeze would quickly dissipate and felt the passenger floorboard, happy it remained dry given the rotting heater core. He turned his attention to the fading light of the afternoon, knowing it represented the leading edge of a long, cold night ahead. A couple flurries drifted through the open window and landed on the faded and cracked dashboard. They lingered before melting which confirmed the hundred-mile journey back to Salem would be a frigid one indeed. Getting out, he looked under the front of the truck relieved nothing was dripping from the radiator.

One of those new electric cars with heavily tinted windows for the Tanned gentry quietly whizzed by and he watched it disappear over the hill. *Hills and rotting cores—that pretty much sums it up.* After the visit yesterday with Jenny, Griffin petitioned him a dozen times on the ride home to stop for a drink. Thinking it over, he should have caved since wading into whiskey waters were the only thing this side of the grave that made the wheelchair disappear for both of them. However, he was on a mission and deposited his frustrated and thirsty friend with Gracie before driving to the hospital. Todd was awake and did not seem surprised by the visit, though given his condition, it was impossible to tell.

"I know visiting hours are almost over but thought I would stop by and see how you're doing," he began awkwardly. *"I asked the nurse, but she didn't say much, except I'm the first visitor you've had."* He stood

at the foot of the bed and hesitated. "I'm sorry about your dad," he offered gingerly.

Todd's glossy eyes remained fixed on him.

I should have come better prepared, maybe rehearsed what I would say, especially since this will be a monologue instead of a conversation, he thought. *Now the timing feels wrong, though I will beat myself up if I leave without beginning the dialogue.*

"Look man, as a kid I was concerned with two things: milk in the fridge so I could float whatever out of date cereal was in the cupboard and keeping Momma safe from the varmint that liked to knock her around."

Todd closed his eyes.

"After what's gone down, I'm revisiting things." He cleared his throat. "When we met, I reacted like I did because of the way things were framed for me. It's like one of those magic tricks where you watch a woman being sawed in half and if you aren't allowed to look in the box afterwards, you'd think it really happened. My momma," he paused, realizing again he shouldn't call her that, "well, she's a master in black magic and blamed you for deserting us. Given that, I would have clapped pretty loudly after she sawed you in half and fed the pieces to the dogs." His hands began trembling, and he hid them in his pockets. "I know you're trying to make sense of it all. In the end, it's about Momma feeling betrayed. It's as simple or complicated as that. Add to that her mother needing a boatload of money for nursing home care and she rationalized a reckoning of sorts. Some stuff we have to talk about when you're feeling better." He knew the man on the ventilator needed additional strength before learning his son wasn't his at all.

Todd's eyes glistened and pulled at his restraints. His head motioned toward a tray with a pad of paper and pen. Cotton untied one hand and held the paper steady as one shaky word was scribbled.

Sorry

He turned away as the tears came. After waiting his entire life, the apology came from the wrong man.

Cotton looked up and down the street and cleared his thoughts by admiring a long line of birch which must be a godsend in the hot weather. Their branches were stripped clean and he could make out a squirrel nest in the crook of one high branch. He wondered if its furry resident ever looked out from its simple abode when the winds howled, and the temperatures crashed, and stared at those tiny buds lining the fingers of each branch promising spring would come someday... *Someday.*

He took a few steps toward the elevated sidewalk. Driving this afternoon, he pictured a large estate with a colossal wooden door leading to his *real* father. Instead, he found himself staring at a crop of condominiums, with fifty identical front doors. *How appropriate! All uncles-to-be except one.*

Surveying the grounds, he noted how everything was meticulously maintained. Not a single fugitive leaf could be found on the sleeping lawns of this Tanned neighborhood. Cotton compared it against the carpet of leaves and pine needles blanketing Nana's yard. He hoped Mother Nature would show a little sympathy and give him another month before sending snow. He took a deep breath. Regardless of DNA, Nana would always be his dear grandmother.

He slowly inched his way toward the big reveal but hesitated at the doorbell. Would Jonathan Picard recognize his first born appearing appropriately enough at sunset? He bit his lip still unsure whether to introduce himself as Emmet, Cotton or Raymond.

His stomach rebelled but he stood his ground, hoping his father wouldn't be too disfigured from the fire. Maybe after a long bear hug, Dad would excuse himself and return teary-eyed carrying a worn leather photo album and gush for hours about their happy, but short family life. Then he would hum a few bars from the lullaby his true mother sang, and it would strike a chord somewhere deep inside and quiet all the dragons. Sunrise would come and they would still be talking about the lost years. He would share his feelings about Jenny and how he missed her terribly. Although he might blush recounting the past, he would tell his father how he was determined to live a purposeful life—how he planned to cut the top off the burnt orange soda can and plant a violet inside for Jenny as proof. He would hold his breath waiting for his father to confess how his burns were nothing in

VINCENT DONOVAN

comparison to the ache of separation...how he never gave up hope...never stopped loving him.

A cold breeze cut across his face and made him realize reality rarely matched one's hopes. "Worthless has been my adopted name since Raymond disappeared," he whispered feeling Darlene's presence on the stoop beside him. He put his hand in his coat pocket and felt where the smooth jar of honey resided before he threw it in the Spicket River. Knowing Darlene, the contents would still have enough potency to do a lot of damage. He looked down half expecting to find himself standing in a green puddle. Instead, his eyes spotted an acorn hiding under the doorstep. He rolled it out with the tip of his shoe then crushed the nut with his heel. He kicked the tiny pieces of debris off the landing.

He was ten-years-old in a cold kitchen on a Saturday morning. All he craved was cereal and cartoons, but Uncle—this one with enough hair on his back to braid, stood in front of the sink in stained boxer shorts. Uncle gave him a dirty look as he polished off the last of the milk, straight from the carton. He thought of grabbing the container away from him until Momma came staggering down the hall with one eye swollen shut. Their eyes locked and he knew he had to be the man of the house this time.

Cotton opened the pantry closet and pushed aside a board covering her "special hiding place" and retrieved the jar of honey. The white bread sat in a rusting metal drawer below the stove and he quickly took out a slice, tore off a small green piece of mold, and slid the rest into the toaster. Before the toast got too burnt, he slathered on the honey nice and thick. When he looked up, Momma was standing beside him watching. She took the knife away from him and for a second, he thought she would throw the toast away. Instead, she added a little more of the golden gooey spread and carefully made sure it touched all four corners.

They both sat at the table in silence and watched Uncle eat his special breakfast treat.

Later that night, after diligently counting the hours, his mother appeared in black silk stockings, a low-cut red blouse and short black skirt. Using a generous application of cover-up on the black eye, she

255

looked almost normal. Uncle felt a little queasy by then, but she whispered something in his ear that always revved men up. A few minutes later, he watched them drive away in her car. Hours later she returned alone like she always did.

Taking a deep breath, Cotton pushed the doorbell and heard the chimes ring. Footsteps from the back of the house approached. He hoped his intuition was wrong and his real father would quench the longing he carried for so long.

Please, don't hide behind a litany of excuses and a fake smile, he thought as the breeze strengthened. That would be a deadly combination he could not forgive and the reason he threw away the poisonous honey before coming. No matter who was on the other side of that door, he would never consider himself an orphan. He glanced at the buds on the birch tree and they appeared to nod as he thought of Jenny and the promise of spring. "Bend, but don't break," he whispered.

When the door opened, he came face to face with a thin middle-aged man sporting a crew cut and outfitted in blue jeans and a sweater. He thought if the police did an age enhanced sketch, he might look the same in about twenty years but hopefully minus the heavy bags around the eyes and the drooping shoulders.

"Can I help you?" he asked.

Does limbo have an exit? The weird thought short-circuited this back of the envelope plan and he felt like he did when visiting Todd in the hospital. He weaved his way through that painful monologue, but now he was in the dark and terribly lost.

He needed a moment to quiet the panic before pressing on. "My truck broke down and wondered if I could use your phone?"

The man glanced toward the street and then back at him.

"Twenty other doors are closer. What made you knock on mine?" The tone was more inquisitive than suspicious.

Cotton remembered how Nana always said the truth will set you free. He licked his chapped lips, tired of wandering in the desert. "Actually, the truck is sick most days, but it gets me from point A to B. Are you Jonathan Picard?"

The man's eyes narrowed at the sudden detour. "Yes, and who are you?"

"Actually, that question pretty much sums up why I'm here," he replied hoping for a foothold. His hands were trembling and he hid them in his pockets. "My given name is Emmett...though most everyone calls me Cotton because I was a towhead as a baby. The last name doesn't matter either because I just discovered it's based on a lie." He took a deep breath. "My real name is Raymond. I'm here because I'm your—" he stopped, too exhausted to reach the summit.

Their eyes locked as he watched a look of terror mixed with hope practically erase the bags under the man's eyes. "That's impossible!" Picard muttered more to himself than the stranger facing him on the stoop. He took a step back and began to close the door. "I don't know what type of sick scam this is, but—"

Bend but don't break, he whispered to himself as a lifeline. He reached in his back pocket and pulled out the remnant of the baby blanket and held it up. "The fire was spreading so quickly in the hall; your next-door neighbor didn't have time to pack my bag or gather any family pics before abducting me."

Picard eyed the exhausted scrap of material and reached for it. He studied it for a long moment as his face contorted. "Marie's mother made the blanket herself... I used to think it had some magic sewn in because it stopped the baby from crying."

His father looked up and his face broke. He pulled Cotton in and hugged him tightly as they were cleansed in a shower of tears.

CHAPTER THIRTY-SIX

Darlene waited until Emmett entered the condo before she left the side street and parked behind his ailing truck. If not for the tinted windows, she would have been surely busted in the ill-timed drive-by. She stretched across the cockpit of the rented car and retrieved a business-sized envelope from the glove compartment. *Nana's Nursing Home Funds* were written in black cursive. She knew Emmett loved her mother deeply no matter the family tree and would never let her go homeless or be shipped off to some state facility. Consequently, he would follow the enclosed instructions and tap the safety deposit box for the cash Nana needed.

After leaving the envelope on the driver's seat of the truck, she got back in her car and realized how well she felt. The cancer was MIA today, and she felt the entire length of the sumac vine tattoo and smiled when nothing ached. She wondered if the good vibes were the result of listening to her mother and making a small ripple by not finishing Todd off. Even so, if the hospital heroics succeeded in nursing him back to health, she would choose the day and time of his demise. Next time she would be more discreet and with less fanfare.

Putting the car in drive, she remained curious about Emmett and glanced at Picard's front door.

"Go ahead and try, but you can't go home again," she whispered. "I'll always be your Momma and you'll come to realize that someday. I raised you right and demonstrated again and again what a reckoning requires." Her face soured. "But you never appreciated any of it or the sacrifices I made. You turned out to be no mama's boy."

ACKNOWLEDGEMENTS

Like millions of others, I'm a big fan of the creative genius and insights of Malcom Gladwell. I remember reading *Outliers* and being fascinated by his theory that with some degree of talent, it takes ten years and approximately 10,000 hours to master a skill.

I mention this because Mr. Gladwell crossed my mind as I dusted off *Only Dead Leaves Fall* after a long hiatus. When I first wrote the novel, I remember feeling over-the-moon excited about completing the manuscript and successfully landing an agent. The book made the rounds, but when it was not picked up, I put it aside and started another project. I learned over the years that it takes passion and discipline to face what at times feels like a 10,000-hour commitment with every book given the endless polishing.

After publishing *Chasing Mayflies* and *A Difficult Crossing*, I prepared for some heavy demolition to incorporate lessons learned on this previous effort. To say I wasn't disappointed is an understatement. After diving back into the story, I questioned what propelled a much younger me to write such a dark tale. After much reflection, I found the elements that continue to motivate me—tell an interesting story with an epiphany or two. Given the level of instant communication today, I also decided to change the setting by overlaying the effects of a solar storm to make this "fictional dream" more plausible. Ironically, this addition was completed before COVID-19 commenced, though it made the final revisions feel like I was writing about current affairs. As with *A Difficult Crossing*, I also found time had changed my perspective. I decided to further mine Darlene's sense of abandonment which fueled, but did not absolve her actions. I also took a much harder look at Todd and his self-serving view of the world and whether he truly recognized what he did to Darlene. This also led me to contemplate the ethics regarding his level of guilt for rejecting Cotton given circumstances that come to light in the big reveal near the end of the story. I do not want to spoil it for those that may read this section first, but suffice it to say I heard echoes of Flannery O'Conner's *A Good Man is Hard to Find*. In that masterpiece, the misfit has the takeaway line of the story: "she would of been a good woman ... if it had been somebody there to shoot her every minute of her life." The same might have been said of Todd's journey. I have higher hopes for Cotton since he rejected the darkness and desired to lead a purposeful life.

Tackling the final edits, I had a good laugh thinking I could have entitled this story "Cicadas" as it remained underground for seventeen long years. It found daylight thanks to the love, friendship and support of many. Special thanks to my wife and best friend Robin for sustaining this passion of mine for over forty years. No words can capture the love and support provided by my daughters Heather and Taylor as well as son-in-law Michael. I am also blessed beyond measure with the love and support of family and friends. I could fill many more pages with additional kudos but want to specifically thank my agent and friend Kimberly Shumate for her many years of insight and support of my three novels. I am also especially grateful for the support and professionalism of publisher Reagan Rothe and the entire BRW team. Their critical feedback and quality standards brought this story to its full potential.

I have come to appreciate the true reward in bringing a book to life are the people you meet and the feedback received. I look forward hearing from you on my author website at **vincentdonovanbooks.com.**

ABOUT THE AUTHOR

Vincent Donovan, a two-time quarter-finalist in the highly competitive "Amazon Breakthrough Novel Contest," graduated with a B.A in English from Merrimack College and an M.B.A from Rivier University. For over twenty-seven years, Vin worked in various leadership positions in the biopharmaceutical industry. His debut novel *Chasing Mayflies* was a 2017 finalist for the Christian Small Publishers Association Book of the Year Award for General Fiction. He is also the author of *A Difficult Crossing*. He resides in Haverhill, Massachusetts with his wife Robin. They have two grown daughters and two adorable grandsons.

NOTE FROM THE AUTHOR

Word-of-mouth is crucial for any author to succeed. If you enjoyed *Only Dead Leaves Fall*, please leave a review online—anywhere you are able. Even if it's just a sentence or two. It would make all the difference and would be very much appreciated.

Thanks!
Vincent Donovan

We hope you enjoyed reading this title from:

BLACK ROSE
writing™

www.blackrosewriting.com

Subscribe to our mailing list – *The Rosevine* – and receive **FREE** books, daily deals, and stay current with news about upcoming releases and our hottest authors.
Scan the QR code below to sign up.

Already a subscriber? Please accept a sincere thank you for being a fan of Black Rose Writing authors.

View other Black Rose Writing titles at
www.blackrosewriting.com/books and use promo code
PRINT to receive a **20% discount** when purchasing.

We hope you enjoyed reading this title from

BLACK ❦ ROSE
writing

www.blackrosewriting.com

Subscribe to our mailing list – The Rosevine – and receive FREE books, daily deals, and stay current with news about upcoming releases and our best authors.

Scan the QR code below to sign up.

Already a subscriber? Please accept a sincere thank you for being a fan of Black Rose Writing authors.

View other Black Rose Writing titles at
www.blackrosewriting.com/books and use promo code
PRINT to receive a 20% discount when purchasing.

CPSIA information can be obtained
at www.ICGtesting.com
Printed in the USA
LVHW040609230122
709144LV00006B/683

9 781684 337989